'*Merry Christmas*!' the elves shouted in joyous farewell, throwing their hats high into the air.

The reindeer charged away down the tunnel; the beautiful hand-carved sleigh with its precious load flew forward as if it were shot out of a cannon. Hooves echoed ringingly on the tunnel floor as the reindeer picked up speed. Launching themselves, their gleaming hooves surging, they soared on and up into the sky, leaving a trail of magic stardust behind them. The cheers of the elves followed them out into the night.

The newly-proclaimed Santa Claus gaped at the reindeer flying ahead of him through the air; gazed from side to side and down at the frozen wastelands far below, his face alight with amazement and sheer delight. The wind whipped his beard, and he began to laugh. The hearty, heartfelt laughter that would ring down through the years, to fill countless children's hearts with happiness, echoed out aross the silent, silver fields of snow for the first time.

a novel by Joan D. Vinge
based on a story by David and Leslie Newman,
screenplay by David Newman

SPHERE BOOKS LIMITED
London and Sydney

First published in Great Britain by
Sphere Books Ltd 1985
30–32 Gray's Inn Road, London WC1X 8JL

TRADE
MARK

Set in Century

Printed and bound in Great Britain by
Collins, Glasgow

To Andrew and Martin with love

*In a certain time, in a certain land
once there lived and once there was...*

ONE

The icy wind swept over the dark pine forests, bearing on its back yet another blizzard to be dumped on the rudely-built dwellings huddled among the trees below. It was midwinter in the Middle Ages, and the late afternoon sky was already as dark as night – as dark as the precarious lives of the peasant folk became when the Northlands' winter buried their fields and houses under snow.

The bitter wind probed the cracks between the ill-fitting logs of an isolated, rough-hewn barn on the outskirts of a tiny village. The barn was home to not only a variety of farm animals, but also to the large peasant family who owned them. People and animals occupied the space indiscriminately, sharing precious warmth and companionship as well – especially today. This was Christmas Eve, when all the people of the village put aside the problems of their daily existence for a brief time. Winter still ruled the land, but Christmas brought them a promise of new hope and rebirth, bringing spring into their hearts. It also promised a time of quiet celebration... and a very special visitor. Already the older children were beginning to grow restless, waiting for him, although the younger ones still sat in a circle listening raptly to one of Grandmother's stories.

A circle of children ranging in age from toddlers to almost-teenagers, all dressed in the same drab, much-mended clothing, had gathered around their grandmother in front of the blazing hearth. Some sat straight-backed and wide-eyed on top of the

3

woodbox, some snuggled on pillowed quilts or sprawled across a warm, patient husky or a woolly lamb while Grandmother told her traditional Christmas tales. (The farm beasts gathered near the hearth too, although whether they enjoyed the story, or simply the warmth, more, none of the children were really sure. Grandmother was the best storyteller anyone had ever heard, and she had told them that even the animals could speak and understand, on this one miraculous day of the year.) Most of the young ones had heard before the story the old woman was telling now, but anticipating what came next only made it more fun.

'... suddenly the ice mountains cracked open, and beautiful, beautiful lights shone in the sky.' The old woman spread her arms, smiling as if she could see the wonderful lights herself, hidden inside the soft gleam of a candle flame. 'And out came the *vendegum*, hundreds of them in their brightly-coloured clothes!'

The younger children gasped in amazement, seeing the beautiful lights and the great crystal mountains of ice just as clearly as the old woman seemed to, somewhere in the wonderful land of their imaginations. 'Granny, what's a *vendegum*?' little Else piped. She was only three, too young to remember last year, and not certain exactly what her imagination was supposed to be showing her.

The old woman drew her shawl closer about her shoulders, and smiled again. Reaching down to stroke Else's fair, downy hair where it curled out from beneath her cap, she said, 'The *vendegum*, those are the little men who live in the ice mountains way up at the top of the world, under the North Star.'

'*Inside* the ice?' Else asked, awed. 'Are they as little as me?'

'Almost.' The old woman nodded. 'And they love children, who are small like them ...' Her eyes filled with her wonderful vision again, and she returned to her story once more.

4

'This is the same story she told last year,' Hans murmured to himself, over by the window. He was thirteen, and had decided that he knew too much to listen to children's fairy tales. With a chilly hand he wiped away the fantastic frost-flowers that covered the tiny, crowded windowpanes every time he breathed, and peered out again. He could barely see an arm's length out into the farmyard; the snow-storm was as bad as ever. He had been sitting by the window, watching and waiting, for what seemed like hours. He turned back to his father, a tall, bearded man named Axel who sat quietly on a bench beside him, enjoying the day of rest. 'When is he coming?' Hans said impatiently, his voice rising. 'When is he going to get here?'

'On a day like this, he'd be crazy to come this far,' Axel said. He pulled his grey cloak closer about his neck, and adjusted his warm leather cap. The adults were scattered around the room, the women peacefully working at the spinning wheel or the hearth (for their work was never done), while most of the men huddled around the long wooden table, drinking holiday cups of hot ale and mulled cider, trying to keep warm from the inside out. They wore the same drab homespun clothing their children wore, with here and there a leather jerkin or fur hat for the men, and a neat white cap or apron, embroidered by hand and carefully saved to wear on holidays, for the women.

'The road from the village must be blocked,' Uncle Viktor added, listening to Hans's complaint from his place at the table. 'Even those reindeer of his couldn't make it through.'

Hans frowned unhappily. Seeing his disappointed face, his mother, Marta, shook her head in reassurance. 'It wouldn't be Christmas without him, would it?' she said, and glanced at her husband. 'He hasn't missed one yet.'

Stubbornly Hans peeped out through the thick glass panes again, squinting into the storm. This time he made out a vague, dark shape that had not been there before. He grinned, as all at once a sleigh took form in the shapeless whiteness of the farmyard. 'It's them!' he shouted triumphantly. 'Here they come!'

Even Grandmother forgot about her story now, as all the children leapt up together and rushed to the window to look out.

In the farmyard an open sleigh drawn by two reindeer pulled up before the barn door. A stocky man in his late fifties climbed down from its seat and tethered the reindeer in the lee of the barn's log wall. He had a short, full beard; its grey was already almost white beneath its sparkling frosting of snow. He wore a heavy, fur-lined wolfskin coat over peasant clothing as drab and rough as any worn by the expectant watchers inside. He had pulled his hood up high in an attempt to keep himself warm, but he scarcely seemed to notice the unpleasantness of the weather, or the difficulty of travelling through it. He turned back to the sleigh, offering his hand to its other occupant.

His wife, Anya, pushed aside her travelling rug and climbed down to stand in the snow beside him. She was almost ten years younger than her husband, and although her form was almost completely hidden beneath layers of shawl and a fur-trimmed elkskin coat, her round, rosy face was still lovely. She smiled too, as she saw the anticipation in his eyes; but her smile was tinged with a private sorrow as she glanced towards the light spilling now from the opening door before them.

Claus pulled a large canvas sack from the sleigh. Settling it on his shoulder, he started towards the barn with Anya at his side. Their heads down, struggling against the wind, they waded through the snowdrifts towards the welcoming warmth and light.

As they entered the barn the waiting children swarmed around them, laughing and shouting. Before the barn doors were even closed again, the clamoring children were hugging Claus, and pulling at the bulging sack he carried. Claus smiled, and then began to laugh, caught up in their infectious delight.

'What did you bring?' Hans cried. 'What have I got?'

Claus raised his free hand to silence them, still laughing his deep, hearty laugh. 'Wait, wait – don't I hear something first?'

The wave of children subsided as they abruptly remembered their manners. In a grinning chorus, they cried, 'Happy Christmas, Uncle Claus!' Several of the older children moved forward again, to help him lower the heavy sack and carry it to the hearth.

'All right now,' Claus said, as he pulled open the bag. 'Everybody stand back!' Beaming with pleasure and pride, he began to take from the bag, one at a time, a wonderful assortment of hand-carved wooden toys. Soon a pile of hoops, ninepins, balls and animals covered the wide wooden planks of the floor, within the ring of breathless children.

The adults stood by, watching with broad smiles. Axel shook his head in wonder. 'Cutting wood all day for the whole village is enough to exhaust any man. How does he find time to make all those things?'

Anya watched her husband with the children, her eyes shining. 'He makes time, Axel,' she murmured fondly. 'What can I tell you? It gives him pleasure.' She smiled, but there was a melancholy in it that no one but Claus would have recognised. 'Tomorrow, believe me, he will begin making the toys for *next* Christmas.'

'How lucky you are, Anya,' Marta said softly.

Anya did not answer; the trace of sadness that touched her smile crept into her gaze as well. *Lucky?* she thought. *To be married for thirty years to a wonderful man who loves children so, and never be blessed with one of our own? Spending the long winter evenings making toys for other people's children?* 'Yes ... lucky ...' she murmured, remem-

7

bering herself at last. She looked back at the children again.

Most of the little ones were already scattered about the vast, beam-ceilinged room, playing with their new toys. Grandmother led little Else up to Claus as the crush of older children loosened. Claus smiled down at the little girl, marvelling at how much she had grown. 'Little Else,' he said, reaching into his sack again. 'Here. For you. Especially for you.' He pulled out his favourite among all the toys, which he had saved especially for his favourite little girl. He handed her a wooden carved elf about a foot tall.

Else took it shyly, her eyes wide and shining with excitement. 'What is it?' she asked.

'It's the *vendegum!*' Grandmother said, delighted. 'It's just what I was telling you about.'

Else hugged the toy elf to her, dancing with her own delight and amusement. Claus smiled, his broad face filled with love. He looked around the room, at all the other children playing happily in the candlelight and fireglow with their new blocks and hoops and toys and stilts. His handmade toys brightened their dreary winter like a thousand candles, and their happiness filled the room and the spirits of their elders with warmth and light. The joy his Christmas gifts brought to others was the greatest pleasure in his own life. Despite all the time and effort they required, he always felt, as he worked through the long year on his toys, that he was repaid in riches even a king could not possess by the shining happiness of a single child's smile.

Anya and the other adults had gathered around him now, drawing him back into their company. They sat down together at the long table, laughing and talking. The gloom and chill was forgotten as the women of the household began to serve the holiday dinner they had been preparing since yesterday. On this one special day of the year, with the old year passing away and the promise of a new one ahead, they filled everyone's bowl to the brim with warm and hearty food.

The evening passed swiftly for the happy adults and children, with much laughter and little thought of the worsening weather outside. Only Claus's reindeer, tethered to a post in the farmyard, were aware of the rising wind, the deepening snow. Donner, the younger and always the more skittish of the two, tossed his head and pawed nervously at the drifts rising about his knees. His companion Blitzen, older and always more stolid, rooted contentedly in the generous serving of fodder that had been put out for them, oblivious of the elements.

At last the merriment inside began to die down. The children played quietly now, some of the smaller ones already curled up asleep on the floor, clutching their toys close. Claus and Anya began to gather their things together, pulling on coats and shawls. 'Well, time to go on,' Claus said, nodding in farewell.

Axel went to the window, rubbing away the frost to peer outside. He frowned and shook his head. 'Claus, stay the night,' he urged, looking back at their guests.

But Claus clapped a hand to his forehead in mock dismay, 'Stay the night!' he cried. 'Listen, you great fool, that little boy of Pyotor the Blacksmith, the one who broke his leg – he's waiting for a Christmas toy just like these children did!' He shook his head incredulously. '"Stay the night" he says...' He looked at his wife.

Axel turned to Anya. 'Anya, convince the stubborn man –'

Anya shrugged with good-natured resignation. 'Me?' She lifted her hands. 'I've been married to him for thirty years and I can't even convince him to come to the dinner table on time.' She began to pull on her own coat, with Marta's help.

Marta moved to join her husband at the window, and looked out. 'You can't see your hand in front of your face out there,' she said worriedly. 'You won't get through.'

'With my reindeer?' Claus laughed, trying to reassure her. 'Donner and Blitzen can get through anything!'

'One of them has already got through two bags of feed,' Axel's brother Viktor remarked, a bit ruefully, from the doorway.

'That's Blitzen,' Claus said, his smile turning wry. 'The only reindeer in the world who's half-pig.' He put his arm around his wife. 'Come, Anya, the boy is waiting for his present, and it's all the way to the other side of the forest.'

Axel nodded in surrender. 'You really *are* a good man,' he said, smiling again.

'Good?' Claus shook his head. 'Good has nothing to do with it. It's what's fair, that's all.' But the compliment warmed him, and he smiled too, letting a rare feeling of pride fill him. 'But you're right,' he murmured, considering what he knew of human nature, 'as men go, I'm not bad.'

Axel shook Claus's hand, and clapped him warmly on the shoulder, as Anya said her goodbyes and gave quick hugs to her women friends. The couple left the barn, carrying the warm wishes of the others with them into the stormy night.

Claus helped Anya up into the sleigh and untied the reindeer. He settled himself on the snow-covered seat again. Donner and Blitzen snorted and shuddered as he tugged on the reins, turning their heads into the storm. Anya pulled her shawl across her face and Claus felt a fleeting moment of doubt as the blizzard drove stinging snow into his eyes and whitened his beard again. But a promise was a promise... With a final wave to the friends still gathered in the doorway, he started the sleigh on its way down the nearly invisible track.

Anya huddled close beside him, sharing what little warmth they had between them as they drove on. Claus smiled at her, still filled with the warmth of remembered laughter. 'Did you see those faces when they saw the toys? They love their Uncle Claus, eh?' he said contentedly.

Anya's murmured reply was lost in the gathering storm, her voice muffled inside her heavy shawl.

Claus drove on. The windblown snow was sweeping out of the blackness directly into their faces now. He shielded his eyes with a hand, not even certain he could make out the road at all. He had driven this way so often that he was sure he could do it completely blind... but he admitted silently that he had never in his life tried to travel on a night like this. He slapped the reins. 'Come on, Blitzen, pull harder!' he shouted, too sharply. He glanced over at Anya and tried to lighten his voice. 'He's got so much food in him it's weighing him down –' He broke off, seeing the look on her face. 'Anya,' he said, 'don't be sad.'

All at once tears glimmered in her large brown eyes. 'Is it fair that you love children so and we have none of our own?' She couldn't help herself, thinking on this happy, holy day of how many prayers had gone unanswered...

Claus sighed. He too had borne that same sorrow in his own heart for more years than he cared to remember. 'What's meant to be is meant to be,' he said gently. He broke their train of thought by slapping the reins again on the white-coated backs of the reindeer. 'Donner! Don't drag your hooves! Yo!'

The reindeer lunged forward, startled, jerking the sleigh uncomfortably. They struggled on, their wide, splayed feet sinking into the powdery snow.

Claus and Anya travelled on without speaking through the stormy night. Claus would not have thought the snow could fall any more heavily; but soon he could scarcely see the backs of the reindeer ahead of him. The blizzard enfolded them in an eerie, smothering whiteness, silent and without boundaries.

Claus could no longer see even the faintest trace of a track. Anya sat mutely beside him, glancing at him from time to time with unspoken concern. The small seed of doubt that had sprouted inside him as

11

they left their friends began to grow, although he tried very hard to ignore it. They had been travelling for a time that was beginning to seem endless. He wiped the snow from his eyes once again. Surely by now he should have seen some familiar landmark, something he could recognise... at least the fork where the East Road joined this track? Surely they had been travelling for much too long –

He peered ahead, unable to ignore the feelings of confusion and alarm that filled him now. *'Where's the East Road?'* The words burst out with far too much force. 'It should be here, somewhere around here!'

Anya stirred, looking at him with frightened eyes. 'Are we lost?' she asked, giving voice to the fears that had been silently growing in her mind as well.

'No, no,' Claus said, hastily and unconvincingly, 'we just have to follow the road and turn before –' He broke off, peering ahead again, squinting as more windblown snow stung his eyes. 'I can't find it, Anya! I can't see the road!' His own fears took on the terrifying reality of words, as he suddenly realised that the sleigh had stopped moving. 'Hey! Come on!' he shouted, snapping the reins and getting no response from the reindeer. 'Must be stuck in a drift,' he muttered, as much to calm himself as Anya. 'Yo! Yo! Hi-up!' he shouted again, his voice rising. The sleigh still did not move. The reindeer, barely visible through the snow, did not even seem to be trying to pull the sleigh free.

'Blast!' Claus climbed down, sinking knee-deep into the snow. Furious with the reindeer, their predicament, and most of all himself for getting them into it, he waded through the snow to his animals.

As he reached the pair of familiar, velvet-antlered heads, he stopped short, feeling a chill far sharper than the freezing air. The team of reindeer stood motionless, their dark eyes glazed with a strange torpor. As he watched, Blitzen suddenly slumped in his traces and fell to his knees.

Claus caught hold of Blitzen's harness, trying with all his might to drag the reindeer to his feet again. 'Blitzen! Get up!' But even the strength of his sudden panic was not enough to force the heavy animal to stir.

'What is it? What's wrong?' Anya's frightened voice reached him from the sleigh.

'Nothing, nothing –' he called distractedly. He could not even see her from where he stood. 'Look,' he blustered, trying now to bully the torpid animals into action, 'do you want to stay here and freeze to death? Or do you want a nice warm barn and food, eh? *Eh?*'

Suddenly Donner slumped to his knees beside Blitzen.

Claus backed away, his concern deepening into real fear. He looked around him again, willing himself to see something – the outline of a building, a familiar landmark, anything that would guide them to safety. But all was as before – the same dark, half-seen forms of trees wherever he looked, shrouded in the suffocating whiteness of the blizzard. The wind howled ominously through the brooding pines and he felt the icy chill creeping into his bones. They were lost in a winter storm, far from shelter, and now they had lost their reindeer too. He had not lived all his life in the Northlands without knowing what terrible peril they were in now.

'*Claus!*' Anya's voice cried, rising with her own fear, '*Come back, I can't see you!*'

'Anya, wait –' he called tensely, rubbing Donner's head and neck briskly, trying to rouse him. 'Come on, boy,' he urged cajolingly, 'try to get up, come on my good boys...' But Donner's head only fell forward into the snow. Blitzen sagged further into the drifts beside him and lay motionless.

'Claus!' Anya cried.

Claus ran back to the sleigh, struggling against the wind, frightened by something he heard in her voice. He climbed up into the seat beside her. He put

13

his arms around her, pulling her close to warm and reassure her. But even as she lifted her head to meet his gaze, a great drowsiness seemed to overwhelm her. Her eyes dimmed and flickered shut and she sagged against him, unconscious.

'Oh my God! Anya –' Claus gasped. He hugged her tightly, rubbing her arms, trying frantically to warm her even as he wondered how a strong woman and two hardy reindeer could have succumbed so quickly to the cold.

But even while he wondered it, the same creeping lethargy began to lay its icy fingers on him, stealing up through his limbs, stealing away his strength. He shook his head, struggling to keep his eyes open, telling himself that this couldn't be happening to him, not on Christmas Eve, when he had not yet delivered his last toy ...

Claus slumped over in his seat, his eyes closing, his arms still holding his beloved wife against his heart. The relentless wind and snow closed in about them, covering them with a blanket of white, until they were utterly lost in the greater whiteness of the storm.

TWO

Donner woke with a snort and raised his head,
shaking off the clinging blanket of snow which
covered him. He opened his eyes cautiously, one at a
time, and blinked. He was not certain why he had
been asleep, when the last thing he remembered
was drawing the sleigh; nor certain why he had
awakened, except that there was suddenly an
absence of the howling wind and snow. He looked
around him, pricking up his ears, startled into
alertness. The storm, the wind, the snow had
disappeared – and with them, the forest. The air was
perfectly still and clear now, and amazingly cold.
Donner struggled to his feet. He stood on a frozen
plain that was completely devoid of trees, beneath a
sky glittering with stars of incredible brightness.

Donner lowered his head and nudged his still
silent companion with his nose. Blitzen opened his
heavy-lidded eyes slowly, shaking off the effects of
the mysterious sleep which had so suddenly
overtaken him. As his eyes registered the strangeness of their surroundings, he scrambled to his feet,
abruptly alert and staring.

Reassured of the reality of things, Donner looked
back over his shoulder at his master and mistress.
They sat slumped together in their sleigh, asleep
just as he had been. He snorted loudly, trying to get
their attention.

Claus started awake at the sound, blinking with
astonishment, just as his animals had done. As his
eyes focused, something more incredible than the
open plain and the stars filled his vision, and he
stared at it in wonder. Gently he shook Anya, and

she woke too, shaking her head drowsily. 'Anya!' Claus whispered. Anya raised her eyes and they widened like his own.

The North Star hung directly overhead, far brighter than it had ever looked before, twinkling like a beacon. The finger of its light seemed to point downward towards the snow-covered plain ahead of them... where now a glorious array of twinkling lights filled the space between heaven and earth. It had something of the magical aurora borealis about it, and the fluid, shifting form of a great forest tree decorated with Christmas candles. It was neither of those things, and yet it was both of them, and more. And below the unearthly glowing display were more lights, hundreds of flickering flames moving slowly over the snow towards their sleigh.

Claus and Anya sat where they were, clinging to one another, paralysed with terror and awe. 'What...?' Anya whispered tremulously.

As the streaming lights came closer, they began to see that each light was a separate candle, set into a candlestick that resembled a snow-clad fir tree. And each candle was held aloft by a small being that looked very much like a miniature human... and even more like the wooden elf that Claus had carved for Else. Each and every one of the small men coming towards them wore just what the tales said that elves wore – a pointed hat, a woollen tunic, leather belt and felt jerkin, boots with turned up toes, all in a riotous rainbow of brilliant colours.

A strange, melodic chanting drifted ahead of them over the snow. Neither Claus nor Anya could make out any words until the elves had almost reached them; and then they realised that they were hearing the sound of hundreds of voices murmuring together, 'Welcome. Welcome.'

Claus and Anya still sat without moving, completely mesmerised. Donner and Blitzen exchanged curious glances, wondering what in the world was happening as the tiny people began to gather about their sleigh.

16

One of the elves stepped forward. He was an elderly man, with sparse white hair and a ruddy wrinkled face framed by long mutton-chop whiskers. He had a look of bespectacled efficiency and the manner of a spokesman about him. The other elves stood behind him, seeming almost breathless with anticipation. Their expressions mirrored curiosity, a hesitant shyness, but also an undeniable warmth and friendliness as they gazed at the frightened couple in the sleigh.

'Welcome!' the white-haired elf cried.

Anya gave a small, muffled shriek, as one of these strange creatures out of myth and fairy-tale actually addressed them.

'The... the... *vendegum?*' Claus gasped, barely able to speak. He was sure now that he must be dreaming. The *vendegum* did not exist – they were fancies out of a children's story.

'The little people?' Anya echoed, glancing at him wide-eyed.

'We prefer to be called elves, if you don't mind,' the small white-haired man said pleasantly.

'You... you... you...' Claus began, and couldn't finish it. He blinked again and again, still unable to believe his eyes.

'I'm the one called Dooley,' the spokesman continued, smiling. 'We've been expecting you.'

'Expecting us?' Claus echoed.

'For a long, long time.' Dooley nodded, his eyes shining. 'We almost gave up hope.'

Claus shook his head. 'Where are we?' he whispered.

'Home,' Dooley said, smiling, and gestured towards the lights.

'No, no, no,' Anya protested, lifting her hand to point. 'Our home is far from –'

'Not any more,' Dooley interrupted gently. 'This is your home now.'

'What?' Anya turned to Claus, more frightened and more befuddled than before. 'What does he mean?'

17

'You don't understand,' Claus insisted, looking back at the small man. 'We live in a village a long way from this place.' He waved his hand as his wife had done.

'You'll see, you'll see...' the elf murmured good-humouredly, shaking his head, still smiling but explaining no further.

Behind them, as they spoke, four elves slipped away from the larger gathering and moved quietly around behind the sleigh. The leader of the foray was an impulsive young elf called Patch – because, as the bright green patch on the knee of his trousers suggested, he had more important things to think about than the state of his clothes. His quick, creative mind was as bright as a star, but as undisciplined as it was unique. Because he was not like the other elves, it was sometimes hard for the others to understand him. As a result, he was frequently in trouble ... and always the last to admit he might have been wrong.

Following him as he circled the sleigh – at his side as they always were – were the elves Boog, Honka and Vout, his self-proclaimed personal entourage. The three of them didn't really understand him any better than any of the other elves did; but they sensed that he was something special. Their admiration for him was real, if vaguely un-comprehending. And, as far as Patch was concerned, he welcomed all the attention he could get.

Patch's right-arm man was the elf Boog, who had mechanical skills almost as impressive as Patch's own, and a ready supply of tools at his belt; he was always willing to work out a method for producing Patch's latest creative design or brainstorm. Patch's second inseparable companion was Honka, whose overwhelming enthusiasm for Patch's every inspiration (however impractical) or joke (however feeble) was second only to Patch's. Completing the trio was Vout, who trailed behind the others now, a bit slower on the move both physically and mentally. He was often left in a fog by whatever joke

18

or idea filled the others with sudden laughter or excitement; but Patch liked him for his unshakeable good humour, and he liked being a part of Patch's constant boil of activity.

Patch bent down as he reached the rear of the sleigh and then slid deftly beneath it to inspect its underside more closely. The others gathered around his protruding feet, patient and expectant.

'Bits of old rope?!' Patch's muffled voice muttered in dismay. 'Single-hinge runner connectors?! Unbelievable!' The elf began to wriggle out from under the sleigh again. 'I can see I'm going to have a lot to teach him –' the words caught in his throat as two extremely long legs suddenly appeared on either side of his head. 'Whoops,' he murmured, his dismay suddenly genuine, as he suddenly found himself staring up into a large, completely alien-looking face; it stared back at him with equal incredulity, its hair standing on end, with its wide blue eyes where its mouth should have been.

Patch blinked and shook his head, as he realised that he was only seeing their guest upside down. Caught in an awkwardly compromising position, he grinned hastily, trying hard for congeniality, since dignity was clearly beyond reach. 'Hi, there!' He scrambled to his feet, his tongue already running, 'Welcome aboard, sir. Speaking for the boys and myself –' He looked up, away at his friends, back, waving his hands like an amateur magician trying to cover an awkward move. 'You must be the missus!' he almost shouted, as Anya stepped down to stand beside her husband.

'Me?' Anya said dazedly, still at least as flustered as the small figure before her.

'Well!' Patch smiled his most disarming smile and nodded his approval as he saw her face for the first time; utterly sincere for once beneath his flattery. 'We knew you'd be nice, but we didn't expect someone so young and pretty, pretty and young, did we, boys?' He glanced again at his companions, with a quick nod. Honka and Boog nodded eagerly

19

and sincerely, and so did Vout, once he had seen what they were nodding about.

'Oh my...' Anya said, and blushed becomingly. She had not heard such a compliment in some time and she had never expected to receive one from the *vendegum... elves!* she corrected herself hastily.

Patch touched her arm. 'Now, now,' he said, grinning. 'You mustn't be elf-conscious.' Honka, Boog and Vout nodded on cue, witnessing his wit. Anya smiled at last, still uncertain, but utterly charmed.

Dooley pushed forward, deciding that it was time to reclaim his position as spokeself. He separated Patch from their dumbstruck guests with a deft nudge. 'My friends, let us show you your new home,' he said to Claus and Anya, turning them to face the distant lights. He glanced over his shoulder with a nod of dismissal. 'Patch, take charge of the reindeer.'

Patch turned to Boog in almost the same motion. 'You heard him, Boog. Take care of the reindeer.' He waved blithely, opting himself out.

Obediently Boog began to unhitch the reindeer as Dooley guided Claus and Anya back into their sleigh.

'I don't understand,' Claus murmured, as he climbed back into his seat. 'You said our new home? But there's nothing here.' He waved a hand at the shining plain.

'Look again,' Dooley said, smiling.

Claus and Anya looked out again dutifully at the empty wastes of snow. And as they watched, an incredible transformation began to occur before their wondering eyes. Where moments before there had only been the light of countless flickering torches below the magical pyramid of stars, there was now a vast snow-covered mountain. And below it, truly as if by magic, an entire village suddenly shimmered into existence.

Claus caught Anya's hand in his and held it

20

tightly, feeling her squeeze his own in return. They gazed, speechless, at this new miracle, heaped upon far more wonder than they could even begin to comprehend.

A broad pathway marked by fir trees and warmly glowing lanterns led across the snow to the distant village. The village itself was not made up of separate houses, but seemed to be one enormous structure, like the barn-home where they had shared in a perfectly normal Christmas celebration so recently. But this structure was something far more remarkable and sophisticated, built on a far larger scale – for far smaller people. They could see countless tiny separate eaves and turrets and chimneys protruding everywhere, all thickly frosted with snow like an enchanted gingerbread house. Something about the brightly-painted village, so cheerful and perfect and beautiful, made Claus think of the toys he made. It was as if he were seeing a toy town brought to life. Donner and Blitzen, being led aside from their traces, gazed at the vision with equal wonder, glancing at each other for reassurance that they actually saw the same thing.

'Where... where did it come from?' Anya asked, in a voice so small it was barely audible.

'It was always here,' Dooley said reassuringly. 'But it can't be seen by just anyone, y'know.' He turned away and called out to the gathered elves, 'Come, fellow elves! Take them to their home! Lead and follow, follow and lead!' The waiting elves gathered around eagerly and took up the empty traces of the sleigh. Claus and Anya, perched high on its seat, clung to the sleigh and each other, wide-eyed, as the elves began to draw it towards their village. The elves looked up constantly at their guests as they marched along, their faces shining with excitement.

Patch walked next to the sleigh, as if its occupants were under his personal protection;

21

Honka and Vout followed him as usual. Vout looked up at Claus, and back at his friends. 'He's nice, isn't he, Patch?' he murmured.

Patch beamed as if all this had been his idea. 'I tell you, boys, the man gives me a real feeling of elf-confidence.' Honka and Vout chuckled obediently.

Anya glanced down at the sound of good-natured laughter; looked out again at the sea of elves around them, and the approaching village. 'Isn't it funny,' she murmured, 'I'm not afraid?' She looked back at Claus again. 'What's it all about?' she asked, not really expecting an answer that made any sense.

'Maybe it's a . . . ?' Claus held out his hand to her. 'A dream.' Anya tweeked his skin hard; he winced. 'No,' he said weakly, shaking his head. 'We're awake.'

They had reached the village gates at last. Claus and Anya climbed down from the sleigh at Dooley's invitation and followed him, while Boog led the reindeer along behind them.

Dooley stopped before the village gates, which were still closed, beaming proudly. He raised a hand, ready to begin the official welcoming speech he had been rehearsing for centuries in preparation for this long-awaited moment. Patch's bright cap popped up behind him, unnoticed, as Dooley opened his mouth.

'My friends, it's moments like this that make an elf feel humble and proud . . .' Dooley took a deep breath, because over the centuries he had thought of quite a lot of things to say on this auspicious occasion. Patch made a face, having heard Dooley speak before. 'Proud to have this golden opportunity to welcome –'

Patch stepped forward, seizing Claus and Anya each by an arm and drawing them aside towards the entrance. 'Right this way, folks,' he interrupted smoothly. 'Sixty rooms, hot and cold running ice cubes and a southern exposure in every direction.' He grinned congenially at Dooley. Claus and Anya were beginning to shiver; it was far too cold to keep them waiting outside... and far too boring.

Dooley closed his mouth with a huff, controlling his indignation out of consideration for their guests. He dutifully opened the great main door as Patch commandeered his visitors and led them towards it. Claus and Anya stopped short as the elves ahead of them began to pass through the doorway. As each elf stepped over the threshold, he suddenly pivoted an entire 360 degrees. Claus and Anya looked at each other, their amazement somewhat benumbed by now. No one offered an explanation for the strange behaviour, or even seemed to realise how strange it looked. Claus decided it must be a little known superstition. They *were* at the North Pole, after all. He wondered briefly, as he reached the threshold, whether he should attempt the feat himself. But he was not as light on his feet as he used to be... and he was not an elf, after all. He stepped through the doorway in a normal fashion and Anya followed the same way, smiling strangely.

Claus and Anya stepped through the doorway into another world. A panorama of dazzling, dizzying delights filled their eyes as they entered the elves' home. What had seemed from a distance like no more than a wonderfully detailed hand-carved toy was actually an enormous dwelling-place for hundreds of elves. Vast rooms stretched away from them in every direction or rose level upon level, all laboriously and lovingly built of hand-hewn logs, their walls decorated with brightly-painted toy-like sculptures. In spite of its size, the building reminded Claus more than ever of the toys he made... the workmanship and the charm of this huge structure filled him with heartfelt admiration.

And yet this was clearly a real, functioning village, with a place for all the necessities of life and work. They stood now in a high-roofed central hall which was large enough to hold two humans and hundreds of elves. On the wall facing them, high above their heads, was a spectacular rainbow-coloured cuckoo clock marked, oddly, not with hours

23

but with WINTER, SPRING, SUMMER and AUTUMN. Over to one side as they stared around them was a great stone hearth two storeys high, which held the most tremendous bronze cauldron either Claus or Anya had ever seen. Looking away in another direction they saw workbenches, racks of tools, shelves of unrecognisable wooden parts, cloth and coloured yarn. Claus had never seen anything like this before, and he could scarcely begin to imagine what use they could have for so many tools.

But not the least of the remarkable things about this village was the number of its inhabitants. From every corner, from behind benches and doorways, leaning over railings on the stairs and peering eagerly down from the balconies, hundreds of elves gazed back at him. Young and old, bearded and cleanshaven, they all wore the same eye-boggling outfits, striped and polka-dotted and combining more colours than Claus had ever dreamed existed. Their faces were alight with fascination to match his own; but more than that, they smiled with undisguised joy, as if they had been waiting all their lives for this moment. He could not for the life of him imagine what it all meant.

Another elf, whose rumpled hair and bright, slightly protruding eyes made Claus think of a good-natured pigeon, stepped forward to greet the new arrivals. Bobbing his head and beaming carefully, he cried, 'Welcome, welcome! I'm the one called Puffy. We've been expecting you.'

Claus barely heard the words, still so over-whelmed with wonder at his surroundings. He nodded absently. 'Isn't this something?' he murmured to Anya, his gaze wandering up into the rafters again. She answered him with a silent nod of her own.

'Did you hear that?' an elf whispered, delighted, from behind a nearby pillar. 'He said it was "something"!'

A second elf nodded eagerly. 'He did, he did!'

'Oh my!' Anya breathed, following Claus's

wandering gaze, and finding her voice at last.

Up above them two other elves chortled, hanging over the rail to catch the visitors' every word. 'She said, "Oh my"!' one of them gasped. 'She likes it, she likes it!'

'She does, she does!' His companion offered a hand and they shook with hearty congratulations.

Dooley bustled forward to take charge of his awestruck guests once again. Taking them politely by the arm, he began to lead them on into the building for his carefully planned tour. They crossed the wide hall and he guided them up a winding flight of stairs at the far side. At the top of the stairs was a huge dormitory, where countless tiny wooden beds, each with an elf's name carved at its foot, lay side by side in long, orderly rows. Warm, hand-sewn quilts and goosefeather pillows rested neatly upon each bed. A great open fireplace filled most of one wall, with a warm cheery blaze leaping in its hearth.

'Isn't this something!' Claus murmured, for the dozenth time.

'Is it warm enough for all of them?' Anya asked, looking about the enormous room with the practical eye and kind concern that Claus appreciated so much.

Dooley opened his mouth to reassure her, but before he could utter a word, Patch slid in front of him again, interrupting eagerly, 'It's exactly what I've been saying, mam. Now I've got an idea for a way to heat this entire place using pipes. Pipes? You know?'

Claus and Anya looked at him blankly, just as most of the other elves did.

Patch waved his hands in a circle. 'Cylinder thingies.' He raised his eyebrows, as if by sheer willpower he could get them to see what he meant.

Dooley pushed forward again, his patience beginning to wear thin. Officially Patch was only Chief Stablehand, and yet he was always butting into everyone else's business. Dooley wished the young upstart would learn to control himself and stop being so elfish. 'There's much more to see, folks,' he said briskly, leading Claus and Anya on towards the exit.

He took them downstairs to see the immense dining hall. At one side, above the orderly rows of tables and benches, the tremendous cauldron they had noticed before hung above its great firepit, its contents steaming and bubbling. A platform had been built around the cauldron's lip, large enough for six or seven elves to stand on at once. But at the moment only one elf was up there, stirring, walking patiently around and around as he pushed an enormous spoon. He wore a high white hat that looked like a chef's hat instead of the elves' usual floppy cap; an immaculate white apron and white sleeves protected his clothing from splatters and stains.

'That's Groot, our head cook,' Dooley said, waving to him.

Groot looked down over the railing at the circle of elves and their two human guests. He smoothed his neatly-waxed moustache and pointed beard, smiling graciously, welcoming them into his domain. 'Here, missus,' he called, taking to Anya immediately, as most people did, 'you must be cold and hungry.' He ladled a huge spoonful of stew into a bowl and leaned over the railing with it, passing it down to Dooley, who presented it to Anya.

Anya, who was indeed very cold and tired, took the steaming bowlful of stew gratefully. The elves stood around her, watching – Groot seeming almost to hold his breath – as they waited for her reaction.

Anya ate a spoonful rather self-consciously, and swallowed. 'Oh...' she murmured, blinking. 'It's very... um...' She glanced at Claus.

'Warm?' Dooley suggested.

'Oh yes, it's warm, all right.' Anya smiled, wanting desperately not to hurt the feelings of her hosts. Looking up at Groot, she sensed that what she said next would be vitally important to his self-

26

esteem. 'And it's very -'   'Bland?' Patch said, with a bit of a smirk.

'Bland, eh?' Groot shouted, his face reddening with anger as his over-sensitive ears picked up the insult. 'You try cooking for three hundred and forty-seven elves and see how much you can do!' His indignation began to rise and so did his voice. It was clearly an old wound. 'Some want salt! Some want spice! Some want barley, some want rice!' He began to stride the platform again, stirring the cauldron with abrupt, jerky motions that suggested he would rather be using the ladle on Patch.

'I was going to say it's very good,' Anya called gently. Groot stopped stirring abruptly and looked down at her again. He smiled, and his expression said that his heart was hers for life. Anya glanced at Patch with a smile that was equally warm, but still an admonition. He reminded her of some young humans that she knew, so bright and curious and full of life... and so hungry for some recognition of their talent that they sometimes made pests of themselves. Patch subsided with a guilty grin at her look. Already she couldn't help taking to this eager young elf more than anyone she had met; but he certainly needed to learn some good manners to match his good intentions.

At last they circled back into the elf village's great central hall, where a spiral staircase they had not climbed before led upwards to an oddly oversized cottage perched like an eyrie in the middle of the compound. It was built of the same wood as everything around it, but its lines and form looked much more familiar to Claus and Anya, and it had clearly been constructed on a much larger scale. Dooley stopped before it and stood looking at them expectantly.

'What is it?' Claus asked.

Dooley puffed his chest with pride, spreading his arms. '*Your* house,' he said. At his words all the elves around him broke into smiles and applause.

'Our house?' Anya raised her hands to her cheeks

in disbelief. They had always been as poor as church mice. She had never dreamed of having such a beautiful house of her own... even at the North Pole. Why in the world should the elves have made one for Claus and herself, out of everyone in the world? Why in the world had they been brought here? And how long were they expected to stay? She bit her lip and kept silent, telling herself that surely it would all be explained eventually.

Dooley led the wondering couple up the spiral stairs onto a small balcony and opened the solid wooden door of the house. Claus and Anya followed him inside wordlessly. Inside, the cottage was even more pleasant and cosy than Anya had imagined. Two high-backed wooden rocking chairs sat side by side, facing the living room's large fireplace. The mantel above the fireplace was decorated with small wooden animal figures and carved fir trees. Barrel-shaped storage cabinets were built into the cottage's walls and a large kitchen, already with wooden table and chairs, lay beyond. A separate bedroom with eiderdown quilts on its bed waited behind a door. After the draughty, one-room hut they had always lived in, this seemed to both Anya and Claus as wonderful and spacious as a palace. And, like the rest of the elves' village, it had a lovingly hand-crafted personality.

'Oh, it's sweet!' Anya said, still hardly daring to believe that all this had been done just for them. She clasped her hands, thinking privately that, wonderful as it was, the cottage still lacked a certain something...

'Bit drab, hmmm?' Patch murmured, sidling up to her.

'What?' Anya asked absently.

'Paint it,' Patch whispered. He hid his words behind a raised hand, pretending to yawn.

'Well, it *could* do with some colour,' Anya admitted softly, glancing around again and seeing only unadorned wood. She had always liked bright colours, but in her often bleak village, they had been few and far between. The elves certainly lived in a far more colourful world. Perhaps they could be persuaded to lend a little paint... Anya followed Claus to the window at the far side of the room. 'And some little curtains, maybe?' she added tentatively, thinking of the privacy question.

'How do you like the view?' Puffy asked, encouraging them to look out and down. Below them they saw another vast room, filled with a confusion of seats and tables and a mind-boggling variety of tools. 'That's where we make them,' he said, with a grin.

Claus glanced at him. 'Make them?' he asked blankly.

Patch winked at Anya, still following unshakeably at her side. 'He still doesn't understand, does he?'

She looked down at the grinning elf and shook her head slightly; not understanding any more than her husband did, but not quite daring to say so, since everyone seemed to think she should. She looked back at Claus, who matched her shrug of confusion with his own.

'Well, good people,' Dooley said, oblivious of their obvious puzzlement, 'we'll leave you now to a good night's sleep.' He smiled, looking as relieved and content as if his own duties had at last been fully discharged.

Claus and Anya looked at each other now with expressions that bordered on panic. After this entire fantastic tour, they still had no idea at all of why all this was happening to them... even though the elves seemed to know and Dooley clearly seemed to believe that they did too.

But now even the elves around Dooley were glancing at each other in surprise. Some of them began to whisper among themselves. Patch moved away from Anya, making small half-hidden motions with his hand, hissing through his teeth, 'Pssst, pssst!'

'What?' Dooley said, looking at him with a

mixture of concern and exasperation.

'You forgot,' Patch said, raising his eyebrows and glancing towards the window. The old elf was really getting embarrassing, he thought to himself.

'Forgot?' Dooley said.

'*You* know,' Patch urged. 'The tunnel!' he whispered. 'The tunnel!'

Dooley continued to look at him with complete incomprehension.

Patch formed the last vital clue silently with his lips and jerked his thumb at the window again. 'Toys,' he mouthed. 'Toys.'

Dooley's eyes brightened at last. He nodded briskly, his face reddening, huffing a bit to cover his embarrassment, as he took his guests in hand once more. He led them out of the front door again and down the steps for the grand finale of their tour.

They went back across the Great Hall once more, stopping this time before a set of massive wooden doors at its far side. Dooley gestured and two teams of elves hurried forward. Seizing the door handles, and each others' waists, the two chains of elves began to haul the great doors open. The doors were so tremendously high and heavy that it took nine or ten elves pulling together just to swing them outwards.

The doors moved ponderously aside, revealing what lay beyond. Claus gasped. He had thought that after all he had seen nothing more could ever astonish him. He had been wrong.

A great tunnel lay beyond the door, stretching for what seemed like miles, its far end lost from sight. From its walls and ceilings hung toys ... countless fantastic, brightly-painted toys in all shapes and sizes: dolls and wagons and musical instruments, balls and wooden animals, puppets and hoops - every kind of toy that either Claus or Anya had ever seen, and far more besides, dazzling in their profusion. Claus and Anya stood silently side by side, awestruck once again. The tunnel seemed to go on forever; they could not see any end to it.

'What are they?' Claus whispered at last, his eyes on the countless toys; asking far more than just the question his words expressed.

'Christmas toys,' Dooley said.

Claus nodded and waved his hand. 'But what are they doing here?'

Dooley began to smile. 'Waiting for you.'

'For *me*?' Claus said, incredulous. 'What have I to do with them?'

'You're going to *give* them.' Dooley raised his arms in a sweeping gesture. 'Deliver them. To the children.'

Anya flushed. 'There must be a mistake,' she murmured. 'We have no children.'

Dooley smiled again, his face filling with warm understanding. 'You do now. You have all the children of the world.'

Claus and Anya stared at him for a long moment. 'But how can I deliver so many toys? It would take *years*,' Claus said. 'Even with my reindeer – and they're pretty fast – I'd never live long enough to give out so many toys.'

Dooley shook his head ruefully. 'Still you don't see it.' He took a deep breath and looked up at them again. 'Both of you will live forever like us.'

THREE

Claus lay beneath the eiderdown quilt on his comfortable new bed in his fine new home, snugly warm in the red-striped flannel nightshirt and cap he had found waiting on a peg by his bedside. He closed his eyes for the hundredth time; found them wide open and staring into the darkness again before he knew it. He sighed heavily and changed position yet again. What was he, a simple woodcutter, doing in a place like this? Would he and his wife truly live here... forever? Would he spend forever carrying toys to children all over the world?

Dooley had finally explained to them how the elves kept watch over everything that went on in the human world that bordered on their own magical, northern land. They were fond of humans, and particularly of children, who were the only ones with the ability to see elves, because their own world still had soft edges of wonder, and not the hard edges of fact that their parents' world had. Because the elves loved children, and loved to make things, they had been making toys for human children for centuries and leaving them where the children would find them. But as time passed things changed and it grew more difficult and dangerous for the elves to venture too far into the human world; more and more of the toys they made could not be given away and were left unused in their storeroom.

Then, one long-ago long winter's night, the eldest elf of all, their venerable Ancient One, had a vision. He foretold that there would come a human who loved children as much as the elves did – who would become the one who would deliver their gifts for them to all the world.

They had been waiting – and preparing – for centuries for the day when the prophecy would come about. At last they had found, in Claus, its fulfilment. Claus felt his mind still reeling as he thought about it. His brain seemed to echo Dooley's words over and over again, refusing to let them go.

He heard his wife sigh and shift position again restlessly beside him. 'Anya?' he whispered.

'Mmmm?' she said softly. Reaching for his hand beneath the covers, she gave it a gentle squeeze.

'Me too,' Claus said. 'I can't fall asleep either.'

'I don't want to fall asleep,' Anya murmured, and he heard a smile in her voice. 'This mattress is so comfortable I hate to miss a moment of it.' They had never even dreamed of having a goosefeather bed; they had always slept on a mattress of lumpy pine boughs.

Claus sighed and rolled over again. Anya had the right idea . . . if you were going to have insomnia, at least you should enjoy it. But somehow all this miraculous good fortune simply frightened him. He had been chosen by the elves as their special messenger to the children of the world. Was he really up to such a responsibility and honour? And what about the people of his village? He supposed they would find a new woodcutter . . . He wondered curiously and a little sadly whether he and Anya would ever have reached home again through the storm. Somehow he thought he knew the answer.

And then he thought of Donner and Blitzen. They had been transported here too, but he had not seen them since they had all entered the elf village. If he was going to deliver toys, he needed his reindeer and sleigh. He ought to find out what had become of them and whether they were being well taken care of. His mind seized gratefully on the idea of something so basic and sensible. He slipped out from under the covers. Anya made a small, questioning sound and he murmured, 'It won't take long, I'll be right back.' He took a lantern from the wall and lit it.

Holding the lantern before him, he made his way tentatively down the spiral stairs, across the Great Hall, and on in the direction he remembered the elf taking as he led away the two reindeer. Almost by instinct Claus chose a way through the maze of unfamiliar log-walled corridors, ducking his head as he passed through the low, narrow doorways. All the elves seemed to be soundly asleep, and he met no one in the quiet halls.

At last he found the entrance to the stable. As he approached, he suddenly heard a familiar voice – the voice of the elf Patch – speaking softly and soothingly from somewhere inside.

'Easy, boy. It's all right, easy now...'

As Claus entered the stable, he found an unfamiliar reindeer standing in a stall to his left, peering with great interest at something he could not see. More steps showed him more reindeer, also watching something intently.

At last he saw what all the reindeer were looking at. The stable was a circular structure, with eight spacious stalls ringing its inner wall, facing into the centre. There was a reindeer standing in each of the stalls and at the front of each stall was a large wooden manger filled with hay, with each reindeer's name carved prominently on its side. At the far side of the room, instead of another stall Claus saw someone's sleeping quarters, complete with a bed. The name *Patch* was carved on the bed's footboard.

And in the stall nearest the bed, on the far side of the dimly-lit circle, Donner stood, trembling with fright. Patch, dressed in a blue and white striped nightshirt and cap, was standing beside him, offering him a hand to sniff, speaking gently and reassuringly all the while. 'I know how you feel, boy,' Patch said, with a smile. 'Strange place. Strange companions. But we're all friends here.' Carefully he stroked Donner's quivering neck and scratched him behind an ear. 'Look at old Blitzen, now – does *he* look worried?'

Claus and Donner followed Patch's glance and

34

saw Blitzen standing in the shadows beyond his friend, quite oblivious to the strangeness of it all, happily munching his way through a generous portion of feed. At the sound of his name he looked up briefly at Donner and Patch, then went back to his meal.

'Why don't you eat a little something, hmm?' Patch urged. 'It's great food, believe me. See, look, even *I* like it – Yummm!' He scooped up a handful of oats and stuffed it into his mouth, chewing gamely, like a worried father urging his infant to eat.

Claus smiled, warming to this impulsive, unpredictable young elf, who clearly cared as much about his reindeer as he did. 'He's like me, I guess,' Claus said ruefully. 'A little confused.'

Startled, Patch spun around to face him. 'Oh! I didn't –'

Claus started slowly across the wide, creaking floor. 'He's always been a fidgety type.' The warm scent of animals, feed and wood was homely and reassuring.

'He'll be just fine, sir, just as soon as he gets used to the place,' Patch said, with the assurance of someone who knew and loved animals. 'He just needs a little elf-control.' He grinned.

Claus smiled and nodded in agreement, glancing around at the other reindeer admiringly. 'You certainly seem to know reindeer. These are fine specimens.'

Patch straightened up proudly. 'Hear that, boys?' he said to the reindeer. 'You've made a good impression on your new boss.'

'Boss? Me?' Claus said, raising his eyebrows.

Patch nodded. 'Let me introduce you.' He moved to the first two stalls. The two reindeer standing behind the carved feedboxes bore a remarkable resemblance to one another. And in fact, Claus realised, they even *did* everything together. They raised their heads in unison to look at Patch, turned back in unison to study Claus with dark, equally placid eyes. 'Those two are twins,' Patch said, unnecessarily, 'Prancer and Dancer.'

He moved on to the next stalls, where two more reindeer stood side by side. Patch pointed them out. 'That's Comet,' he said as the object of his introduction casually scratched his antlers against a beam, 'and the next one is Cupid.' Cupid, graceful and large-eyed, ducked his head shyly as if he were embarrassed by the attention.

'That one is Dasher,' Patch said, moving on to the next stall. Dasher, a restless, sturdy-looking animal, raised his head eagerly, pricking up his ears. 'He loves to run, he does,' Patch grinned. 'He'd rather run than eat.'

Claus chuckled. 'Hear that, Blitzen?'

Blitzen flicked his own ears unconcernedly, not even bothering to look up from his food.

The last of the reindeer to be introduced stood snorting and muttering impatiently, as if he felt he was the victim of an oversight. Patch shook a finger at him in good-humoured admonition. 'And this noisy one here is Vixen. Keeps me up half the night with his snorts and whinnies, whinnies and snorts.'

'You sleep here?' Claus asked, both surprised and impressed that Patch should be so diligent in his care.

Patch nodded, pointing towards the one empty stall. 'Over there,' he said. 'Where I do my other work,' he added significantly. He might be just a stablehand to most of the elves around here, but he knew he was destined for better things. This was a perfect opportunity to make himself and his ideas known to their new boss, before the others could dismiss him as just a reindeer-keeper.

'They keep you busy, eh?' Claus asked politely. He stared, while trying not to seem as if he were staring, at the remarkable jumble of projects that littered Patch's quarters. A bright-red storage cabinet and a mirror bedecked with wooden reindeer antlers dominated the decor of Patch's small, hay-floored room; but draped over them both, and over every other available surface, were elaborate

36

blueprints, half-finished toy mock-ups and odd random pieces of wood and leather.

'That's the way I like it!' Patch cried enthusiastically. 'Sometimes I get so many ideas I don't know where to keep them in my head.' He turned away, rummaging through the mess on his worktable, searching for examples of some of his favourite projects, the ones that were sure to make the best impression. He held up a carefully sketched blueprint. 'A clock that wakes you up in the morning, how about that?'

'Not bad...' Claus nodded, studying the drawing; he was taken by the novelty of the concept, though he suspected privately that a cock crowing could do the job just as well.

Patch jerked out another sketch and held it up. 'A plate that whistles when the food is too hot!'

Claus scratched his beard, peering at it. 'I like the first one better,' he said frankly.

Patch shrugged and smiled, undaunted. 'One thing about me, I don't lack elf-assurance,' he said, his grin widening. And he had a million more ideas where those came from. Some of them were bound to be winners. Now that his new boss had seen his potential, he was sure he'd finally have the chance to prove what he could do.

Claus looked around him at the circle of reindeer again. 'But what do I need all these reindeer for?' he asked. Donner and Blitzen had always been quite enough to draw his sleigh. He couldn't imagine needing eight, or even four.

'You'll see,' Patch said, with a small, secret smile.

'Humph... well...' Claus bit his tongue, growing more than a little frustrated at all the coy hinting. It was rather like being given a present in January and then being forced to wait until Christmas to open it. But he didn't quite dare to demand an explanation. He was still too new and unsure about all of this – and still just a little bit afraid of hearing the answers. '... This is a very curious kind of place,' he finished weakly.

'Oh, this is nothing now.' Patch shrugged. 'Wait till you see how it gets during Season's Greetings.'

'... "Season's Greetings",' Claus repeated. 'What's that?'

'You'll see.' Patch smiled again like the cat who'd swallowed the cream. Claus gave a snort of exasperation.

But Patch was already turning away again. 'Look, sir! Now he's having a bite!'

Claus followed his glance and saw Donner standing by the feedbox, munching away at his moss and hay at last. Reassured by the presence of his master, he had finally begun to relax and eat.

Claus smiled, more to himself than to Patch, and sighed. He was still the master of his own reindeer, at least, if not of his life. He had done what he had come here to do - seen that his reindeer were in good hands. He realised that he really did *not* want to get any further into this mystery tonight, after all. He was suddenly exceedingly weary. Stifling a yawn, he nodded, bidding Patch and the reindeer a muffled 'good night'.

Leaving the stable, he started back through the halls towards his warm, waiting bed. It seemed to him this time that he could hear a faint, rhythmic sound echoing through the halls, almost as if the building itself were asleep and gently snoring.

Claus climbed the steps to his new house and went back into the bedroom. He settled into bed beside Anya, who had already fallen asleep. This time his eyes closed willingly of their own accord, and stayed closed. Soon his peaceful snoring had joined the regular sighing rhythm of the sleeping elves. The enchanted village and all its inhabitants lay peacefully at rest at last, beneath the endless, star-filled winter night.

The time flew by for Claus and Anya as they settled into their new life at the North Pole. No one offered them more explanation about their curious new existence than they had already been given, but somehow as the days and weeks passed, that no longer seemed to matter. They quickly grew to love the comfort – and the bustle – of their new home, the warm friendliness of the remarkable elves.

The elves quickly took care of the changes and alterations Claus and Anya had requested in their new house. In no time they had painted its exterior and interior with bright colours, made comfortable cushions for the rocking chairs, quilted a warm felt rug, hung up curtains – which they carefully matched to the colour of the cushions and table-cloth, all under Anya's practised supervision. They even provided the delighted couple with new clothes, in eye-catching colours to match their own.

Meanwhile, Claus grew more and more familiar with the elves' workshops. They showed him their many skilled techniques for creating a seemingly endless supply of toys, all the while politely and earnestly asking him for any suggestions he might have to improve their workmanship and designs. He marvelled at the elves' dedication, at their creativity – at the pleasure they took in creating, and their love for all children, which truly rivalled his own.

Claus also found himself gradually introduced to more inexplicable activities, by an insistent Dooley. He accepted the mysterious goings-on good-naturedly, telling himself, as Anya had done, that at least the elves seemed to know what he was doing and that surely some day he would know too.

By far one of the oddest things he was asked to do was to learn to drive a sleigh. He had protested that he was quite proficient at it already; but Dooley had insisted that Claus had never driven a sleigh like *this* one. And when Claus had been confronted by the curious arrangement of chairs, pulleys and reins that Dooley presented to him, he had to agree.

'This?' he said in disbelief, staring at the bizarre scene in Dooley's private study. A chart of the reindeer he had been introduced to in the stable, their places in harness, their names and dis-

39

tinguishing features, had been set up for him to study. But small green rocking horses took the places of reindeer before the model sleigh, and a backdrop of the starry night sky substituted for the real world outside. It struck him as especially strange that there was no ground visible in the painting.

'Only a mock-up,' Dooley had assured him. 'To simulate flight.' He watched Claus cautiously for a reaction.

'Flight?' Claus echoed, his eyes widening in disbelief. 'A flying sleigh?'

Dooley nodded. 'Drawn by eight reindeer. Obviously we can't train you in the air on the real thing.'

'Eight?' Claus repeated again. He shook his head. That explained the other reindeer in the stable... sort of. 'Well...' he murmured dubiously. He sat down in the proffered chair and took up the reins. After all he had seen here, even a flying sleigh would not really surprise him; but he thought to himself silently that he would believe it only when he saw it.

In the hours that followed he discovered to his dismay how very little he knew about driving a sleigh – at least, a flying sleigh drawn by eight reindeer. Driving in three dimensions, or even pretending to, was a subtle art and a dizzying challenge.

'Don't pull too hard or they'll bank too sharply,' Dooley called out, standing to one side as Claus manipulated the mock-up's reins. 'Just a tug.'

Claus loosened his hold on the reins, then drew them in more slowly. 'Now I'm climbing?'

'That's it,' Dooley said, nodding, 'but gently, gently. And always into the wind...'

Claus closed his eyes and tried to imagine the wind in his beard. He sighed and wiped his brow.

While Claus began his unique flight training, Anya stood in the elves' sewing room, studying their latest creation. They had wanted to make a

40

fine outfit for Claus to wear on his mysterious gift-giving journey, one that would keep him warm and comfortable as he flew through the icy winter night. It was to be a surprise, their special gift to him, and they wanted it to be something that would please and perfectly suit him.

Anya studied the dressmaker's dummy, which had been altered to suit Claus's considerable size and girth, and shook her head at the outfit draped upon it. '... No... not really... no...' she murmured. She frowned uncertainly. She liked the design very much – the long, flowing fur-trimmed coat, with trousers and cap to match, the wide black leather belt. But something was just not right... Her fists clenched in her apron pockets as she tried to decide what was missing.

She looked back at Gooba, the elves' chief tailor, and his assistants. Gooba was a neat, stylishly-clad elf who wore a tasteful blue ribbon woven into his beard; he stood by nervously, twirling his scissors on their own ribbon at his belt. 'It's nice,' she added hastily, as his face began to fall. 'Please don't think I'm criticising, but... well, green's just not his colour.' She tapped a finger thoughtfully against her lips. 'What about...?'

'What about brown?' Puffy said quickly, pushing forward, eager as always to say the right thing.

Anya hesitated.

'Red!' Patch cried, having invited himself along with her to the showing, as usual.

Anya glanced up, her eyes sparkling with pleasure as she pictured the suit before her in a new colour. '*Yes!*' she said, delighted. 'Red! Perfect. Matches his cheeks and everything.'

Puffy glanced at Patch with a slightly peevish frown, as Patch beamed proudly, having proved himself indispensible, as usual. Gooba nodded and his assistants set to work immediately, dismantling the suit to re-cut it from new cloth.

The weeks and months flowed past in a timeless

41

routine that the elves had followed for countless years, and which quickly became a comfortable rhythm for Claus and Anya as well. Weeks seemed scarcely longer than hours, so easily did they pass.

But at last a sense of unspoken anticipation began to spread among the elves, like a whispered secret passing from ear to ear. Eventually, one crystal-clear evening found them all gathered together at once, crowding into the Great Hall in front of Dooley's library, murmuring softly among themselves as they stared expectantly at the ceiling. Claus and Anya stood on their front porch, gazing down in curiosity at the scene below.

Patch stopped looking upwards as he began to develop a crick in his neck and called impatiently, 'Well?'

Dooley stood alone in the centre of his suite of rooms, which served as the information centre, library and astronomical observatory for the entire elvish community. In one of its rooms, filling the great bookcase which covered two walls and was designed to resemble a great book itself, were the numerous volumes of ancient and practical lore that the elves had collected over centuries.

Another room was given over to the comfortable chairs and great oak desk of Dooley's private study, warmed by a blaze in a vast stone fireplace. And in the centre of that room, on a raised pedestal, stood a large telescope. Dooley stood beside it now, peering into its sight as he aimed it upwards through an opening in the roof. 'Coming closer now...' he murmured to himself as he worked, '...not just yet... two more degrees north by northwest...'

He had the telescope trained on the North Star. Through the scope's eye he could follow its progress as it moved slowly through the heavens, almost directly above the elf village. He stopped mumbling, and almost stopped breathing, as it moved ever so slightly further towards... '*Now!*' Dooley shouted.

The two elves standing high in the rafters of the Great Hall, eagerly awaiting his command, began

42

to haul on heavy ropes, setting the large wooden pulley up above them into motion. Ropes and lines grew taut as the pulley began to move, and with a great creaking and racheting, something overhead began to part. The two elves hauling on the ropes looked up at the ceiling, as all the other elves were already doing, to see the centre of the roof high overhead begin to open slowly, like a flower. As the midnight sky was revealed little by little, a radiant, magical light began to beam down through the opening, suffusing the hall and the breathless watchers below with a wondrous glow. The North Star stood directly overhead, shining its light upon them as though a heavenly sign were being given.

'*Season's Greetings*!!!' Patch shouted ecstatically, at the top of his lungs. The other elves echoed his shout, until the Great Hall and the entire village rang with their joyful cries of celebration. Claus and Anya looked at each other, smiling in spite of themselves, moved and amazed by the spectacle, in spite of still having no idea whatsoever of what these cries of 'Season's Greetings' meant, to the elves or to themselves.

Claus had thought the elves were tireless workers, but in the days and weeks that followed their level of activity seemed to increase a hundredfold. The village was an endless hubbub of frantic preparation as Christmas Eve drew near again; its corridors and halls rang with hammering and talking and – music.

Patch, being only a stablehand, had no official role to play in the toymaking. But, never at a loss for ideas, and determined to make himself visible, he had decided that everyone worked more happily and efficiently to music. He loved music and played the organ well, if he did say so himself. He gathered together a small band of other elves who were equally musically inclined and set about making music while the others worked.

He sat playing the large pipe organ in the Great Hall, a remarkable instrument whose pipes were topped by tiny castles and whose keys were guarded by toy soldiers; the organ was pumped by two other elves standing on bellows at each side, playing on flutes as they pumped. They were surrounded by a zither player, another elf on mandolin, one who played a trumpet and two who, together, managed an enormous cello. All their instruments looked familiar to Claus as he and Anya looked down from their balcony, their feet tapping in time... and yet the instruments were also unique in odd ways, made from wood and brightly coloured in what he had come to think of as elf-style: beautifully functional music-makers which managed to look charmingly, deceptively like simple toys.

The band played day in and day out, its musicians varying according to their work schedules, but always with someone playing to fill the air with a bright holiday spirit while finishing touches were put on countless toys. Venerable elvish painters – the last practitioners of an art that had long ago been lost in the outer world – dipped their specially-tended beards into pots of paint and painted happy faces on wooden dolls, bright manes and saddles on horses, intricate, colourful designs on toys and building blocks. Other elves carried vast loads of finished toys on their backs to the toy tunnel, where they would be carefully stored until Christmas Eve. In the sewing department, gaily printed cloth flowed off bolts and through the hands of the industrious stitchers, becoming stuffed rag dolls and animals, or brightly-coloured dolls' clothes.

Meanwhile, Groot and his assistants worked overtime in the kitchen to feed the hungry workers. Two elves pumped the pair of enormous bellows that fanned the cooking fire from each side, day and night. Between the two bellows was a see-saw like contraption that Groot had devised, and the two elves perched on its ends. As each rode up and down in turn, they squeezed the air from one of the bellows, fanning the flames high. An almost constant train of elves carried enormous round loaves of freshly-baked bread away from the oven, balanced skilfully on their heads. And above the flames hung the great, fire-blackened cauldron where Groot cooked endless batches of his hearty and filling – but, as even Anya secretly admitted to herself – bland stew.

At last one day Anya arrived on the cooks' platform to stand beside Groot, watching him and six of his assistants pass the great stirring spoon around from hand to hand, mixing the contents of the cauldron. She held a crock of herbs in her hands and she glanced inquiringly at the sceptical-looking Groot, awaiting his final nod of approval. She was determined to make herself into a useful part of this community, having grown restless with nothing official to do while Claus oversaw the making of toys – and as far as she could tell, the greatest need the elves had for a skill of hers was in their kitchen. She had been known back in the village as an excellent cook and baker, and although she did not wish to offend the elves' kindly chef, she was certain she could only improve on his stews.

Groot nodded somewhat reluctantly and Anya stepped forward to dump the large pot of herbs into the cauldron. The elves stirred obediently. Groot ladled himself out a spoonful, sipping at it cautiously, and his eyes widened. Much to his amazement, the flavour was excellent. He smiled broadly and gave Anya the ages-old raised thumb of approval. Anya beamed, content at last.

The success of Patch's music in improving the elves' productivity brought him new attention and many compliments, especially from Claus – and from the other elves, when they saw that Claus approved. The elves respected Claus greatly; for his knowledge about toymaking, and because he was their long-awaited messenger to the world outside. They had made it very plain that he was indeed their new boss, that they looked up to him for guidance and leadership. And they had never had a

45

Season's Greetings like this before, one with such an ambitious goal at its end.

So, with Claus's approval, the elves began to initiate more of Patch's efficiency-orientated innovations. At his suggestion, the elves began working round-the-clock shifts, and in their dormitory he installed his new invention, the alarm clock. He had taken a classic hand-carved cuckoo clock and redesigned its works so that its tiny toy figures marched out as the time arrived for every shift change, and chimed the hour. The night-shift elves sleeping soundly in their beds would wake promptly, yawning and stretching, just as the weary day shift began to file in to get some much-needed sleep. The freshly wakened, well-rested elves hurried towards the newly-installed sliding-poles at the far end of the room, and slid down through the new openings in the floor like eager firemen, to begin their night shift in the factory below.

Gone were the days of relaxed, easy-going toymaking. And gone too were the beds with each elf's name carved at the foot. Now the tired elves reached down as they stood ready to slide under the covers and turned a knob on the footboard; changing the occupant's name like a bus driver changing the sign for the bus's destination. Then the exhausted elves dropped into their beds in unison and within moments they were asleep and snoring.

As a result of his successful efficiency projects, and because of Claus's respect for his skill, Patch was also given the plum project of designing a new sleigh to carry the toys on their Christmas journey. Patch had argued that Claus's old sleigh was much too small and hopelessly outdated, and Claus had rather wistfully agreed. With Claus's go-ahead, Patch called Honka, Boog and Vout together and got to work on a new sleigh that he already knew would be a work of art as well as a marvel of technological expertise. He had long ago drawn up plans, and now he oversaw the project of making his dream into a reality. He was busier, and happier, than he had ever been in his life, now that his creativity had a positive outlet.

At last Christmas Eve arrived and the final preparations for the Great Event began. An elf stood above a vast conveyor belt and, under Patch's careful supervision, poured the contents of a mysterious bag into a sieve, grinning with anticipation. As the contents spilt out and down, they appeared to be pure glittering stardust.

Below Patch, looking up, another elf loaded ordinary reindeer feed – a mixture of grain and moss – onto a lower level of the conveyor belt. Between the two levels, a third elf began to shake the star-filled sieve. Stardust drifted down through the sieve and settled onto the moving pile of feed, which began to glow and twinkle as if it were somehow transformed by the touch of magic. A small amount of the glittering dust remained when all the feed was treated; Patch scooped up the precious residue and put it back into a bag for storage. The leftover stardust regenerated magically, so that it never ran low.

Claus strolled through the toy factory with a smile, looking over busy shoulders, making final adjustments: correcting a painting error here, fixing a joining there. Everywhere he nodded his approval and open admiration at a tremendous job well done.

He stopped along the way to watch an elf with a bucket of stardust, who stood before a wide sheet of paper that had been dyed green to brighten up the dreary season of winter. The elf reached into the bucket, grabbed a handful of stardust, and flung it at the paper. As it touched its surface the stardust seemed to fuse there, becoming one with the paper, adhering in graceful patterns of red and gold snowflakes to delight the eye, a symbol of winter's own beauty. This was the wrapping paper that would transform gifts into a bright surprise to be opened on Christmas morning by happy children everywhere.

Back in the stables, Patch and his assistants groomed the reindeer with extra care as the animals ate their ration of specially treated feed. As Patch and his comrades finished grooming each reindeer, polishing every hoof and horn, Patch held his antler-framed mirror up before them so that they could admire themselves. They were special and fortunate creatures indeed, and well-loved, and he wanted them all to know it. The reindeer snorted softly, nosing at their reflections as if they approved of, and appreciated, the splendid effect. And then they were led from their stalls to be harnessed up in their new, perfectly-fitted, traces of red and green leather, decorated with their names and covered with merrily jingling sleighbells.

Inside the toy tunnel the elves stood on high catwalks and began to take down the countless toys suspended from the ceiling and lining the walls, attaching them to pulleys and sending them down to the tunnel floor. A large canvas sack lay there, gaily decorated with green Christmas trees on a background of red felt and edged with more bright brass bells. No matter how many toys the waiting elves dropped into the sack, its capacity seemed limitless, and it never was completely filled.

Claus went back to his waiting house and patient wife as the day of Christmas Eve drew to a close. Anya fed him a hot hearty meal to keep him warm and give him energy on his historic journey. After dinner he went into the bedroom to change. For the first time he put on the new suit presented to him that day by the elves.

'Northwest crosswind, point left of land. South-east crosswind, point right...' he murmured, hardly seeing his reflection as he pulled his new fur-trimmed hat on firmly to keep it safe from the wind. But no matter how often he thought about it, he still found it difficult to believe that he was actually going to be *flying* a sleigh tonight.

Anya stood in the doorway, smiling, wearing her own new holiday outfit which the elves had presented to her, to her delight, along with Claus's. She wore a bright red jacket over a ruffled blouse and apron of canary yellow with green polka dots, and a black skirt striped with yellow ribbons. She loved bright colours and this was far finer than even her best holiday clothes had ever been. She wore a cap of red and green with trailing ribbons over her neatly-plaited blonde braids. She moved to stand before Claus, beaming as she gazed at the results of the elves' sewing skills and her own good taste. 'You look *wonderful*,' she said.

Claus stood back from the mirror, studying himself full length now that his outfitting was complete. He smiled in spite of his nervousness. The figure who stood reflected before him was undeniably impressive. His full white beard was magnificently displayed against an eye-catching bright red coat and trousers trimmed with white fur, a wide black belt and leather boots. 'It does suit me, doesn't it?' he murmured.

Standing beside him, Anya folded her hands before her. 'A handsome man looks good in anything,' she said, her eyes filled with love. She came over to him and kissed him on the cheek. 'I'm so proud of you.'

There was a knock at the door.

Claus looked up, all his nervousness instantly back again. The door opened and Dooley stepped into the room, his normally cheerful face wearing a very serious expression. 'It's time, sir.'

'Oh,' Claus said, swallowing the lump in his throat. He stood rooted where he was.

'They're waiting,' Dooley said, and gestured encouragingly towards the front door.

Claus nodded. 'Right, right, coming...' He started out of the house with a strained smile on his face. Anya took his arms as they crossed the Great Hall below, reassuring him.

Waiting inside the echoingly-empty toy tunnel were all of the elves who had worked so long and hard to make this moment happen. They had lined up in silent rows along each side of the tunnel – not murmuring or chattering, as he glanced in through the vast door, but only looking on, hushed with an almost reverent expectation. An atmosphere of great seriousness hung over the hall, as if a coronation were about to begin.

Claus barely had time to be surprised at the size of the gathering before his eyes settled on something which lay waiting for him in the empty centre of the tunnel. In the middle of the strangely vacant space sat a magnificent sleigh, the one which Patch had lovingly designed for him, covered with exquisitely hand-carved Christmas decorations – toys and trees and holly, all painted with the reds and yellows and greens and blues the elves loved so much. The eight reindeer stood in a line before it, proudly wearing their newly-made harnesses and looking about expectantly.

As Claus entered the tunnel with Anya and Dooley, a murmur spread through the crowd of waiting elves.

'He looks *wonderful!*' Puffy exclaimed.

Gooba, who had overseen the sewing of the outfit personally, preened and fluffed his beribboned beard. 'A perfect fit, if I do say so myself,' he murmured.

'The colour, the style,' Patch raved, never for a moment forgetting his own part in it all, 'I'm telling you, that outfit is *him*, it's just *him!*'

Claus moved out into the centre of the tunnel to stand by his new sleigh; Anya took her place alongside Patch and Dooley at the front of the crowd, her cheeks flushed with delight.

The crowd fell silent again and for a long moment the vast room was filled with a breathless expectancy. Claus stood waiting, still not certain what he was waiting for.

Then suddenly a strange, haunting music began

to echo softly through the empty tunnel. A golden light began to suffuse the hall, radiating outwards from the seemingly infinite distance of its far end. The watchers began to murmur once more, as a retinue of elves appeared out of the light and began to proceed solemnly down the tunnel towards Claus.

First came six elves who bore like a ceremonial train an immensely long beard, its ends neatly braided. As they emerged from the light, Claus saw that the beard belonged to a tremendously impressive and ancient-looking elf, who walked slowly and with great dignity behind them. There was an aura of wisdom and goodness about him that was as tangible as the light and music. Claus and Anya knew at once that this was the Ancient One, the elves' true spiritual leader, who had guided them in this selfless project. As the ancient wise man proceeded down the tunnel, the elves bowed their heads, removing their hats and clutching them to their chests. It was the only time Claus or Anya had ever seen them remove their hats; the gesture was one of profound respect. Even the reindeer bowed their heads as the ancient elf passed. Donner and Blitzen, seeing the others bow around them, lowered their own heads respectfully.

Claus, standing alone beside his new sleigh, pulled off his own hat, awed and a little frightened, as he saw the Ancient One approach. Anya, standing at Patch's side, took hold of the young elf's hand and squeezed it tightly, because she could not reach Claus's hand.

The majestic, mystical music swelled in the hall, bringing tears of emotion to Anya's eyes, as the elvish wise man stopped before Claus. The gathered community of elves held their breath, until the Ancient One spoke at last. 'The prophecy has come to pass,' he said, his voice like parchment crinkling, 'that there would come to us a chosen one to carry our gifts to the world.' And now the elves began to murmur, chanting with the music, intoning a soft background note that harmonised with his quavering words. 'That having no child of his own,' the Ancient One said, 'he would love *all* children.' The elves chanted another sonorous tone as he paused again, shifting and modulating each time the ancient paused in his ritual recitation. 'That he would himself be an artisan, a craftsman, a skilful maker of toys,' the Ancient One continued. 'That the joy of giving would be alive in his heart, and the wish to bring joy would be embodied in his spirit.'

Anya tore her gaze from the ancient elf to look again at her husband, feeling as if she would burst with pride.

'And finally that he... um...' The ancient elf paused, scratching his head, as his memory suddenly failed him under the stress of the auspicious occasion. '...er...'

Dooley twisted his hands together anxiously, wondering whether he should prompt the old man.

'Ah, yes!' The Ancient One brightened, remembering. He smiled at Claus. 'That he should be a good driver.'

Claus felt his own mouth try to form a smile and he kept his face straight with an effort, as the Ancient One said solemnly, 'Now Chosen One! Come forward!'

Claus stepped forward with bowed head, suddenly filled with a great and humble pride.

'From this day on, now and forever, you will bring our gifts to all the children in all the world. And all this is to be done on Christmas Eve.' The elves had chosen Christmas Eve because Christmas was the holiday on which Claus himself had always given his gifts, the most special day in the year for him, his village and the people of the northlands they were most familiar with – and because it was the time of year when many other people around the world had their special holidays.

Claus drew a deep breath. 'May I speak?' he whispered, lines of sudden worry furrowing his brow. The ancient elf nodded. 'How can I do so much in just one night?' At last he dared to ask the

52

question that had been secretly plaguing him for months.

The ancient elf smiled and raised his hands. 'Know then that Time travels with you. The night of the world is a passage of endless night for you until your mission is done. This is your legacy, as is the gift of flight.' He reached up and placed his gnarled hand firmly on Claus's right shoulder. His voice rising strongly until it filled the hall, he proclaimed, 'Let all within the sound of my voice and all who live on the earth know that you will be called ... Santa Claus.'

'*Santa Claus*,' the elves echoed, all together, their voices hushed with awe. It was a title that bore the highest honour the elves could bestow.

Anya's eyes filled with tears again as she was caught up in the wonder of the moment. Patch, ever alert and exceedingly fond of her, passed her a handkerchief.

'And let us all say – Merry Christmas,' the Ancient One proclaimed.

'Merry Christmas!' the elves shouted, the words echoing with happiness and joy.

The ancient elf turned away then, taking his leave, and went slowly back down the tunnel, with his train of beard-bearers following behind him. He disappeared at last into the distant golden light.

Patch, Boog, Honka and Vout stepped forward then, with four other elves behind them. Each of them carried a large bowl filled with specially treated reindeer feed, each bowlful glittering subtly. They offered a bowl of feed to each of the waiting reindeer, who ate it eagerly.

The effect on the reindeer was immediate, and remarkable. As Claus watched, he saw their eyes brighten and their chests expand; they almost seemed to glow themselves with a magical energy made visible. They began to paw restlessly at the floor, tossing their heads and snorting, impatient now to be off on their night's adventure.

Claus – Santa Claus – climbed into his waiting

sleigh at last and blew a kiss to his wife. Anya waved, her eyes still shining as she gazed at him with a wide, happy smile. Claus waved back to her and to the assembled multitude of elves. He picked up the reins and collected the reindeer, collecting his thoughts at the same time. He took a deep breath. 'Yo!' he cried, signalling the reindeer to start forward. The reins tightened as the reindeer leapt into action.

'MERRY CHRISTMAS!' the elves shouted in joyous farewell, throwing the hats they still held in their hands high into the air.

The reindeer charged away down the tunnel; the beautiful hand-carved sleigh with its precious load flew forward as if it were shot out of a cannon. Hooves echoed ringingly on the tunnel floor as the reindeer picked up speed. Halfway down the tunnel they turned sharply, heading down the specially constructed exit ramp. Like a ski run, it sloped downwards and then up, giving them momentum and lift. The reindeer ran down its length and then, swooping upwards, sprang out into empty air. Launching themselves from its tip, their gleaming hooves surging, they soared on and up into the sky, leaving a trail of magic stardust behind them. The cheers of the elves followed them out into the night. The sleigh continued to gain altitude as the reindeer galloped strongly onward, rising through the clear, frigid air of the winter night.

The newly-proclaimed Santa Claus gaped at the reindeer flying ahead of him through the air; gazed from side to side and down at the frozen wastelands far below, his face alight with amazement and sheer delight. The wind whipped his beard, and he began to laugh. The hearty, heartfelt laughter that would ring down through the years, to fill countless children's hearts with happiness, echoed out across the silent, silver fields of snow for the first time.

Back in the elves' village, Dooley rushed into his study to peer through his telescope. He aimed the lens rapidly across the sky, tracking the fast-disappearing sleigh. "Atta Santa!' he chortled, as he found the man in red in his sights. 'Perfect... That's it, pull back - now bank left - right, that's the way!' His own hands pulled back and let out on imaginary reins, soaring through the sky in his own imagination along with his pupil, as he watched the flying sleigh grow smaller and smaller in the distance...

The sleigh sailed on through the star-filled sky. Santa Claus watched the team of eight reindeer galloping tirelessly ahead of him, Dancer and Prancer synchronised in every motion even now.

'Faster, boys!' he cried gleefully, having more fun than he had ever imagined was possible. 'Feel the wind in your faces!' The reindeer leapt forward in eager response and the sleigh soared even higher.

But not all the reindeer were enjoying themselves as much as their driver was. Donner, as skittish as always, was realising to his dismay that vertigo was a fear he had never even thought of before... but the moment they shot out of the toy tunnel he had become suddenly, terrifyingly aware of it. He looked down... and down... at the snow far below. He shut his eyes, swallowing hard.

Claus, seeing Donner's obvious distress, called, 'Come on, Donner - forward ho! Nothing to worry about,' he said reassuringly, 'it's only flying.' He shook his head, as the words registered in his brain. 'It's only flying???!! What am I saying?' he cried. Clutching his hat wih a mittened hand, he laughed again, this time in disbelief.

Donner opened his eyes and took a deep breath, finding the courage to continue, reassured by the sound of a familiar voice - and by the fact that he was not the only one astonished to find himself in this position.

'All right -' Claus called, pulling himself together again, 'bank to the right. Ready?' He pulled back and up on the reins and felt the team respond beautifully. All his training had certainly paid off and he appreciated at last how good a teacher Dooley had been. The sleigh banked to the right and soared higher still, until it seemed to him that he could reach out to catch a star from the crystalline bowl of the sky and tuck it into his pocket.

'That's it!' Dooley said, turning away from his telescope to make his report at last. 'Picture perfect!' He smiled, still seeming to hear the joyful echo of Santa Claus's laughter filling the night.

FOUR

Santa Claus travelled in that one night far beyond
any lands he had ever known, to places he had
heard of only in legends and stories... and further
yet. And everywhere he left a gift for each child
whose home he saw. His bag of toys never grew
empty, his reindeer never grew weary and neither
did he. Even though the night seemed endless, still
it seemed to be over almost before it had begun, as
he finished his circuit of the world that the elves
knew, and the reindeer headed northwards once
more with the light of a new dawn trailing behind
them.

He returned to his North Pole home, to the
jubilant elves and the welcoming arms of his wife...
and only then did he feel his weariness. He ate a
good hot meal and slept long and deeply – dreaming
all the while of the happy, wondering faces of
children around the world as they woke and found
his gifts. And the next day, the elvish toymakers
began their work again, already preparing for the
next Christmas.

And after that the weeks, months and years passed
with a magical rhythm that made them seem
scarcely longer than days. Every year, as Christmas Eve drew near – as another old year passed
away and another new year was born in the world
outside the elves' enchanted land – people all over
the world rejoiced in the celebration of their holiday
customs, so varied, and yet so full of the same spirit
of good will. And each year Santa Claus set out on
his journey, bringing gifts and happiness to every

child he could find, wanting no other reward than the right to go on sharing his love and the elves' love with the children of the world... and always richly rewarded just the same, by the very privilege of brightening their lives.

And as the years passed, the world outside began, slowly but surely, to change. The toys the elves made began to change as well, reflecting the new interests of the children Santa visited, and also their growing variety, as he extended his toy-giving journey farther and farther beyond the edges of the elves' domain.

But Claus and Anya, gazing at their own faces in the mirror, saw no signs of change at all. Just as time never touched the elves, it no longer touched the two humans, or even their reindeer. Year after year husband and wife turned as one to gaze at each other, smiling; still amazed at the miracle that had brought them here, still grateful that they had been chosen out of all the world's people for this rich, rewarding life.

But even as they were always conscious of the good fortune that had brought them here, they began to feel as if they had always lived here among the elves, who had become like one vast family to them. The traditional routine of toymaking, the comfortable patterns of day to day life leading towards and culminating each year in Santa Claus's Christmas journey, was a comfortable and fulfilling one.

More and more, Claus found his view of the world broadening and changing with the passage of time, with each fresh experience as he visited the far reaches of the earth. And his presence, touching the lives of children everywhere, changed their lives as well. He became a figure of wonder-filled tales and legends, a symbol of goodness and generosity in a world which often had not enough of either. And more and more, as the world and its people gradually became more sophisticated, the children began to reach out in whatever way they could to communicate with their beloved Santa Claus.

Santa Claus entered Dooley's office at the start of a new day, as yet another Christmas Eve was drawing near, to find a stack of strange looking messages piled on the chief elf's wide desk top. Dooley sat in his comfortable high-backed chair, reading one of the letters.

'What's that?' Claus asked curiously.

Dooley looked up over his spectacles and smiled. 'More and more are learning to write now,' he said, 'asking for what they want.'

Claus raised his eyebrows and took the proffered letter from Dooley's hand to study it. The calendar on Dooley's wall said that it was already the fourteenth century in the world where he had once lived. The letter had been scrawled on a sheet of dried sheepskin by a resourceful boy who had apparently used the glowing tip of a stick from the fireplace. 'Dear Santa Claus,' it read, 'I would like a ball-and-cup toy. I would be most happy if the ball could be blue and the cup yellow...'

Claus smiled, nodding, and handed the letter back to Dooley, who slipped it into his new *Out* basket. Santa Claus had instructed that all special requests be filled if possible because of the extra effort the children had made to write to him. Puffy, the elves' painstaking production chief, was in charge of making certain that all the requests were carefully filled by the carvers and beard-painters of his industrious production line.

As more years passed, every Christmas season brought more special toy requests for Santa Claus to fill. As the number of letters grew, Claus kept his habit of reading each one personally; miraculously, he found that his memory only improved as their numbers increased, so that he was able to deliver each child's most-wanted toy on his Christmas flight.

And over the years the requests changed and

changed again, along with the lives and imaginations of the children, until sometimes even the elves were hard-pressed to fill their special requests:

Julio, a gypsy boy, scribbling on parchment with a nail dipped in berry juice, wrote, 'My father makes music with a guitar and my uncle with a fiddle, but I can't play anything. So could you send me a box with music in it? Then everybody would see I, too, can bring songs to the caravan.'

Santa (everyone in the elf village called him 'Santa' now for short, except his wife) scratched his head and tugged thoughtfully on his beard as he put the letter down. A box filled with music ... even he could not imagine how that could be done. He called over a nearby elf and sent him to find Patch.

Through the years, Santa Claus had become a firm believer in Patch's ingenuity and creativity. Patch still oversaw the tending of the reindeer, for no one had a better way with them – but more and more Santa recognised and encouraged Patch's amazing ability to create new toys and gadgets. The young elf responded to Santa's appreciation of his work with an overwhelming eagerness that filled both Claus and Anya with fond amusement, and sometimes still caused them to shake their heads. He was as dear as a son to them, but they often thought, in their private moments, that he would never stop running at top speed, or learn to stop and smell the flowers. Of all the elves in the village, he seemed to be the only one who was never satisfied with the way things were; he was always looking for a new way to do things even if the old way worked perfectly.

But over-eager as he sometimes was, Patch was an undeniable creative genius. He had never failed yet to come up with a solution to any request. In almost less time than it took Santa to summon him and show him Julio's letter, he was back with a hand-cranked music box, the answer to the gypsy boy's dream. Santa grinned and nodded as Patch turned its handle and it played a tinkling tune.

Patch beamed, basking in the approval he could never get enough of.

More years and more Christmas Eves than Santa Claus cared to count flew by. His legend grew, and so did the flow of letters from children everywhere. As always, each year's letters brought some new challenge to be solved. And sometimes the problem was not simply a creative one...

In the stately dining room of a manor house in one of the Thirteen Colonies (of what would soon become the United States), the dinner table was set with crisp linens and fine silver for a Thanksgiving feast. But over by the hearth a young boy in knee breeches and a powdered wig was holding a squalling cat down on the hearthstones while he tied a stick to its tail. His little sister Sarah pulled at his arms, crying, as she tried to make him stop. The boy pushed her away, laughing cruelly, until their sturdy nanny came back into the room and separated them with an angry scolding.

During dinner Sarah picked fitfully at her turkey, staring unhappily at her brother, too worried about her favourite pet to enjoy the feast. And after dinner she hurried to her room and scribbled a letter, her tears dripping onto the parchment as she wrote, making the ink run and blur.

'Dear Santa Claus, I do not ask for any present for myself this Christmas. I ask only that you make my brother stop being cruel to my cat Tabby...'

When she had finished, she blotted the ink with sand and left the letter on her writing table. She put on her nightgown and climbed into bed; curling up with Tabby safe in her arms, she was quickly asleep.

And as she slept, a gentle breeze slipped down through the flue of her bedroom's fireplace. Catching up the piece of parchment in invisible hands, the magical breeze, which searched the world each night for letters like hers, bore the parchment sheet back to the fireplace and straight up the chimney.

61

The letter soared up into the sky, borne on the back of the wind, until it disappeared into the clouds high above.

The breeze-borne letter sailed on through moonlit clouds, always northwards, until at last it reached the point at the top of the world where all directions were south, and all things were touched with magic.

Then, far above the elves' village, the letter began to fall, spiralling down until it was sucked in through the flue of Dooley's own fireplace, to land squarely in a bin marked *Incoming Mail*.

Dooley's new assistant, perched on a ladder, glanced up from the enormous ledger that now reached from ceiling to floor, and in which he carefully recorded every child's toy request. He sighed and shook his head. Soon he was going to need an assistant of his own. He looked back at the ledger page, which was far taller than he was, and went on carefully recording, *598 dolls, 74 hoops*...

Dooley entered the room behind him and scooped the latest pile of letters from the basket, carrying them away to read.

Late in the day Anya and Claus sat finishing a meal of hearty soup and freshly-baked bread, enjoying a quiet evening together in their snug kitchen. They glanced up in surprise as someone knocked on their door. Claus answered the door and found Dooley there, clutching a single letter in his hand. The elderly elf said respectfully, 'I hate to disturb you, sir, but I think this letter needs some extra attention.' Claus beckoned him inside as Anya appeared in the kitchen doorway, wiping a clean dish.

Claus sat down in his armchair before the crackling fire, put on his spectacles, and began to read the letter. A frown of concern spread over his face and he held the letter out to Anya. He sat pensively while waiting for her to read the letter in turn.

Anya sat down and began to read, and her own face grew pink with indignation. '"... I'm sure he hurts the poor little kitten,"' she read aloud, unable to keep silent any longer, '"and when I cry, he just laughs at me. Yours most sincerely, Miss Sarah Foster."' She looked up again, her eyes shining with outrage. 'You were right to bring this to our attention, Dooley. That little boy should not get a present.' She looked back at Claus expectantly.

Claus pulled at his beard. 'No present for him?' he said, his forehead wrinkling with the expression of a man caught in an extremely painful dilemma. 'But every child gets a present,' he protested.

Anya lifted her head, her own face set with determination. 'It's time to change that rule,' she said firmly, her sense of fairness and justice kindled.

Claus shook his head uncertainly. 'You'll have folk saying that Santa Claus rewards only the good little boys and girls.'

'And isn't that as it should be?' Anya asked, raising her eyebrows.

Claus was silent for a long moment. At last he nodded. 'All right,' he said, looking up at his wife. There were times when one had to make a difficult choice and stand by it. Through their many years together, he had grown to trust implicitly Anya's instincts of right and wrong. 'Dooley,' he said. 'You will have to keep track of who is good and bad.'

'Yes, sir.' Dooley nodded and started for the door.

'And be careful,' Santa called. 'I'll be checking your list more than once.' This was a matter so important that he could not afford to make a single mistake in that list.

Dooley nodded again, with a smile, and closed the door behind him.

Santa sighed, looking back at Anya with a weary smile of his own. He wished for a moment that things could remain as they had been in the beginning. Why did everything always have to change and grow more complicated? But then, he had to admit that his arrival here had been the biggest change he would ever know – and it had certainly been a good one. He smiled again at his wife and reached out to pat her hand.

More years flew past and the inevitable changes still came, faster and faster now. Not only in the styles of toys and their numbers, in the always-difficult judgements of who deserved to receive them – but also in the widening of the territory which Santa covered in his one extraordinary night a year. His fame had now spread to nations far beyond the lands the elves knew or were known in. Now he received letters in countless different languages, from children whose backgrounds and faces were as different and diverse as their letters were. The toys they asked for, and the homes he delivered them to, were marvellously strange and different as well. Even the toy houses the elves made took on new and different forms; new games were created each year to keep young minds growing; dolls now had black hair as well as blond and brown, curls, plaits and topknots – round blue eyes and brown almond-shaped ones, and skin of many different colours. Discovering the infinite variety of the world's children was one new change that never failed to delight Claus and set him to remembering the misty, distant time when he had been only a simple peasant, never even dreaming of the vast and varied world which lay beyond the boundaries of his own village.

There were, as always, changes he was not as fond of, however. 'All this progress may be a fine thing, but the way people are changing is not such a fine thing,' he remarked to Anya one evening, just before the start of his latest Christmas flight. He sat finishing his second helping of dessert, as Anya kept him company at the table, having long since finished her own dinner. She nodded in agreement, but her gaze wandered to the buttons of his bright yellow polka-dot shirt, which were straining over his more-than-ample girth. She had noticed that he always left his favourite red waistcoat unbuttoned these days, and she knew that he could no longer fasten his favourite green jacket. She was glad that he still enjoyed her cooking after so many years, but secretly she was sad to see him losing his handsome figure.

'People don't trust each other the way they used to,' Claus went on unhappily. 'Years ago, the doors were always open. Now they lock 'em, afraid somebody's going to steal what's theirs.'

Anya raised her eyebrows. 'How do you get in?' she asked.

Claus shrugged. 'Windows, when I can. But mostly chimneys, and I don't much like it. I don't like the going in –' In his mind's eye he saw himself squeezing his ample form into the narrow opening of a chimney, high on top of a crochet-and-grillwork bedecked Victorian rooftop. 'And even less do I like the going out.' He sighed, picturing the inevitable plate of now-traditional delicacies waiting for him on the mantel when he had finished setting presents beneath a gaily decorated tree. The snacks were always so good and he knew that the children who left them there would be terribly disappointed if he didn't eat them... And each time he climbed back into the chimney to leave, it was just a little more difficult. As it became increasingly difficult, he was forced to use his magic to go in and out of the chimneys.

Anya bit her tongue, on the verge of saying something, but lost her nerve and only nodded sympathetically. Perhaps tomorrow she would think of a way to mention such a touchy subject...

The next day, however, fate saw fit to take the matter gracefully out of her hands. As Santa made his rounds of the toy factory, Dooley came up to him, holding out an English newspaper. As the other elves gathered around curiously, Dooley cleared his throat and began to read aloud:

> *"Twas the night before Christmas*
> *and all through the house,*

Not a creature was stirring,
Not even a mouse.'

Santa chuckled appreciatively, as he began to listen to this new retelling of his annual journey. Anya came up beside him and took his arm, smiling as she saw his face. 'What is it?' she asked.

'It's a poem, about me,' he said. 'They say it's a very big hit.' He beamed proudly, forgetting as he did that pride usually went before a fall. He turned back to listen as Dooley continued reading.

'He had a broad face and a
little round belly,
That shook when he laughed
like a bowl full of jelly.'

Claus froze, the smile and all the colour disappearing from his face. '... *What was that?*' he gasped in disbelief, feeling suddenly utterly mortified.

'Pardon?' Dooley glanced up absently.

'What was the last part?' Claus asked again, his voice barely functioning.

Dooley looked at the page and read unsuspectingly, '"*He had a broad face...*"'

'Broad? A broad face?' Claus huffed, his face turning red with indignation now. He turned to Anya frowning. 'Do I have a broad face?'

Anya looked down, twisting the hem of her apron self-consciously. 'Well... your particular bone structure, darling –' She glanced up at him again, her own cheeks reddening with the awkwardness of the moment.

Claus turned back to Dooley, glowering. 'Yes, yes, go on,' he said gruffly. He waved a hand.

'"*And a little round belly,*"' Dooley read, his own voice barely audible now, as even he finally realised his dreadful oversight.

Claus's face had grown as red as his jacket now. Anya stared worriedly at him, expecting to see steam coming out of his ears any moment. 'Go on,' he said, between clenched teeth.

Dooley cleared his throat, wishing fervently that somehow the floor would just open up and swallow him whole. '*"That shook when he laughed/ Like a bowl full of..."*'

'Jelly,' Claus finished grimly.

Dooley glanced up at him, his shoulders hunched with unspeakable chagrin. 'It's...just...a poem...' he wheezed.

'Is that how they think I look?' Claus asked querulously, not even listening. He put his hands on his hips, turning back to Anya again.

Anya moved her hands in the air, then clasped them together. 'Well... you know,' she murmured unhappily, 'the snacks...'

Claus turned and stalked away through the circle of embarrassed elves, huffing wordlessly, trying to save what little of his dignity remained intact.

That evening, in the privacy of his own kitchen, Claus sat down to a Christmas Eve dinner which consisted entirely of four carrot sticks, two celery sticks and an olive. He stared at his plate for nearly as long as it would have taken him to eat his usual five-course holiday meal. Anya stood motionless by the stove, thinking sadly that she had never seen her husband look so grim. Was such misery really necessary? she wondered. She would still love him if he were twice as fat... and so would the world's children, for he would still be their own Santa Claus. She sighed and shook her head.

At last Claus picked up a carrot stick and began to crunch it loudly, like the reindeer in the stable down below munching their magic fodder for the evening's flight.

That night Santa Claus flew out into the darkness feeling like a paragon of restraint and resolve. He promised himself that he would not eat a single thing tonight and by next year he would be so fit and trim that elves or people would hardly recognise him.

His resolve lasted all the way across the frozen

polar wastes and onto the first rooftop of a house, down the first chimney... until he saw that first plate of biscuits waiting for him on the mantelpiece and the sign beside it, lettered in a child's awkward scrawl: FOR SANTA CLAUS.

Santa started towards the chimney; then stopped and stood for a long moment before the mantel, trying to draw his eyes away from the sight. He shook his head, started towards the hearth again; looked back. And then, in a moment that verged on sheer panic, his will-power collapsed utterly. He swept the biscuits from the plate – all of them – and began to cram them into his mouth, chewing and swallowing like a starving man. He was still chewing as he made his way up the chimney and climbed back into his sleigh to start on his way once more.

Swallowing the last bite of the last biscuit, he smiled contentedly as he flew on, thinking how pleased that child would be to know that Santa Claus had enjoyed her biscuits more than any he had ever eaten... 'Look, boys,' he called to his reindeer (who were glancing back at him in mild disapproval), 'here's how it is: I'm sure there are some skinny, meagre, wasting-away men who are perfectly good fellows, but...' he shook his head as he thought of what terrible things abstinence was doing to his good nature, 'the world wants a jolly Santa, well-fed and laughing.' And he began to laugh, a great, joyful, rolling *Ho-ho-ho*! as he realised that he was perfectly happy with himself just the way he was. He looked down at his stomach in satisfaction. 'And it did not shake when I laughed like a bowl of jelly, you silly poet you.' He patted his wide black belt, which was let out to the last notch, exonerated.

The sleigh and reindeer soared up over the rooftops of the sleeping village and on into the night, leaving a faint trail of laughter and sleigh-bells echoing in their wake.

FIVE

Santa, Dooley and Puffy stood together in the elves'
busy workshop, eyeing Patch's latest toy proposal
with something less than their usual level of
enthusiasm.

'It looks like just another hoop,' Santa said,
letting Patch down gently. 'What's so special about
this one? I can remember those things centuries
ago.' It was the twentieth century by now, and he
was slightly surprised to see the forward-looking
Patch so far behind the times.

Patch held up the unusually large, brightly-
painted hoop, shaking his head at their lack of
imagination. 'No, this isn't just one of those hoops
you roll,' he protested. 'Watch!' He flipped the hoop
over his head and shoulders. When it had dropped
halfway down his body, he began to gyrate his hips
wildly, as if he were doing some strange new dance.
Instead of falling to his feet, the hoop began to circle
around and around his slender middle. In another
few decades, almost any child would know it as a
Hula Hoop. Patch was still very much ahead of his
time – unfortunately, too far ahead for the isolated
world he lived in ... as was so often the case.

Santa Claus pursed his lips, trying to gauge his
little friend's intentions. 'What's the point of it?' he
asked.

'It's fun,' Patch said breathlessly. 'And,' he
puffed, having saved its real selling point for last,
'it's good exercise.'

Santa stared at the wildly gyrating elf a moment
longer, and shook his head. 'No, no,' he murmured
at last, reluctant as always to turn down any
workable idea. 'I don't think so really, Patch.' He

turned and began to walk away.

Patch let the hoop drop and leapt out of it, hurrying after Santa to catch his arm, his mouth open to protest. In all the centuries they had been together, he had never quite learned how to take *no* for an answer gracefully.

Santa turned back. 'I honestly can't see people going wild about a hoop,' he said briskly before Patch could continue. 'Take my word for it, Patch. I was a "people" myself once.'

Patch closed his mouth, pressing it into a line of brave acceptance as he nodded, this time acknowledging defeat. But his disappointment still showed clearly in his dark eyes.

Santa patted him on the shoulder, wanting to make the hurt look disappear; wanting to reassure Patch, whose creative mind was far too sensitive for his own good, that he was still the best inventor around. 'I hope I haven't filled you full of elf-doubt,' he said gently. 'Keep up the good work.'

Patch lifted his chin, putting on the brave front he always affected in situations like this. After all the years, and all his successful inventions, he still felt as insecure as ever deep inside – as so many creative people do. Somehow he was never able to convince himself that absolute perfection was beyond his, or anyone's grasp. He nodded, turning away, his eyes downcast as he said, 'Well, back to the drawing board.' He picked up his hoop and walked out of the workshop.

Santa sighed as he turned back to Dooley and Puffy, who were still standing at the other end of the workshop, watching all that occured. As he drew closer, he saw the smile on Puffy's face – a smile that was not in the least sympathetic. 'As for you, Puffy,' he said, with unaccustomed sternness, 'don't look so elf-satisfied. At least he *tried*.' Santa was well aware of the unspoken rivalry between the two elves, knowing that Patch envied Puffy's responsible position, while Puffy was secretly envious of Patch's creativity. Puffy was a good, careful worker, but he was as stolid and uninspired as Patch was brilliant and unpredictable.

Chastened, Puffy hastily wiped the smirk from his face and hurried off to his duties. But secretly he continued to feel just as smug at Patch's defeat, and just as jealous of his successes.

The twentieth century continued to ripple by, years passing like waves on the great sea of time. Dooley now had a globe of the entire world (which looked, not inappropriately, like a gigantic jigsaw puzzle-ball) in his study, for plotting Santa's gift-giving journey each year. His office walls were cluttered with the countless slots of a filing system for letters that would have put the largest post office in the world to shame. But most things continued to be done in the same careful, time-tested ways in the elves' village. And as technology – and the number of human beings – continued to grow with dizzying speed in the world outside, Santa Claus and his devoted helpers began to feel the strain on their traditional methods of production and delivery. Patch constantly suggested ways of updating their systems; but Santa, not entirely pleased by what he glimpsed of progress – frequently at the expense of people – in the outside world steadfastly refused to introduce any more newfangled innovations into their own timeless village. And yet even he knew, in his heart of hearts, that some day something had to give...

Patch, Boog, Honka and Vout stood waiting expectantly in the toy tunnel as Santa and his sleigh returned from yet another journey through the magical night before Christmas.

Santa Claus guided the reindeer into the tunnel with the skill of very long experience and pulled them to a stop on the runway. The reindeer halted gladly, their tongues lolling with exhaustion as they pulled up before Patch. Santa leant back in his seat and sighed, every bit as exhausted as his animals were. He thought longingly of the time when both he and the reindeer had made this journey easily...

'Welcome home, Santa Claus,' Honka called, his wide-set eyes crinkling with his usual enthusiasm.

Santa Claus mumbled an inaudible response, the best he could manage as he climbed heavily out of the sleigh.

Patch checked the reindeer one by one, his face filled with concern. 'Oh boy, they look like they've been through the mill.'

'Mill!' Santa said, a bit gruffly. 'I can't remember the last time I saw a good old-fashioned mill. Now it's all apartment blocks and skyscrapers. You think it's easy navigating through those sky-scrapers?' He waved a mittened hand as he trudged off down the tunnel. 'Not to mention the wind current from those jumbo jets.' He shook his head, his voice trailing behind him as he went muttering-ly on his way, still getting the complaints out of his system.

He plodded wearily across the Great Hall, which this morning seemed endlessly wide, nodding mutely as various elves called out greetings and congratulations. He reached the bottom of the spiral steps leading up to his own house at last. He stood staring up at the final long climb that awaited him before he could rest. He sighed in resignation and started upwards.

Anya greeted him at the door with a welcoming hug and kiss and led him directly to the kitchen, where two bowls of steaming pea soup waited for them on the table. Claus sat down obediently in his chair. Anya sat down opposite him and began to eat. But Claus sat unmoving, too weary even to lift a spoon.

'Your soup's getting cold,' Anya urged with gentle concern. Her good hot soup had always been able to restore him, if she could just get him to eat it.

A knock sounded at the door and Dooley entered the kitchen diffidently. 'Welcome back, Santa,' he said, smiling. 'Have a good trip?' He set the folder he was carrying down on the table, almost as if he hoped they wouldn't notice it.

'What's this?' Anya asked, fixing it with an anxious glance.

'Next year's schedule,' Dooley murmured, his voice apologetic. He kept his eyes on the folder, not looking at them.

'Can't it wait for a few days?' Anya said. She rose to her feet, rising to the defence of her exhausted husband.

And as she rose, Claus's eyes closed and he slumped forward, landing face down in his soup dish with a clatter and a splash. Anya let out a startled cry as Claus sat up again abruptly, his face red with embarrassment and green with soup. 'Sorry,' he mumbled vaguely, through his pea-green beard. 'I must have dozed off.'

Hastily Anya wiped the hot soup from his beard and collar with a napkin. 'Darling,' she said, her voice filled with concern, 'why don't you get yourself an assistant?' It was a thought that had often been in her mind over the last few years, as she spent more and more time waiting for him to get back from his endless rounds in the toy factory.

Claus stared at her, his eyes wide. 'What??' he said indignantly, as if the very idea were almost incomprehensible. 'Me, Santa Claus, needing help –?'

Anya shook her head, putting her hands on her hips. 'I don't like to see you pushing yourself like this, Claus. You're spreading yourself too thin.'

Dooley nodded thoughtfully, adding his look of concern to Anya's. 'I'd volunteer,' he said, 'but I'm up to my ears as it is.'

Claus shrugged and shook his head. 'Who'd want the job?' he asked, thinking of all the endless details and headaches that only the pleasure of his Christmas trip could possibly make worthwhile.

But Dooley smiled. 'Two elves spring to mind,' he said.

'One of them practically *bounces* to mind,' Anya added, with a fond smile of her own, as Patch's cheerful, bright-eyed face filled her thoughts.

Knowing exactly whom she meant – Patch being one of the two he had in mind himself – Dooley nodded again. And, thinking of Patch, he suddenly snapped his fingers. 'Oh yes,' he said, remembering at last, 'I'm supposed to show you this.' Reaching into his pocket, he pulled out a small, hollow globe and handed it to Claus.

'What is it?' Claus asked, taking it carefully into his own hands.

'An old idea Patch came up with,' Dooley said, slightly embarrassed as he remembered how long ago he had mislaid it in his office. It must be several decades ago, now,... He wondered with a touch of worry whether his memory was starting to go.

The interior of the globe began to change with its movement from his hand to Santa Claus's. Claus peered more closely at it and raised his eyebrows. Within the globe, suspended in water, floated tiny white flakes of artificial snow. As he shook it gently, the snow whirled in a blizzard around the tiny, cut-out figure of an elegant townhouse. The details of the small picture were perfect, down to its charming white porch and front door.

'Huh, look at that,' Claus murmured, fascinated, as he held it out to show Anya. 'Isn't that a clever thing...' He shook it again, watching the snow-flakes whirl, thinking that it looked so real he could almost be looking into another world...

And in another world, the world that a peasant couple named Claus and Anya had left centuries before, there was now a city called New York, on an island named Manhattan. The snow of the real world, cold and stinging, whirled past a townhouse with a charming white porch and front door that was curiously like the one in the globe. But this elegant mansion lay on a quiet sidestreet in a neighbourhood that lay precariously on the edge of a very fashionable part of the city. An area where the mansions of New York's wealthiest citizens squatted complacently on the fringe of one of the poorest neighbourhoods.

The fact that just around the corner families were wondering where their next meal was coming from was the farthest thing from the minds of the two well-to-do boys walking home from the cinema, warmly dressed in heavy down jackets, wool scarves and caps. Their breath was as white as steam in the night air, as the first boy said, 'Why don't you come over to my house?'

His friend shook his head. 'I've got to be home for dinner. My mum'll kill me if I'm late.'

'You can eat at my house. C'mon.' The first boy shrugged, looking at his friend with raised eyebrows. The other boy grinned and shivered as the rising wind wrapped its chilly arms around them; he nodded eagerly as they hurried on down the street to his friend's home.

They passed the empty-eyed, boarded-over front of a crumbling building that was awaiting renovation, not giving it a second glance; never noticing the small, silent figure huddled in the shadows of its doorway.

As they passed by, the small boy, who was about ten years old, stepped out of the doorway, watching them enviously as they walked on down the street. He pulled up the collar of his own coat – a torn and battered leather jacket, several sizes too large, which he had found in a rubbish bin. Shivering as the wind-driven snow whirled past him, he pushed his mittenless, chill-reddened hands morosely into his pockets.

His name was Joe – Joe was all the name he ever told anyone. He had never known his father and his mother had died more than a year ago. When the social worker had come to take him to the orphanage, he had run away. Since then he had lived out on the streets, surviving however he could, preferring to live on his own rather than live in an institution where uncaring strangers would rule his life.

But a life spent alone, with no home or family, without even the simple shelter and regular meals of an institution, was harsh and frightening even for an adult. A ten year old boy could not afford to show weakness to anyone, for there was always someone older, bigger, or stronger waiting to take advantage of a kid who looked soft. Joe had learned quickly to hide his feelings, to be suspicious of everyone. He was learning to face the world as if it held nothing but enemies and danger. But beneath the tough manner of a boy old beyond his years was still a child who cried himself to sleep sometimes at night, wrapped in newspapers against the cold, and dreamed of his mother's voice and her warm arms around him.

Joe sighed as he watched the two older boys climb the steps of a well-kept house at the end of the road. He imagined the hot meal waiting there in a bright, warm dining room, letting his mind picture all his favourite foods steaming hot on the table, until he could almost taste them... And then he took out the half a stick of gum that was all he had left in his empty pockets. Putting it into his mouth, he chewed it resignedly, getting what nourishment and flavour he could.

If he had known that he was being watched, he would never have let even a moment's longing show. But he did not know, and in the elegant white townhouse across the street, silhouetted in a brightly-lit window, someone stood staring out at him.

A young girl named Cornelia stood inside the tall bay windows, holding the curtains aside, gazing down at the ragged, shivering boy who was just a little older than she, as he stood on the snowy street below. He looked so alone and sad. She knew that poor people lived near her home and she had always felt guilty somehow when she was hurried past the children who had only ragged hand-me-downs to

76

wear, only broken toys to play with, while she had wardrobes full of the latest fashions, shelves and boxes full of toys, all to herself. She had even asked Miss Tucker, her nanny, to let her give some of her toys and clothes away; but Miss Tucker had only scolded her sharply and told her she was being ungrateful and didn't deserve her step-uncle's kind generosity.

As Cornelia watched, the boy glanced up at her house, at her standing in the window, her face dimly lit by the street lamp just outside. Her eyes met his dark, wary ones; he held her gaze for a moment that seemed to go on and on. And in that moment Cornelia felt as if a kind of electric shock tingled through her; in that moment she seemed to understand everything about him ... that he had no home, no parents to care for him. Her hands clenched on the edge of the heavy curtains; sudden tears of sympathy burned in her eyes. She wanted to call out to him, to run out into the street, ask his name and tell him her own ... because she *knew* how lonely he must be.

Because they were so much alike. She had no one who cared about her, either. Her own parents, who had loved her very much, were dead and now she lived with her step-uncle, who barely knew she existed. Miss Tucker, her dour, tight-lipped nanny, saw to her every need, as competently but as coldly as a robot. Cornelia glanced down at the simple, very expensive red and white dress that she had just been given yesterday – and was forced to wear in spite of the fact that she preferred blue jeans. She might be surrounded by every comfort and certainly every toy anyone could imagine – but she was still an orphan, who cried herself to sleep at night and dreamed of her mother's warm arms.

Cornelia sighed, letting go of the curtains again, glancing reluctantly back into the living room as the high, nasal drone of Miss Tucker's voice intruded insistently on her private thoughts.

'I'm warning you, Cornelia. Your step-uncle is not

77

going to tolerate those grades. Imagine! A B-minus in geography!'

'What does he care about my marks?' Cornelia said with quiet defiance. 'He never even looks at my school report. He probably doesn't even know what form I'm in.' She brushed her straight, reddish fringe back from her eyes.

'Young lady, I'm telling you –' Miss Tucker glanced up from her crocheting and saw Cornelia standing by the window. 'Cornelia! Come away from that window this instant before you get a chill!' She rose to her feet, dropping the crocheting into her sewing basket. 'Now come to dinner before Cook starts getting cranky and complains about the soup getting cold.' Cornelia thought sullenly that Miss Tucker, whose appetite she was very familiar with, was far more interested in getting to her own dinner before it got cold, than in whether Cook was angry, or anyone else was fed. Miss Tucker walked stiffly though the doorway into the dining room, her severe, high-necked brown dress rustling with starch.

Cornelia turned away from the window and stared around her at the warm, bright, high-ceilinged room, at the antiques and paintings, the expensive carpets and exquisite *objets d'art*, as if she had never seen them before. She stared at her step-uncle's huge portrait, hung like something in a wood-panelled shrine high on the far wall of the room. She blinked, and looked back out of the window again. But across the street the doorway was empty; the boy was gone.

Back at the North Pole, Santa Claus's distracted thoughts were centred at the moment more on the reordering of his own small, enchanted village than on the injustices of the greater world beyond. He had called together Patch and Puffy, the two prime candidates for the newly-announced position of his official Assistant. Santa sat in his comfortably padded rocking chair, with Dooley standing at his side, as he listened to the two elves' ideas for helping him streamline his unwieldly workload. Anya stood in the doorway, listening too, unobtrusive but intent.

'An assistant!' Patch was saying, bright and breathless with excitement. 'Your assistant!' His eyes shone. *At last!* This was the honour he had been waiting for, for all these many years... the thing that would prove once and for all to the other elves – and to himself – that he was as good as he had always wanted to believe he was. 'With all due respect, sir, I've got ideas that'll turn this place upside down!'

Santa's brow furrowed slightly. 'That isn't exactly what I had in mind,' he said. He was still, in his private thoughts, a bit dubious about this whole business.

Seeing his hesitation, Patch added quickly, 'I'm talking about modern methods of production! I'm talking assembly line! I'm talking wave of the future! I'm talking faster, quicker –'

'– and sloppier,' Puffy interrupted sceptically. He had always been suspicious of Patch's modern ideas... though not always for the best of reasons.

Patch broke off and turned to stare at his rival with undisguised disdain. 'Just because *you* lack elf-assurance doesn't mean that I do, Puffy. I'm not afraid to rock the sleigh.' He put his hands on his hips.

Puffy ignored him, keeping his own eyes on Santa Claus. Smiling ingratiatingly, he said, 'Sir, I have long admired your traditional methods of manufacture. I assure you that I will give the same meticulous attention to quality and detail that –'

Santa held up his hands, cutting off the flow of verbiage with an abrupt shake of his head. 'Boys, boys, don't give me promises. Give me results. The one who gets the job is the one who does the job best.' He raised his eyebrows, looking first at one elf, and then the other, straight in the eye. They subsided, nodding respectfully... But they still stole secret, measuring glances at each other as they turned away towards the door.

During the next few weeks, the activity in the elves' vast factory was even more frantic than usual. The workshops hummed like a beehive from morning to night. But now the elf workers were pitted not against a deadline of Christmas Eve, but against each other.

Puffy continued to oversee the making of toys in the classic tradition of Santa Claus's own exquisite handcrafted, hand-painted creations. He inspected each elf's work, touching up a toy here and there as Santa himself did, giving all his attention to quality, even at the expense of quantity, just as Santa Claus had always done.

But at the same time, in the west wing of the factory, Patch and his handful of loyal friends were hard at work setting up a new, streamlined, fully-automated production line, using ingenuity and whatever supplies Patch could get hold of. The result was an assembly line that would have made Henry Ford shake his head in disbelief. But, guided by Patch's hastily-drawn plans and inspired mechanical genius, it was ready to function in record time – and function it did, with terrifying efficiency by old-fashioned elvish standards.

'What makes it go?' Honka asked when they were finished. He stared incredulously at the red-, yellow-and blue-painted contraption he had helped to build.

'It's got an elf-starter,' Vout said good-naturedly and pointed to Patch.

Patch stood with his hands on his hips, proudly gazing at his new brainchild. It looked like a miniature factory, sitting in a corner of the greater factory, and within it were contained all the automated assembly lines that were about to make the rest of this place obsolete. He lifted a hand, not for even a moment plagued by doubts over what he was about to do. '*Go!*' he cried.

At one end, huffing with effort, Boog began to turn a crank, which started the conveyor belt rolling. Even Patch could not come up with a perpetual-motion engine ... And as the elf in charge of this project, he might start things rolling, but he did not expect himself to supply the brawn as well as the brains. That was what friends were for. He watched, holding his breath, as the first parts of the toys to be assembled began to drop from hoppers. Carried along the moving belt, they disappeared into the maw of the waiting automatic assembly machine.

He rubbed his hands in satisfaction, thinking of the pile of neatly stacked toys that Puffy had accumulated in the North Wing while he had been occupied just with the construction of this enormous machine. Puffy might laugh at him now, and so might all the others – let them stay stuck in a centuries-old rut! The world outside their village was a world of change and new ideas ... and he was the only one here who appreciated it. You had to keep up with the times. He was about to have the last laugh and all of Santa's praise and admiration too. He had always known he was meant for bigger things. To be the personal assistant of that kindly, wonderful old man in the red suit was the highest honour he could imagine, and he had put all of his energy and heart into achieving it. He watched the conveyor belt speed up, moving faster and faster as it carried the toy parts along.

'Isn't it going too fast?' Vout asked anxiously.

'Too *fast*?' Patch chuckled, giddy with excitement. He grinned confidently. 'Welcome to the twentieth century!' he cried, waving his arms.

The automatic toy-making machinery began to roll at top speed, and finished toys – shiny, new and seemingly perfect – began to drop out at the other end, onto another belt, where they were swept off to be automatically sorted and stacked. *It worked*! Patch did a small dance of triumph. Wait till Santa saw this ...

But within the heart of Patch's ingenious machine, where no elvish or human eye could carefully watch over production, things were not functioning as intended. Patch's plans had been drawn up in too much of a hurry and put together with too much haste. And so an automatic screwdriver, screwing two parts of a bicycle frame together, did not turn the screws quite enough times to hold the pieces securely. A tiny red wagon had its handle attached – not quite tightly enough. Pieces of a jigsaw puzzle, pouring into a box, had not been cut precisely, and no human or elvish hand was there to test them, to see whether they really fitted together. Every toy that came tumbling off the conveyor belt had some fatal flaw hidden somewhere inside it, just like the machinery itself. And yet every single toy coming off the line *looked* perfect. No one suspected they were not, including Patch ... or even Santa Claus.

Several weeks later Santa stood in the centre of the vast factory building, studying the enormous pile of completed toys that Patch's machines had produced, all spread out for his perusal on the polished wooden floor. All the elves of the village had gathered here to see who had won the competition. They looked on as Santa raised his eyebrows, stroking his beard as he did when he was impressed. He glanced at Dooley, who nodded in agreement. It was unquestionably an immensely impressive display. Patch beamed proudly as he watched their expressions, putting his arms around the shoulders of his tired but happy companions.

Beyond Santa, Puffy stood with his own, far smaller, assortment of old-fashioned, handmade hoops and balls and dolls. As Santa turned back to look at them, Puffy's shoulders drooped. He could see for himself, just as clearly as everyone else assembled there could see, that Patch had won the contest. Patch had made far more toys, and they all looked perfect. He didn't need Santa's sympathetic but reluctant glance to tell him that he had lost.

Santa smiled apologetically, turning away without speaking because he was unable to think of words that would take the sting out of Puffy's disappointment. He hated moments like this. But then he turned to Patch and his smile widened. He was secretly delighted to offer his hand in congratulations to such an eager and creative elf. Patch had delivered both quantity and quality, and that was exactly what he needed. And Patch was finally getting the recognition he had always longed for.

Santa was still a bit sad to think that his own way - and Puffy's way - of creating toys was now hopelessly outmoded. But he realised that this acknowledgement of Patch's talents was long overdue, and his smile broadened even more as Patch stepped forward. The young elf looked like he would burst with pride in another moment, as his fellow elves raised a tremendous cheer around him. Honka, Vout and Boog cheered the loudest of all. Patch took the red apron with the word ASSISTANT printed on its front from Santa's own hands and put it on. He looked back at his pile of toys and thought of how many more there would be by Christmas to make Santa even more popular with the children of the world... and all because of him.

SIX

The Manhattan street was bright with tinsel and coloured lights. Shoppers hurried by, their arms full of Christmas presents, as Joe stood outside the window of McDonald's with his nose pressed against the glass. His breath made a small patch of white on the cold pane as he watched the people queuing up inside, young and old, black and white, all ordering hamburgers and fries and shakes, slathering their steaming McNuggets with ketchup and hot sauce. He swallowed and swallowed again; his stomach, which had been entirely empty for nearly two days now, gurgled in protest. But he could not tear himself away from the window, from watching, from remembering, from imagining the smell of burgers frying, the sizzle of potatoes plunged into hot oil, the icy, prickly tang of a cold fizzy drink...

He stared wide-eyed at the people eating obliviously right in front of him, separated from their dinners by only a thin, transparent wall – that might as well have been the Great Wall of China. If only one of those people would look up at him and see how hungry he was and offer him that last bite of burger or the half bag of fries they were tossing into the bin...

'Merry Christmas! Merry Christmas!'

Joe pushed himself away from the window, colder than ever from standing still and dizzy with hunger. He pulled the earflaps of the hat he had been lucky enough to find on the pavement yesterday further over his ears, and looked away down the street.

Another in an endless string of fake Santa

Claus's had appeared on the previously-empty street corner. This one was as skinny as a scarecrow. He hadn't even bothered to stuff a pillow into his ill-fitting suit, or to tidy up his obviously phony beard. The sign on the box in front of him read, 'Make it a Merry Christmas for Everybody. Give to the Urban Development Fund.'

A well-dressed man passing by tossed a few coins into the box as Joe watched. He kept on watching and saw the fake Santa look quickly from side to side before he reached into the box and pocketed the change. Smugly pleased with himself, the derelict pulled a bottle of cheap Muscatel wrapped in a paper bag out of his back pocket, and took a long swig from it.

Joe's mouth twisted with knowing disgust. That was predictable. They were all cheats and phonies, the ones dressed up in red suits and beards. They were all just pulling a fast one, and the people who fell for it were fools. There was no Santa Claus.

He turned back for one last longing gaze at the warm, fragrant, tinsel-decked interior of Mc-Donald's. Then he jammed his half-frozen hands into his empty pockets and walked slowly away down the street.

Not far away, Cornelia and her nanny, Miss Tucker, sat at opposite ends of a long, candlelit dinner table. They were in the process of finishing a dinner that would easily have fed half a dozen of their hungry neighbours. The silver bowls and fine china platters that crowded the polished mahogany tabletop were still mostly filled with potatoes and vegetables and rare roast beef – all destined for the dustbin, now that dinner was over. They never ate leftovers.

Miss Tucker mopped the last of the gravy from her plate with a piece of freshly-baked bread and said contentedly, 'I can't eat another bite.' She had had at least three helpings of everything, Cornelia had noticed.

'Me too,' Cornelia said drearily, staring at the mound of scarcely touched food still on her own plate. Somehow she had no appetite lately, no matter how good the food was. She sighed and glanced away at the dining room window, drawn by a sudden, nameless feeling. She started, as she saw the face of the young boy she had watched standing alone on the street a few weeks before. He was peering through the glass at the warm, well-lit room and the heavily-laden table, his brown eyes wide and his thin face filled with longing. But as he looked along the table, he suddenly found her looking back at him. Quickly he ducked down out of sight.

Miss Tucker rose from her chair, just missing the boy's disappearing head. 'Well, I'm going to take my coffee in the library so I can watch television.' She smoothed her greying hair, which was drawn up in an unbecoming old maid's knot, as usual. 'And you, my little miss, had better get busy on those Latin verbs.' She sailed from the room like a heavily-laden ship putting out to sea.

Cornelia sat unmoving in her chair for another long moment, until she was sure that Miss Tucker was not going to come back. Then she began to heap an empty plate high with a little bit of everything on the table. Carrying the plate of food, she slipped out of the dining room and through the kitchen. She crept quickly past Cook, who stood with her back turned, loading clinking bottles of wine into the dumbwaiter in the pantry; her step-uncle had vast racks of wine down in the cellar.

Cornelia reached the servants' entrance at the rear of the house safely and opened the back door. Peering out into the darkness, she called softly, '*Pssst!*'

Joe, still hiding in the bushes, stuck his head up far enough to see the open back door and a girl looking out of it. He crouched down again, uncertain about what was going on.

'*Psst!* Little boy?' she called again.

86

Joe frowned and stayed where he was, his curiosity warring with his irritation at being called 'little boy'.

Cornelia hesitated, sure that the boy must be watching and listening even though he wouldn't show himself. She held the plate of food out before her in the glow of the porch light. Then, very carefully and in plain sight, she set it down on the steps. She turned and went back into the house again, closing the door firmly behind her.

Joe stayed where he was for a long moment, gaping in astonishment. What was going on? Had she really set that food out here for him? Why? He bit his lip, too used to tricks and betrayals to quite believe that something good was really happening to him. But a gust of wind carried the smell of roast beef to his sensitive nose and he realised suddenly that he didn't care *why* – all that mattered was that the food was here. Quietly and cautiously, still on his guard for a trap, he started forward through the bushes towards the doorstep.

Inside the house Cornelia stood frozen, her ear pressed to the door, waiting breathlessly for any sound outside that would mean the boy had come for the food. Her face filled with sudden delight as she heard a soft, distinct footstep, and then another, on the snowy steps. She heard the scrape of a dish being picked up. She pressed back against the door, clasping her hands together because she wanted to clap them, grinning with pleasure. And then she slipped quietly back through the kitchen, and went in search of her school books. Somehow even the thought of Latin verbs seemed exciting to her now.

Out in the shrubbery behind the house, Joe grinned too, for the first time in days, as he gulped down the first real meal he had eaten in longer than he could remember. This was food like he had never eaten in his life; even if it had been stale bread and peanut butter it would have tasted like a feast, but roast beef and gravy was like dying and going to heaven. He didn't know who that little girl was, or why she had done this for him . . . but he was truly grateful to her. Tonight when he slept, alone and cold but at least not hungry, maybe he would dream about her . . .

Meanwhile, back at the North Pole, Santa's factory was a beehive of high-tech activity, elf-style. Newfangled automated devices and Patch-work assembly lines had sprouted everywhere, putting together toys with impersonal speed and regularity. Patch wandered among his machines in his red Assistant's apron, looking knowing and efficient and a bit like a mad scientist – revelling in his new position, happier than he had ever imagined being. Honka followed at his heels, hanging eagerly on his every word and basking in Patch's reflected glory. Patch only took the change in his friend for granted, completely swept away by his new prestige. He had even gone so far as to place a large sign over his machinery that read: PATCH'S TOYS . . . forgetting in his inflated pride who was really in charge of the toys, or why he was really making them. The other elves had to admit, however grudgingly, that he had made their lives easier.

Even on Christmas Eve, as the elves began to load Santa's bottomless sack for another yearly flight, Patch stood by, overseeing everything as usual. By next year, he thought happily, even this bottomless sack would be too small to hold all of the toys his machines could make.

No one – least of all Patch himself – realised, as the toys went into the sack, that precisely the same flaws of sloppy manufacturing existed in every one of those countless toys that had existed in the very first ones his machines had produced. Patch had overseen every bit of the production, but his interests lay in *more* and *faster*. His machines did *more* and *faster* perfectly. He was confident that his designs worked and there were far too many toys being produced for someone to check them for (certainly non-existent) flaws.

And so countless toys went into Santa's bag with loose screws, poorly-made connections, pieces that did not fit – a thousand different, fatal, hidden flaws and errors, all invisible to the eye.

Happy and utterly unsuspecting, Santa Claus guided his team and sleigh out of the tunnel ramp and into the sky for one more Christmas Eve trip. He was in particularly high spirits, feeling completely rested and more confident that he had in years that all the millions of good children around the world would receive toys tonight, and every Christmas from here on, thanks to Patch's ingenuity.

SEVEN

Santa Claus soared on his way, making remarkably good time, as even his reindeer caught his infectious high spirits. His hearty *ho ho ho's* of laughter rang out through the crisp, star-filled night as the sleigh circled the skyscrapers of New York City, very late by local time, as it always was. 'Ah, what a night, my boys, what a night!' Santa cried to his team.

The reindeer bobbed their heads and snorted gleefully, Prancer and Dancer nodding agreement in unison.

'Look down there –' Santa gestured with a mittened hand at the scene below. Donner glanced down obediently, looked up again into the sky as vertigo made him dizzy, and shook his head. Even after all these years, he was still afraid of flying. Just as with most reluctant flyers, his fears never seemed to get any better.

'Decorations in the window, stockings hung by the fireplace –' Santa went on, so happy that he was oblivious to Donner's chronic discomfort. 'Tonight there isn't a child who isn't bursting with joy and happiness and –' He broke off as he saw something down below that rang discordantly with his merry vision. He frowned in surprise and concern.

In an alley far below a young boy huddled all alone by a bonfire of rubbish, shivering with cold. What was that child doing out in the open on such a freezing night, with no shelter, too cold even to sleep?

Santa pulled hard on the reins, banking his sleigh around, as the little boy's plight sobered his joyful mood. 'Just a minute, boys,' he said, 'I think we're going to make an unscheduled stop.'

The sleigh descended, circling adroitly between high-rise blocks, and landed silently on the roof of a building just above the street where the boy was.

Joe stepped back inside the building's doorway, escaping from another strong gust of icy wind as it came sweeping down the street to make his fire gutter and smoke. Hugging himself against his uncontrollable shivers, he looked up in surprise as a large, bulky shape materialised abruptly beside him in the doorway. 'Hey!' he said, anger covering his fright. 'Go away. Find your own doorway. There's no room here.'

The fat old man with the phony beard and the red suit said gently, 'What are you doing out here, boy?' His face was furrowed with concern.

Joe frowned with pained disgust. 'I'm pitchin' a no-hitter for the Yankees, what does it look like?' he said. These drunks got weirder all the time.

'But this is Christmas Eve!' the old man said. 'Don't you know what that means?'

Joe grimaced. 'Yeah,' he said sourly, 'it means you're out of a job till next year. You and the rest of the winos.'

'Winos?' the old man said, looking puzzled, as if he had never even heard the word before.

Joe frowned, almost feeling sorry for the old man: he seemed so confused, and there was something kind about his eyes, in spite of the fact that he must be crazy. 'Look, mister,' Joe said, 'you shouldn't drink that rough wine, it hurts your brain, see?'

The old man's expression turned from confused surprise to utter disbelief and his voice was filled with real distress as he asked, 'Don't you know who I am?'

Joe shrugged. 'Yes, you're a nut.'

'I'm Santa Claus,' the old man said, patting his well-padded front.

'Right.' Joe put his hands on his hips. 'And I'm the Tooth Fairy.'

'I'll prove it to you,' the old man said almost

desperately. He held out his hand. 'Come up on the roof with me.'

Joe jerked away, suddenly frightened. He backed away, glancing anxiously down the dark, deserted alleyway. He was all alone with this old weirdo. 'No way, man,' he said. 'You get out of here or I call a cop.'

Claus let his hand drop, filled with a deep, aching distress as he realised how truly awful this child's existence must be, that he could only see Santa Claus as someone to scorn or fear. If Santa Claus was someone to be afraid of, how could the rest of the people in his life be treating him ...? 'Oh, you poor lad,' he murmured. He folded his arms. 'Well, I see I'm going to have to do it my way.' He pressed one forefinger against the side of his nose, concentrating.

Abruptly the alley was empty.

One moment Joe had been standing in a doorway. And then he found himself suddenly and completely inexplicably standing on a rooftop, with the same crazy old man still beside him. Only, maybe he *wasn't* just crazy... Joe stared around him in disbelief. 'Holy Cow!!' he cried. 'How'd you do that?'

'See?' The old man shrugged. 'What did I tell you?'

Joe's eyes popped out as they caught on the fantastic vehicle he suddenly discovered sharing the rooftop with them. It was by far the most amazing thing he had ever seen, a beautifully carved sleigh that looked like something from the window of an antique shop, and eight strange-looking reindeer that seemed so lifelike... He took a step, and then another, towards the sleigh, wondering suddenly if he had fallen asleep and was dreaming. He stopped again. 'Wait a minute,' he murmured to himself, 'I know what this is, it's one of them Christmas decorations somebody put up here. I seen 'em before.' He clung to the thought, comforted by it.

One of the reindeer suddenly tossed its antlered head, and emitted a sound somewhere between a whinny and a snort of indignation.

Joe leapt back, his astonishment doubling.

'Ever hear a decoration make a noise like that?' the old man asked, a bit proudly.

They were *real*! 'But Santa Claus ain't real ...' Joe protested weakly, still fighting the evidence of his eyes. He looked back at the old man, wavering.

Santa Claus smiled, more determined than ever to win the boy's belief as he saw his doubt faltering. 'Want to go for a ride?' he asked, gesturing at the sleigh; making an offer he had never made to any child in all the years he had been Santa Claus. There was just something special about this boy ...

'A ride,' Joe said flatly, out of habit. 'A *ride*???' he said again, suddenly, as the real implications of the offer struck him. 'On *that*?' He pointed at the sleigh. His mouth dropped open.

Santa Claus nodded, his smile broadening.

'I've never even been in a plane,' Joe whispered, hesitating; still slightly afraid of the weirdness of everything that was happening to him – afraid that he really *was* dreaming. Something this incredible *couldn't* be happening to him. He knew if he said *yes* it would all disappear, only leaving him sadder than ever ...

'Make up your mind,' Santa said, still smiling, but showing just the slightest trace of restlessness. 'I'm in rather a hurry tonight.' He raised his eyebrows, glancing away over the rooftops of all the homes he had yet to visit.

'Gosh ... I mean ... well ...' Joe twisted his hand together, weakening; so tempted, and yet – 'Yeah,' he blurted suddenly, 'I mean, yeah, sure, if it's really awright ...' He blinked, nodding, wide-eyed and suddenly breathless with excitement. 'I mean, yeah. Really?' His voice cracked.

Santa chuckled, the friendliest sound Joe had heard in a long time. Santa led him to the sleigh and helped him climb up into its seat, then climbed in himself. Joe settled in wonderingly, amazed to find that his dream was still holding together.

'Hold on tight now,' Santa said. 'Don't worry, you're as safe here as you would be at home.' Forgetting, for just a moment...

'I ain't got a home,' Joe said bluntly, as reality pushed its ugly face into his wonderful, magical dream.

Santa Claus looked over at the boy, studying his pale, grimy face for a long moment, searching for the cheerful words which, for once, simply failed to come. Then, collecting himself, he put a broad grin back on his face, and said heartily, 'Here we go! Can you say, "Yo"?'

'*Yo!*' Joe shouted eagerly, letting the real world go again with great relief.

The reindeer flung up their heads and bounded forward like one creature. Getting a running start, they raced across the roof and vaulted into the air, drawing the sleigh after them.

Joe gasped with astonishment and wonder. It *was* real! It really was, all of it! He couldn't believe it, and yet at last he *had* to... He was really flying! All the defensiveness and the guardedness he had cultivated for his own survival fell away in a second, and he was simply a ten year old boy having the best time of his life. 'Wow!' Joe shouted. 'WOW!'

Santa Claus laughed, and it was the great rolling laugh that he had always been told Santa Claus would have. Joe let out a yelp of startled delight as the sleigh swooped upward, just clearing the top of a skyscraper.

And that was only the beginning. Under Santa's skilful guidance, the reindeer and sleigh dove and swooped and soared among the glittering towers of Manhattan, and up again into the midnight sky. The reindeer danced across the clouds and wove a path among the stars, plunged back down among the skyscrapers of the sleeping city, galloping among them on feet with invisible wings. Joe laughed joyfully, feeling as if he were caught up in a miracle. Santa grinned over at him, filled with delight at the sight of his happiness.

'You really *are* Santa Claus, ain't ya?' Joe said wonderingly.

The white-bearded old man nodded. 'Yup... but I still don't know who you are.'

'Joe!' he cried gleefully. 'I'm Joe!' And tonight he was the luckiest child alive.

'How do you like it?' Santa asked.

'Neat!' he shouted, the very highest compliment he could give, and whooped again as the sleigh banked and plunged steeply once more, rising again into the sky like an enchanted rollercoaster. 'Wow! Neat! How do you make 'em do it?'

'Like a horse and buggy,' Santa replied matter-of-factly, drawing on the last comparable vehicle he remembered driving. 'You just pull the reins. Both together to go on higher...' He raised his arms and the reindeer began to climb again.

'Can they do anything you want?' Joe asked.

Santa's brow wrinkled slightly. 'Anything but the Super-Dooper-Looper.'

'What's that?' Joe said, raising his eyebrows. It sounded impressive.

'I've been trying for years,' Santa murmured. Out ahead Prancer and Dancer glanced at each other as the same thought passed through their matching minds – *Here we go again*. Blitzen looked over at the acrophobic friend Donner with unspoken sympathy. Donner gulped and closed his eyes.

'Maybe tonight's the night,' Santa said encouragingly. 'What do you say, Donner? Let's give it a whirl!' Claus prided himself on keeping up with the latest expressions. He pulled back on the reins, giving the reindeer the old familiar sign to begin the difficult aeronautical manoeuvre, which amounted to a great flying loop-the-loop. The reindeer and sleigh rose up and up, curving into the first half of the wide arc... higher and higher...

Donner, straining desperately to keep his courage together as he galloped through a steeper and steeper climb, suddenly shook his head and gave in to his panic, plunging forward and down again. The other reindeer, thrown off balance, had no choice but to follow him down. The loop attempt had failed again; the sleigh, after a jolt, was back again on its former straight trajectory. Prancer and Dancer glanced at each other; the look that flashed between them this time was one of disgust. *He messed it up again.*

'It didn't work again,' Santa murmured sadly to Joe. Then he called out loudly to Donner, 'That's all right, boy, you'll get it next time!' He glanced back at Joe again. 'Tell him it's all right.'

Joe, empathising with the unfortunate reindeer's feelings, called out reassuringly, 'Uh... hey, like, man, don't sweat it. It's cool, y'know.'

Santa smiled appreciatively at Joe. His smile broadened as he looked down into the earnest young face and had a sudden thought. 'Would you like to drive for a while?'

Joe gaped at him, hardly believing his ears. 'Me??? Drive???' he cried, dazzled by even the possibility.

Santa Claus nodded. 'It's not too hard. Here – take the reins.' He passed them into Joe's wondering hands. And then, just as he had done in dreams for countless years, for a son he had never had, Santa Claus began to teach Joe how to handle the sleigh and team.

With seeming casualness, he watched Joe's every move like a hawk as they soared into the night; speaking to him constantly, calmly, smiling all the while as he made sure that Joe did not make any mistakes that were potentially dangerous. Joe's movements at first were the awkward, jerky motions of an excited and uncertain beginner. The reindeer responded with gallant patience – if some confusion – and after a time Joe's spasmodic efforts to steer them began to smooth out as he gradually got the hang of guiding them through three dimensions. 'How'm I doin'?' he called out, as he pulled recklessly on the reins, banking so sharply that the reindeer and sleigh swerved in a way that made stomachs turn over.

'Fine,' Santa said gamely, through clenched teeth. After so many centuries, he was finally sharing the experience of every adult who had ever taught a child to drive anything.

'What do you call 'em?' Joe asked, watching the reindeer surge upward.

'Reindeer,' Santa said, a little fuzzily.

Joe shook his head. 'No, I mean what are their names?'

'Oh,' Santa Claus murmured, and shook his head. He began to point them out one at a time. 'Starting from the front, that's Donner and Blitzen, Dasher and Vixen, Comet and Cupid, Prancer and Dancer.'

'On Donner!' Joe cried, shaking the reins. 'On Blitzen! On Dasher! On Vixen!' He called out their names, unconsciously echoing the famous poem which lay in fragments somewhere deep in his memory.

The reindeer responded eagerly, speeding up as they executed a broad, dazzlingly perfect turn. And then at a word from Santa, they started down towards the distant rooftops again.

'Where are we goin'?' Joe asked.

'We can't joyride all night, Joe,' Santa said good-naturedly. 'I've got a job to do, you know.' He took the reins out of Joe's reluctant hands again, guiding the reindeer down and down to a precise eight-point landing on the flat, snowy surface of a dark and silent rooftop.

Joe climbed down from the sleigh, helping Santa lift down his enormous sack filled with brightly wrapped presents. And then, before he could even ask what they were going to do next, Joe found himself standing beside Santa *inside* an apartment; just as he had found himself suddenly on the roof a short time before. Many years ago, the elves had devised a magic spell that would allow Santa Claus to enter and leave any home with only a nod, regardless of the locks and chains and precautions that kept most normal night-time visitors outside.

Joe stared around him at the silent living room with all its holiday decorations, at the Christmas tree in its centre, twinkling with coloured lights and shiny ornaments. The embers of a fire still glowed in the fireplace, and red-and-green striped stockings hung from the mantel. A plate of small cakes sat waiting for Santa on an end table beside the somewhat worn but comfortable-looking sofa. Santa moved to place two red-and-green wrapped presents beneath the tree. Joe sighed, gazing around him in quiet yearning as he found himself standing in a perfectly normal living room, in a real home that belonged to some lucky kid. His gaze fell on a picture sitting on the end table, of a man and woman posing with their arms around a little boy, all smiling happily beside a sparkling blue lake.

'Is this the kid who lives here?' Joe asked.

'Yup,' Santa answered.

'What did he get?' Joe eyed the new packages beneath the tree with curiosity.

'Fishing rod.'

'How come?' Joe glanced at the picture again.

'That's what he asked for in his letter.' Santa Claus began to gather up his sack again, munching on a fairy cake.

'You mean, if a kid writes...' Joe looked up in sudden awe. 'Anything he wants?' he whispered.

Santa Claus stopped and looked back at Joe. 'Didn't you ever write to me, Joe?' he asked gently.

Joe looked down. 'I never believed –' He glanced up again and said, quickly and defensively, 'I mean, I never needed nothin'. See, I usually travel light.' He pushed his hands into his pockets, where they made fists.

Claus stood silently for a moment as more different emotions, and words to express them, welled up in him than he could ever express to this boy... knowing only that this was not the time or place to try to share them. The boy had his pride. It was all he had, and Santa knew better than to wound it. Instead, he took one more little cake for himself and handed Joe the other one left on the plate.

'Well, let's travel now,' Claus said at last. 'Come on.' He picked up his sack, and they were back on the roof again in an instant. And then the sleigh was off again to another stop, and yet another.

EIGHT

Cornelia lay in her large, soft bed, asleep at last
among its lavender and white frills, as weariness
finally overcame her excited Christmas Eve anticipation. Like children all over the world, she had lain
awake for hours, hoping to catch a glimpse of Santa
Claus. But sleep had finally crept up on her and
carried her away to dreamland... where it was
already Christmas morning.

Then, suddenly, a crash sounded somewhere in
the silent house. Cornelia sat bolt upright in her
bed, abruptly wide awake; blinking her eyes, her
heart pounding. She threw back the covers and
climbed down from her bed, tiptoed out into the hall,
heading towards the wide stairway that curved
down to the living room.

In the darkened living room, Joe was hastily
picking up a lamp. He had accidentally knocked it
over while staring in wonder at the huge, wood-
panelled space around him and the fifteen-foot-high
Christmas tree standing in the middle of it. The tree
was a work of art, covered with exquisite blown-
glass ornaments and shining angel hair until it
looked like a vast, glowing spun-sugar confection.
'Hey, I'm sorry,' Joe murmured to Santa, who was
setting another red-and-green package under the
tree, 'I didn't see the –'

'*Oh!*'

They spun around together, caught in the act, to
find a little girl in a ruffled flannel nightgown
standing wide-eyed with astonishment in the
doorway.

'Are you *him*?' the girl gasped, amazed. 'Are you
Santa Claus?'

'Oh, I hate it when this happens,' Santa muttered under his breath. Putting a broad smile on his face, he said, 'Hello, little girl.'

The girl pointed at the new present among the others heaped up beneath the tree. 'Is that my dolly?' Her eyes flickered up again as Joe moved uncomfortably to set the lamp back on its table. 'It's you!' she cried.

Joe really looked at the girl for the first time, and realised that he knew her, too. '*You*??' he asked incredulously. It was the red-haired girl who had left dinner out for him on several different nights during the past few weeks.

'You two know each other?' Santa asked, equally surprised.

Joe and Cornelia stared at each other, frozen in fascination, face to face at last after so much time. She took a few tentative steps towards him as he started uncertainly towards her, the two of them drawn together by an invisible, irresistible magnetic force.

'I'm... Cornelia.' Cornelia glanced down, stopping again, suddenly shy.

'I'm Joe,' Joe said, pushing his hands into his pockets again, equally self-conscious.

'I'm in a hurry,' Santa said, growing a trifle impatient with this young Romeo and Juliet.

Cornelia glanced at Santa, remembering suddenly who else she had surprised in her living room, and remembering her manners as well. 'Oh, it's a great pleasure to meet you, sir,' she said. She pointed towards the plate of fancy biscuits on the mantel piece. 'Would you like some of these? They're delicious.'

Santa peered dutifully at the plate. 'Oh, chocolate chip,' he said, pleased. 'My favourite.' He took two, stopping a moment longer to enjoy their sweet, chocolatey flavour before moving on towards the chimney.

As he paused for his snack, Cornelia whispered to Joe, 'Are you his friend?'

Joe straightened his shoulders, brushing his straight black hair back from his eyes, and shrugged with elaborate casualness. 'Oh yeah, I help him out. Sometimes I drive the reindeer. And... er...' he glanced up, and saw Santa watching him with a twinkling eye, 'sometimes I... don't.'

But it worked anyway. Cornelia gazed at him in wonder. 'Gosh!' she murmured. 'Don't you have to get home?'

Joe shrugged again. 'Haven't got a home.'

Cornelia thought about that a moment and a smile spread over her face. 'You mean you stay out all night and nobody tells you it's bedtime? Lucky!' she said, with envy and yearning. Considering the people she lived with, not having a home at all seemed like just about the nicest thing she could imagine. She looked up at Joe from under her eyelashes, suddenly shy again. He was the bravest and handsomest boy she had ever seen, she thought – and he certainly knew the most wonderful people!

Joe looked back at her, blushing slightly, trying desperately to think of something more to say to impress her. He had always thought girls were kind of yucky, but suddenly tonight he couldn't imagine why. 'Hey, um Cor...' he hesitated, '...what's your name again?'

'Cornelia,' she said.

'That's too fancy,' Joe said, frowning to cover the fact he had trouble pronouncing it.

'Oh.' She looked down, her face falling. She had always hated the name herself.

'I'll call you Corny.'

She looked up again, grinning with delight. She had never had a nickname before, and to be given one under such circumstances was absolutely the best.

'Listen, Corny,' Joe said, suddenly hesitant, his voice filled with gratitude, 'thanks for all the good food you gave me.'

Santa was gathering up his sack of presents. Joe

glanced towards him, and Cornelia realised that they were both about to leave. 'I can get you a bowl of ice cream,' she said hastily, knowing Santa could not stay, but wanting Joe to, desperately.

'Well...' Joe licked his lips, glancing back at Santa, torn.

Santa Claus smiled, seeing his dilemma and quickly offering him a way out. 'I'll tell you what, Joe, you stay and have something to eat. I'll see you again.' He realised, a bit relieved, that it would make parting much easier for both of them this way.

'You will? You mean it?' Joe demanded, both yearning and dismayed.

Santa nodded. 'Santa Claus doesn't lie, Joe. Next Christmas Eve, we've got a date. Okay?'

Joe grinned. 'You bet!'

Santa started towards the fireplace chimney, hesitated. Turning back, he said to Cornelia, 'Thanks for the biscuits.' Then, searching Joe's dark eyes and small, thin face, he said, 'You're sure you're going to be all right?'

Cornelia smiled reassuringly. 'He'll be fine,' she said, looking at Joe too, with a brief, fond glance.

Santa nodded and smiled, satisfied. Then, with a farewell wave, he took a deep breath and vanished from sight.

Joe and Cornelia stood staring at the spot where Santa had been just a moment before.

'What a guy,' Joe sighed, shaking his head with awe.

Cornelia nodded, still smiling until she thought her face would never do anything else again. 'Excellent,' she said.

NINE

Christmas Day dawned bright and cold over the great metropolis of New York, and, hour by hour, all around the world. Back at the North Pole, Santa slept peacefully in his bed, more satisfied than he had been with a Christmas Eve journey in many a year. Not only had he met two exceptional young people who had added fresh meaning to his journey, but he had delivered Patch's mass-produced toys to more children than ever; he was secure in his rest, thinking that next year Patch would meet his ever-increasing needs for new toys easily.

And as he slept, boys and girls around the world were waking up and opening their presents from Santa, and rushing outside to play with them. And, one after another, finding that the toys which had looked so shiny and perfect were actually fraud, ready to fall apart in their hands. Patch's sloppy manufacturing methods were dealing Santa Claus's reputation a terrible, painful blow even as Santa slept, completely unsuspecting. Before Christmas Day was even over, children everywhere would wear frowns at the very mention of his name...

In front of a suburban house on a sunny street, a happy boy wheeled his brand new Christmas bicycle out of the front door and down the pavement. Hopping onto the seat, he rode away down the street, grinning broadly.

But only for a moment. As he rode along, the front wheel was already wobbling unobtrusively, as the poorly-tightened screw that held it to the bicycle frame began to work loose. All at once the front wheel broke free from the frame as the bolt separated. The boy crashed to the ground, scraping his knee and tearing his new Christmas clothes. He sat on the pavement, crying with pain and surprise.

And down the street, a rosy-cheeked little girl pulled her new red wagon up the road, chattering happily to her favourite doll, who was being taken for her very first ride. But as the little girl towed the wagon up the steep hill its handle suddenly came loose. The wagon rolled back down the hill, faster than the little girl could run. As she watched in horror, it bumped down over the kerb into the gutter, just as a bus came roaring up the street. The bus turned the corner, and the wagon and doll were crushed beneath its wheels. The little girl's wails of grief joined the boy's crying in the clear, cold air.

And on down the road a curly-haired toddler sat in his front garden, trying to fit together the pieces of a simple jigsaw puzzle, which had been cut so badly that none of the parts fitted together. He threw the pieces away and began to howl; his shrieks of frustration joined the rising chorus of weeping and sorrow that was already growing in the street.

It was a scene that was repeated on street after street throughout the city, across the country and around the world. Everywhere the suddenness and universality of the toys' failure, and the fickleness of human nature, combined to blacken Santa Claus's reputation.

Dooley sat in his easy chair late one evening a few days after Christmas, peacefully reading in one of his rare quiet moments. A sudden clatter and crash coming down his chimney sent him leaping up from his seat, as several dozen broken toys came hurtling down the chimney to land in a great heap in his fireplace. Dooley stood beside his chair, his eyes bulging in disbelief for a long moment before he could even make himself move. And then he hurried to the fireplace to sort through the broken pieces, frowning and shaking his head. Clutching the appalling evidence of a genuine crisis, he hurried off and ordered the nearest elf to go in search of Patch. The elf's eyes widened as he heard Dooley's sharp, pungent message for Santa's Assistant and saw the broken toys in his hands. Then, carrying the load of broken pieces, Dooley went to report to Santa Claus.

'*Returns*!' Claus cried in horrified dismay, as Dooley stood in his living room and held the ruined toys out to him. 'We've *never* had returns!'

Dooley nodded silently, his face downcast, knowing that Santa Claus must realise just as he did that there could only be one reason for it to have happened this year, when it had never happened before: Patch had been put in charge of the toymaking...

Anya sat in her chair by the fire, stunned, too upset even to speak. Her hands went on knitting rapidly, as if they were searching for a calm rhythm her mind had lost. How could Patch have done such a thing? She knew he had not done it on purpose; but still, to be so careless, to let such an enormous mistake happen... They had *trusted* him so...

Dooley cleared his throat. 'Maybe we should release some kind of statement...?' he murmured to Claus. He was mindful of modern communications and the repercussions they made possible, ever since Patch had insisted that he install a television set in his communications centre.

A timid rapping at the front door made them all turn as one, their faces falling further. Anya rose to her feet at last and moved reluctantly to answer the door.

Patch stood there, as she had known he would. His face was a mask of cheerful greeting, but she saw the dark, haunted gleam in his eyes. He knew as well as they did why he had been summoned here; Dooley's messenger had told him the news. But she could see that he was still doing his brash best to pretend nothing was wrong. Her heart went out to him; she knew how hard it must be for him to learn that he had made such a mistake... But they both already realised that he had caused terrible harm to Santa's reputation. There was no way he could change, or deny, that. She stood aside wordlessly to let him enter.

'Oh,' Claus said, as Patch entered the room.

'Hi there,' Patch said feebly.

'Well,' Dooley murmured, twisting his belt uncomfortably, 'I've got a lot to do.' He hurried to the open door, eager to be gone, knowing what a painful scene was about to follow.

The awkwardness of the situation was so thick that Anya could have cut it with a knife. She wrung her hands, looking from her husband's face to Patch's.

For a long moment neither Claus nor Patch spoke; and then, at the same moment:

'Well, it's quite a –' Santa began.

'You see, the thing –' Patch burst out.

They both fell silent again, looking down in embarrassment.

Patch took a deep breath, his face as red as his Assistant's apron. 'The thing is –' he said again. 'I don't care about *my* image,' Claus interrupted, trying desperately to find something to say that was not the obvious, 'that's never been my –'

'You see,' Patch ran on insistently, his voice straining with the knowledge of what he had to say; desperate to get it out before Santa was forced to say it for him, destroying the last shreds of his ego, 'being tied down to a desk suits some elves, y'know, but others of us are more – well, *free spirits*.'

'I'm sure you had no idea –' Claus forced the words out, knowing they must both acknowledge the grave seriousness of the situation, and sensing that Patch was unwilling, or unable, to do it. After all, it was the children who had been hurt the most by this. He wiped the unaccustomed perspiration from his brow. 'Patch, how can I say this?'

Before he could say the words Patch dreaded to hear, the elf interrupted again, frantically, 'Can we have a man-to-elf talk here?' As he spoke he untied his bright red Assistant's apron with fumbling hands, and began to take it off. Anya turned away from the sight, her eyes filling with unexpected tears.

'I just feel that red really isn't my colour,' Patch rattled on. 'It's just doesn't suit my... um... complexion.' He held the apron out at arm's length, offering it freely to Santa. But his hands twitched, almost jerking it back again, and the words of protest burst out before he could stop them, 'Of course, if you don't want –' His eyes pleaded for forgiveness, for a sign that Santa truly understood.

'No, no, I'll take it,' Claus said hastily. And, before he lost his own resolution, he took the apron from Patch's hand; turning away, he hurried to the cottage door. He opened it and went out without another word, closing it abruptly behind him.

Patch stood frozen where he was, his shoulders drooping, his heart breaking, his eyes glazed with shock. It had all happened so swiftly... He felt as if any moment the world would simply collapse from under him, and he would fall forever.

At last Anya, still standing beside him in the silent room, said softly, 'That broke his heart, you know. It's the hardest thing he's ever had to do.' Her hands were still clasped together so tightly that her knuckles were white. Her voice was both apologetic and faintly reproving.

'It wasn't exactly a red-letter day for me, either,' Patch murmured. He looked up at her, his eyes brimming.

Anya twisted her hands, wanting very much to reach out and hug him, knowing it would be the worst thing she could do right now. 'Will you be all right?' she asked, feeling as if the words were painfully inadequate. Who could even imagine what he would do next, after such a humiliating failure?

Patch pulled himself together with an effort, and grinned with false bravado. 'Me? I couldn't be

happier.' He shrugged and waved a dismissing
hand, shooing the past away like a fly. 'I mean, let's
face it, us free spirits, we can't be burdened down
with all that responsibility stuff.' He broke off
again, seeing Anya's expression, and cleared his
throat. 'Yes. Well,' he mumbled, suddenly looking
down, 'every elf has his place and mine should be in
bed by now so I'll just toddle off. Night, ma'am.' He
touched his hat in polite farewell. Whistling a
brave, shaky little tune, he turned and hurried out of
Santa's home. Anya stood where she was for a long
moment, feeling as if she had simply frozen into an
icy statue. At last she sighed and shook her head,
turning away to the window to look out at the rising
hubbub down below.

Patch descended the spiral stairs from Santa
Claus's cottage on leaden feet. He looked out in the
workshop area, where until today he had been more
important than anyone but Santa himself. And
now, watching, he saw Santa Claus with his back
turned, handing the red Assistant's apron to a
smugly beaming Puffy, as dozens of other elves
looked on. If word hadn't got around already (and
how the elves loved gossip), everyone would know
his disgrace now. Santa certainly wasn't wasting
any time, he thought bitterly. He could not see
Santa Claus's face; see the sorrow that dimmed the
usually-sparkling blue eyes and pinched the once-
merry smile as Puffy took the apron from Santa's
hands. Santa Claus was happy for Puffy, who was
certainly a good and careful worker. But Patch . . .
Patch had always been something special. If only
he had been as responsible as he was clever . . .
Santa sighed deeply as he turned away.

Patch held his face frozen in an expression of
calm indifference, hiding the pain and embarrassment he felt from the watching elves as he hurried
past their stares and away.

He made his way to the stables, where he still
slept and kept his eye on the welfare of the reindeer.
The reindeer watched in silent curiosity as he began

109

to gather up his possessions. Alone at last except for the silent animals, Patch finally let his anger come pouring out. He had thought Santa cared about him. But Santa hadn't cared abut him at all! *One little mistake*, he thought, *and Santa forgot all the good things I have ever done*... All the while knowing in his heart that it hadn't been a little mistake at all... that it had been such a huge, irreparable mistake that no one could ever forgive him, especially himself. It had been such a terrible mistake that he couldn't face admitting it, even to himself...

'Wait till he wakes up and finds his free spirit has spirited himself away,' he muttered to the reindeer, but more to himself. He *had* done a good job – he had given them just what they'd needed here – modernised their toy production. So there were a few bugs in the system... nobody was perfect. Santa could have given him a second chance. It wasn't like he'd done it on *purpose* –

He pulled open the bright red doors of his storage cabinet, looking for a piece of cloth to tie his belongings up in. As he searched the shelves he saw his copy of the *Elf Rule Book*. He pushed it aside impatiently. Behind it lay the glittering sack of magical stardust that he added to the reindeer's feed every year, lying on a shelf in the very top of the cupboard. He stared at it, without really realising that he was staring. 'Oh yes,' he went on, his voice sharp with hurt, 'then you'll hear the crying and moaning, but it'll be too late. "I never appreciated old Patch", he'll say –' unable even to speak Santa's name. '"Why didn't I tell him in time?"' His voice rose, trembling. 'He'll never have an Assistant as good as me!' All the emotion that he had held inside for so long burst out of him at once. 'Let's face it, he just doesn't like me!'

All the feelings he had lived with for so long before Santa had come, feelings of being unappreciated and misunderstood, rose up in him again in a great wave – and with it, the unspoken fear that had always haunted him, that perhaps the elves who had criticised him were really right... He had thought that in Santa he had finally found the one person who truly appreciated him... But now even Santa had rejected him. Because he was too full of hurt and guilt to see things objectively, his grief and disappointment turned outward, and turned into blame.

Patch looked back at the reindeer, seeing the shared sorrow in their wide, sombre brown eyes. They might not really understand all his words, but they certainly sensed his unhappiness, and felt it as their own. A large tear trickled down Donner's furry cheek. He stretched his neck, reaching out to Patch to comfort him.

At least the reindeer really *did* appreciate, and love, him... Patch's angry frown softened as he thought suddenly of all that he was going to be leaving behind when he left here. 'Oh boys, I am going to miss you, you know that, don't you –' he murmured. Reaching out to put his arms around Donner's neck, he hugged him tightly.

Late that night, when all the elvish village lay asleep, Patch crept out of his refuge in the stable again and went silently across the Great Hall to the front gate. Pushing open the vast door he stepped out into the snow, and shut it firmly behind him. Looking resolutely ahead, he started to walk. He carried a single bundle slung over his shoulder on a stick as he left his home like a fugitive, without a single good-bye. The only sign of his departure was the quiet crunching of his footsteps in the snow.

He turned once, when he had walked several hundred yards, and, walking backwards, looked up one last time at the enchanted home he was leaving for the strange new world that lay beyond its borders. As he watched, the great rippling Christmas tree of aurora which only those who truly belonged within the enchanted village could see, slowly began to fade from sight.

Patch stopped, standing motionless with loss for a long moment, his eyes blinking, still searching for something they could no longer see. Then he turned away again, his dark eyes even darker with sorrow. If Santa and the others didn't appreciate his talents, he would find a place where people did. 'I'll show him what I'm made of,' he muttered. 'I'll make him take notice, I will, I will.' He would prove all over again that he was the best toymaker ever. And then Santa would be begging him to come home ... He had no idea where he was going or what he would do, but he was sure he would find his just deserts somewhere in the great world beyond.

He walked on across the bleak, frozen wasteland, turning his back on the village again. And as he walked, the sack slung over his shoulder glittered softly with its own light. It was not, after all, the bag of belongings that he had originally intended to take with him. Instead, it was a bag of the magic stardust. He had violated the final trust of all, turning his back on Santa and his former friends in every sense. He walked on, struggling against the clouds of snow raised by the gusting wind; his small, lonely figure grew smaller and smaller in the night. The last of him that could be seen, if anyone had been watching, was a glittering flicker of stardust.

TEN

The Capitol Building lay as serenely white as the snow-covered lawns and trees of Washington D.C. The city rested peacefully on a crisp, blue-skyed winter day shortly after the New Year.

Within the halls of the Capitol, the minds of the eight Senate Sub-committee members seated at the long curving table were still on the recent holidays – but not on thoughts of good cheer. The press, television crews, miscellaneous aides and a gallery full of spectators filled the vast chamber, all watching and listening with great intentness as the investigator's key figure, the man on the spot, began his testimony at last. The defendent in this particular instance was none other than the president of the B.Z. Toy Company, one of the largest toymakers in the nation.

B.Z. himself was now answering questions at last about the highly questionable business practices of the company he owned. Sitting before the committee members clad in an expensive, conservative-ly-styled business suit and flanked by an ever-alert lawyer, he concentrated on maintaining the appearance of confident respectability and injured innocence that he had worked so hard to perfect before his shaving mirror this morning. It had been hard then, and it was still hard, to make his long, pasty-looking face seem wholesome, or his hard, beady blue eyes look innocent; almost as hard as it was to cover his bald spot with the slicked-down strands of his thinning brown hair. He mopped perspiration from his brow surreptitiously, the strain clearly beginning to tell on him. The committee's questions were coming at him like bullets.

The Chairman of the Sub-committee was not a man to be easily taken in by superficial appearances of respectability. Having been in politics for most of his life, the Chairman had become a fairly shrewd judge of human nature. And he judged the man before him to be greedy, arrogant, abusive, and rotten to the core. This was a man who ran a toy company the way Attila the Hun would run a charity. The thought of one of his own grandchildren possibly receiving one of the toys on display before him now as a gift made his blood run cold.

'Now, sir,' the Chairman said, his voice rising in righteous anger, 'I am asking you if these two toys are manufactured by your company, the B.Z. Toy Manufacturing Corporation?'

B.Z. leaned towards his lawyer – a thing he did so often the Chairman was surprised that he didn't have a permanent list in that direction – and the lawyer whispered in his ear. '... Uh, they appear to be our products, Senator,' B.Z. said, glancing at the toys suspiciously.

An aide stepped up to the table on which the evidence – a sweet-faced doll in a frilly pink gown and a chubby, smiling stuffed Panda – were displayed. The Chairman nodded, and as cameras *whirred* and *clicked*, the aide set an ashtray containing a lit cigarette next to the doll. Within seconds, the dolly's flimsy, highly inflammable dress began to smoke, and suddenly burst into flames. The doll became a blazing torch; the astonished watchers gasped in horror.

'What do you say to *that*, sir?' the Chairman asked, his eyes blazing with the fire of his outrage.

B.Z. pulled at the collar of his neat white shirt, loosening his discretely patterned tie. 'Well, Senator, I always knew smoking was dangerous. Hehhey...' He laughed feebly, groping in desperation for a joke that would distract the opposition and lighten up the heaviness of his miserable situation.

But the Senators were plainly not amused. 'This is not a laughing matter, sir!' the Chairman said sharply. 'This is a tragedy waiting to happen!' He looked up at the spectators in the gallery, at the whirring television cameras. He was sincerely concerned about this problem, but he was also – always – concerned about his own image with the public. This investigation could win him the hearts and the votes of parents everywhere, and he fully intended to take advantage of the opportunity. 'You, sir,' he flared dramatically, 'are a disgrace to your profession!' He waved his aide towards the table again.

B.Z. squirmed under the camera's merciless gaze. With every second that this went on, he was losing millions of dollars in sales. 'With all due respect, Senator –' he protested.

But the aide had already reached the display table again. Picking up the stuffed panda, he yanked its head off as easily as he would have snapped a dry stick in two. He turned the panda over. The eager lenses of a dozen cameras zoomed in as the stuffing came pouring out – sawdust and lint, glittering with sharp nails and shards of broken glass.

'And I believe this toy is advertised as "suitable for three year olds"?!' the Chairman said, his voice heavy with irony.

B.Z. leant even further towards his lawyer, whispering frantically and then listening intently. He looked back at the Chairman again, wiping his face, pulling his features into order like a man playing with silly putty. 'Senator, I'm more astonished than you are to see this,' he said, shaking his head in what he meant to be innocent dismay. 'I can only conclude that one of my employees, in a misguided effort to cut costs, made these errors in judgement. I guarantee that if these are not isolated examples, I'll make sure it never occurs again.'

'Oh, come now –' one of the other senators on the

115

panel interrupted, his tone expressing the scepticism he shared with everyone there.

'You'd better do more than that, sir,' the Chairman snapped to B.Z. 'You'd better recall every B.Z. toy on the market or I'll personally see to it that your licence to manufacture and distribute in this country is revoked.'

B.Z. mopped his brow again with his already sodden linen handkerchief. 'Senator, may I –' he whined.

The Chairman pounded the table loudly with his gavel, drowning out the sound of more feeble excuses from the human slug sitting before him. *'Next witness!'* he called, his gaze still fixed dramatically on the crowd.

At the same time, in a spot unmarked on any map, Santa Claus sat at the table in the cosy home that had once been his refuge, untouched by the trials and difficulties of the greater world. But the problems of the world had intruded even here, and since this past Christmas they seemed to be getting worse with every passing day. Santa rested his head in his hands, leaning on the sturdy wooden tabletop. 'Patch gone, and it's all my –'

'It's *not* your fault,' Anya said, gently but with absolute belief.

Dooley, Boog, Honka and Vout stood before him, their faces long with sorrow as they saw the stunned look on his own. Dooley nudged the other elves surreptitiously, and they nodded their agreement with Anya's words. 'Not *your* fault, Santa,' Honka, Boog, and Vout chorused together. They missed their friend and leader very much; but even they had to admit that he had only himself to blame for everything.

Santa looked up at them again, distraught and unconvinced. If only he had suspected how hard Patch would take this. But Patch had always seemed so full of elf-confidence. Perhaps if he had found the right words, taken a moment more...

'Where will he go? What will he do?' he said, knowing they had no answer either. 'The world is no place for an elf!' He thought of the often harsh realities of the world beyond the North Pole, with its hunger and mistrust and countless varieties of sorrow, which he had worked for so long to brighten in his own small way. The elves had no firsthand knowledge of such things; their world was one of peace and comfortable order ... though no longer of complete contentment.

Boog frowned with confusion and concern. 'The world's a nice enough place, isn't it?' he said, trying to imagine his old friend out in its vastness somewhere.

'I mean, we get such nice letters from there, it must be,' Vout added hastily.

'Don't worry about Patch,' Honka said, his voice firm and confident; trying to convince himself as much as convince the others. 'He can take care of himself. He knows the art of elf-defence.' He grinned, comforted by the thought of how often and easily Patch had tossed him and the others over his shoulder into the hay in playful wrestling matches.

But Santa only sighed, shaking his head, and Anya put her hands comfortingly on his shoulders. Nothing would be the same, now that Patch was gone. He wondered for a moment whether there was some way they could find Patch, and bring him back ... But he only sighed, without even speaking the thought aloud. No matter how much he might blame himself for Patch's running away, or want to bring the missing elf back to ease his own sorrow, the fact remained that Patch had made a grievous mistake. He had not taken his responsibilities seriously enough. He needed to learn a lesson or two about maturity and responsibility ... and perhaps going out on his own was the only way he would ever get it.

Santa hoped fervently that a year which was starting out so badly could only improve ... and in his heart he wished Patch all the good fortune he

117

could find; and added a wish that some day the small, impulsive genius would find his way back to his rightful home and the people who loved him.

But Patch had no intention of returning to the home he had abandoned, at least not until they begged him to, and admitted to what he still saw as *their* mistake. And so, not many days later, the most impulsive of elves found himself walking quite confidently down a street in the centre of Manhattan, studying the windows of department stores and shops with frank fascination. Having left the North Pole behind did not mean that he had left his magical abilities behind, and he had made good use of them to improve his travelling time, setting an unmarked land speed record from the North Pole to Civilisation – in the form of the Big Apple. This was New York City, the legendary hub of commerce, where it was said that the best and the brightest gathered to become successful; and that was certainly what he felt he was, and definitely what he intended to become. He'd prove to Santa, and all of them, that they needed him.

Blasé urban dwellers swirled past him, hurrying home through the evening rush hour, barely sparing him a second glance. A remarkably small man dressed like something out of a Christmas window display was the least of the strange things to be seen on the winter streets of New York; and even if it did strike some of them as odd, the sophistication of the city dweller demanded that they did not mention it, even to themselves.

Patch was not in the least offended by their lack of curiosity, since the way he looked did not strike him as odd in the least, and it never occurred to him that they might find him unusual. He stopped short in his wanderings, as something in a store window suddenly caught his eye. Beneath a banner bearing a distinctive logo and the slogan 'B.Z. TOYS – FOR HAPPY GIRLS AND BOYS' was a vast assortment of toys, stuffed animals and dolls. As he watched,

118

an assistant began systematically to sweep them from the display window in armloads and carry them away. Patch watched in amazement, astonished to think how wonderful a line of toys must be to be disappearing so rapidly. He turned to the nearest human on the street, the only one who seemed to be standing still beside him. 'They must be very popular,' he said, pointing at the toys. 'Look how fast they're selling—'

The shabbily-dressed wino lounging against the building wall glanced up over the rim of his bottle in surprise as he realised that someone was actually speaking to him. He looked over at the bizarrely-clad adult scarcely larger than a twelve year old who was standing nearby, looking at him with a congenial smile. All of a sudden he disappeared. The wino looked at where the elf had stood a moment before, looked down at the bottle clutched in his hand, and back at the empty spot again. The old derelict shook his head and pitched his bottle into the gutter. He turned and shambled away down the street without a word, still shaking his head.

At the same moment, that B.Z. fellow was brooding in his townhouse not terribly far away, getting ready to visit his company headquarters in the morning, for the first time since the catastrophic Senate hearings. He knew that a financial disaster of major proportions was already in the process of occurring at the B.Z. Toy Company; for the past few days he had been desperately trying to think of a way he could worm out of the responsibility of it. Unfortunately, he had so far failed to come up with one; or with anything that would get his money back, either.

But the next morning, despite his depressing lack of inspiration, he boarded his private helicopter and flew out to his company headquarters. B.Z. wasted no time as the helicopter set down on the pad of the Long Island heliport. Muttering to himself, he strode the few steps to his waiting limousine, which

119

bore the same corporate logo as the helicopter. A hulking, heavyset man in a chauffeur's uniform held the car's door for him. The chauffeur's name was Grizzard, and his nose seemed to have been broken in several different places, at several different times. He looked more like the bouncer at an extremely questionable nightclub (which he had been, among other things) than like a chauffeur of a respectable business man. But then, his employer was hardly respectable.

B.Z. settled into the wide, leather-upholstered back seat of the car. A built-in bar and a television set awaited his interest . . . and also waiting for him, with all the enthusiasm of a condemned man awaiting the executioner, was his chief assistant and Head of Research and Development, Dr Eric Towzer.

Towzer cringed visibly as B.Z. dropped heavily into the seat beside him. B.Z.'s glowering countenance turned to him, and his own face became a pale, harried mask of nervous dread. An ingratiating toady by nature, Towzer had found his ecological niche working for the President of B.Z. Toys. He was utterly loyal to his boss – and utterly in his thrall, a relationship in which he normally thrived, like fungus on a rotten log. But that was when everything had been going fine . . .

'Okay, Towzer,' B.Z. said grimly, 'give it to me straight.'

Towzer squirmed and tugged at his collar. 'The retail outlets are pulling our toys off the shelves so fast you'd think they were disease carriers.'

'Cowards,' B.Z. muttered, disgusted. He glared at the suburban homes passing by outside the tinted glass of the limousine's window, where dozens of children were not happily playing with B.Z. toys – all because of their faint-hearted parents and the paranoid United States Government.

'An article in the *Times* said that anyone who gives his child a B.Z. toy should be arrested as a child molester.' Towzer's voice took on a faintly nauseating whine of anxiety.

'Swine,' B.Z. snarled. 'Cancel my subscription.'
He did not suggest sueing for libel.

'We've got to meet a payroll by the end of the
month for two thousand factory workers –' Towzer's
voice actually began to quaver, like a defective
record.

'Commies...' B.Z's frown grew even darker, as
the storm clouds of his temper gathered.

'– and our cash flow is flowing the wrong way,'
Towzer finished breathlessly, 'right down the
toilet.'

B.Z. glanced at him and said sourly, 'You sure
know how to cheer a guy up, Towzer.'

Towzer pulled in his head like a turtle. 'What'll we
do, B.Z.?' he whined, hoping desperately that the
'we' would be enough to keep the axe he knew was
waiting in B.Z.'s brain from falling on his own neck.

B.Z. stared at him for a moment that stopped his
heart. And then, 'Fire Simmonds!' B.Z. ordered, in
an explosion of inspired fury. 'Tell him he's got one
hour to clean out his desk.'

'*Simmonds*?' Towzer said blankly. 'Vice-President
of Operations, Simmonds?'

B.Z. nodded in satisfaction. 'Put the blame
squarely on him. Put out a statement.' He had never
liked Simmonds anyway. You couldn't trust a man
who wore a bow tie. He was sick of looking at it.

'But...' Towzer said feebly, still reeling from the
suddenness of B.Z.'s decision, still barely able to
believe that his own neck was safe. 'Simmonds has
been with the firm for thirty years.'

B.Z. grinned with evil satisfaction. 'If you can't
stand the heat,' he gloated, 'don't work in hell.' It
was the credo he lived by, and it had always served
him well.

The limousine stopped briefly at the security
guard's hut at the entrance to a large industrial
complex, and then started on into its grounds. The
car drove up and stopped before the single office
building, flat-roofed and graciously landscaped,

121

which lay among the sprawl of the much larger buildings that were clearly used only for manufacturing. A large billboard sign towering above the complex read, 'B.Z. TOYS – FOR HAPPY GIRLS AND BOYS.'

B.Z. launched himself from his limousine and entered the offices like a charging rhino. He swept through the reception area, not even acknowledging the startled employees he passed, or their obsequious greetings. Taking the lift to the top floor, he headed straight for his own private office, which was hidden discretely behind heavy mahogany doors at the far end of the corridor.

'Miss Abruzzi!' he roared, as he neared his secretary's desk, just outside his office.

'Yes, B.Z?' Miss Abruzzi chirped, instantly on the alert. Neatly and conservatively dressed, like her boss, she was a still thin, tense, pale-looking woman; her physical appearance was mostly the result of having been the personal secretary of a raging bully for years – as was the permanent nervous tic that jerked at the corner of her mouth.

'No calls!' B.Z. stormed, in passing. 'No visitors! No nothing!' He jerked open the door to his office and barrelled through, slamming it so hard behind him that the pictures on the wall rattled and swayed. Miss Abruzzi sighed and rose to set them straight once again.

B.Z. crossed the vast solitude of his office, his heavy footsteps making little sound on the deep rust-coloured pile rug. He looked neither left nor right, ignoring the wood-panelled space around him, which had recently been expensively redecorated in black and gold, his favourite colours. One wall was covered with photos of himself in better days, in grinning proximity to the wealthy and powerful; as well as the wide range of plaques and awards his company had been presented with over the years, by people who had mistakenly taken B.Z.'s pronouncements of quality and craftsmanship at face value. On a shelf below the plaques and pictures was a display of the former best-selling toys in the company's catalogue – including a special display case featuring an award he had been given for the now-notorious inflammable doll and infamous nail-and glass-stuffed panda.

B.Z.'s heavy black-and-walnut desk was over-sized, and rested upon a subtly raised platform, so that anyone who sat across it from him was seated considerably lower, with the accompanying psychological feelings of powerlessness and smallness which that position represented. (Behind his back, his employees muttered that his office had been designed by the well-known Mussolini School of Interior Decoration.) His vast black leather desk chair sat with its back turned to him, as if it were looking out of the tall windows behind his desk.

As B.Z. entered his private sanctuary, letting his face go slack, and thinking that he was alone at last, a voice said suddenly and quite distinctly, 'Keeping banker's hours, eh? I thought you'd never get here.' The leather chair swivelled around.

B.Z. stopped short, gaping in disbelief. There, smiling confidently and even putting feet shod in pointy-toed boots up on *his* desk top, was an apparition out of one of his catalogues, a toy elf come to life.

'Who the hell –' B.Z. began indignantly. 'Miss Abruzzi!' he bellowed. But his voice could not penetrate the solid walls and door of his office. Realising it, he rushed forward, reaching out for the intercom switch on his desk.

The elf waved a hand casually, as cool as an ice cube in December. 'Don't bother with that,' he said pleasantly. 'If anybody comes in, I'll just vanish.'

B.Z.'s eyes bulged; his face struggled to look more outraged than it did already. 'You'll what??' he snarled, suddenly becoming certain that this oddly-dressed stranger must be some kind of madman.

The elf shrugged. 'Vanish. Like this.' And he disappeared.

B.Z. swayed, wondering whether he was going

blind, or merely losing his own mind. He stared around the room. 'Hello?' he said uncertainly, almost hoping there would be no answer. It must be the strain getting to him...

But from somewhere off to his right the cheerful voice said, 'Hi!' And abruptly the elf reappeared, perched now on the smooth brass mantlepiece of the office's decorative, nonfunctional fireplace. He smiled his same benignly amused smile.

'How did you do that???' B.Z. demanded, finding it difficult to speak with his jaw still agape.

The elf shrugged, not bothering to answer. 'You make toys, right?' he asked.

B.Z. squinted, suddenly on his guard as a new and worse possibility than his own insanity, or his visitor's, occurred to him. 'Are you from the Federal Trade Commission?' he asked nervously.

The elf shook his head. 'No, I'm from the North Pole.'

B.Z. frowned, his relief changing instantly back into prickling irritation. 'Look, junior, I've got enough on my mind without having to deal with an escaped lunatic.'

Patch raised his eyebrows, a bit taken aback that this seemingly ignorant human should know about what he now saw as his daring departure from Santa's realm. His legend must be travelling even faster than he was, he thought with satisfaction; having no idea at all what a lunatic was.

'*What are you?*' B.Z. bellowed, losing all patience.

Patch shrugged again. 'Isn't it elf-explanatory?' He gestured down at himself, at his colourful clothes, with a sweeping gesture.

'Howzzat?' B.Z. snapped, thoroughly nonplussed and thoroughly exasperated.

'I'm an elf.' Patch held out his hands, shrugging.

B.Z. grimaced. 'An elf. You mean like a fairy?'

Patch drew himself up a bit huffily. There was really no comparison, as far as he was concerned. 'No, I'm not a fairy. I'm an elf,' he murmured. Maybe

124

that comment about his escape had just been a lucky guess, after all.

'What's your game?' the toymaker demanded, looking and sounding a little frightened now. B.Z. had somehow expected this whole scene to dissolve like a bad dream at any moment; but it just wasn't happening.

Patch found it odd to be asked about his taste in sports at an important moment like this, but these humans were nothing if not peculiar. 'Ninepins,' he answered politely. 'Do you play?'

B.Z. struck himself sharply on the forehead, as if trying to shake something loose. 'Why are you here?' he asked, trying desperately to ask a question which would elicit a rational response.

Patch brightened, and smiled again. 'I gather you're a great toy-giver. I'm a great toy-*maker*. We should get together.'

'Why should I do that?' B.Z. growled, instantly suspicious again. He didn't care if this guy could disappear or not – these parasites and hangers-on were always coming around, looking for a way to snatch a piece of his profits.

'Well, you know the old saying –' Patch said whimsically. '"Heaven helps those who help their elf."'

B.Z. shook his head. 'Why *me*?'

Patch held out his hands. 'I want to help you.'

'Why?' B.Z. asked sharply, knowing there was no such thing as a free lunch.

To his surprise, the elf's face fell. His voice dropped to a tremulous murmur as he said, 'So Santa Claus will appreciate me.'

B.Z. grunted in disgust. 'I was right. You *are* a lunatic.'

Patch raised his head indignantly. 'Don't you believe in Santa Claus?' he asked. 'Surely a toymaker, of all people ...'

'Why should I?' B.Z. said petulantly, staring at his feet. 'He never brought me anything.'

125

Patch nodded to himself, understanding now. Santa never ignored a child unless there was a good reason. 'That's because you probably were a naughty boy,' he said, with mild reproach.

B.Z. didn't answer for a moment. A slow smile began to spread across his face, as he remembered wings pulled off countless helpless flies, kittens dropped into sewers, little girls' new party dresses pelted with oily mud... 'Yeah,' he said musingly, 'I guess I was no angel.' His mood brightened by the happy memories of his childhood, he looked up again, and said more congenially, 'What did you have in mind, elf?'

Patch hopped down from his perch on the mantle. 'Just let me use your factory,' he said, his eyes shining with sudden eagerness.

'To make what?' B.Z. asked bluntly.

Patch grinned. 'Something special. Here's the idea. First you stop making all your regular toys –' He gestured at the display of scandal-ridden objects on the far wall. 'I'm sure they're fine and dandy, dandy and fine,' he said placatingly, certain that this would be a point of strong resistance, 'but we won't need them any more.'

B.Z. brightened, his own eyes lighting up at the prospect of something – anything – that would replace his own suddenly notorious and unsaleable line. If this oddly-dressed nut had anything like a good idea, he'd brought it to exactly the right place. He sat down in the nearest chair, pulling it closer attentively, his mind racing with possibilities.

'Tell me something,' the elf said, his face suddenly pulling down with a frown of concern, as if something had been bothering him that he hadn't admitted until now. 'You're a man of the world and I'm just an elf of the top-of-the-world. How can we tell all the people about my "something special"?'

B.Z. grinned. 'Advertise,' he said simply.

Patch scratched his head, trying to remember if he had ever heard the word. 'How do you do that?'

'In my line, television works best,' B.Z. said, his

mind beginning to turn over the possibilities for a new ad campaign to restore his tarnished image.

Patch nodded suddenly. 'Oh...' he said, remembering. 'Those little picture box thingies? Can we get on those?'

B.Z. snorted. 'With money, a horse in a hoopskirt can get on television.'

Patch grimaced, trying to keep up with this flood of new concepts. 'Money,' he muttered. 'I don't know much about that.'

B.Z. grinned again. 'Good. Let's keep it that way.'

Patch nodded happily, relieved not to have to worry about all the messy little details himself. This B.Z. was clearly a man who knew what he was doing; he'd put his trust in the perfect person. 'You just fix it so I can be on tele-whatchacallit.'

'When?' B.Z. asked.

'Christmas Eve.'

Well, that wasn't too soon, at least... 'For how long?'

Patch thought a moment. 'Is a minute all right?'

That wasn't too long... B.Z. nodded. 'What channel?'

The elf looked confused, as if he had suddenly lost track of the conversation again. 'I've read about the English Channel. Is that one of them?' His face brightened as his mind caught up once more with the gist of the conversation. 'Ah, you mean, what tele-thingamabob in what country? All of them.'

'*All of them?*' B.Z. gasped, his face falling like a ton of bricks.

The elf nodded. 'All the countries. All the channel thingies.' Patch cocked his head. 'Well, it's only for a minute,' he said, wondering why the toymaker was staring at him as if he had suggested something akin to stopping the planet in its tracks.

'That would cost a fortune!!' B.Z. held his own head; the very thought of it made his brains ache.

Patch shrugged again. 'If you give extra kisses, you get bigger hugs. That's what Santa's wife always says.' He thought fleetingly and fondly of

127

Anya's smiling face, and felt a twinge of home-sickness.

B.Z. was staring at him in open wonder, now. 'You really *are* an elf, huh?' he murmured. Nobody, not even a lunatic, could be as ignorant of the world as this character, unless he really was from the North Pole. The thought was almost too mind-boggling to believe; and yet somehow, he believed it.

'Anyway,' Patch said soothingly, trying to re-assure the flabbergasted human, 'that's all the "advertising" you'll ever need.'

B.Z. pulled himself together with an effort, concentrating on the practical again. 'It had better be,' he said sourly. 'How many workers does this ... eh ... this product require?' He still didn't know what it was, but now he was almost afraid to ask.

'Just me,' the elf said, smiling.

B.Z.'s mouth dropped open; he looked like a dog eyeing the prospect of a particularly meaty bone. 'No payroll?' he asked.

'My needs are small,' Patch said modestly. 'A bowl of stew – heavy on the dill – a cold place to sleep –'

B.Z. rubbed his hands together, nodding tentative agreement. This really sounded promising ... 'How much will this cost?' he snapped, asking the one thing he really wanted to know, at last.

'Cost?' Patch said blankly. 'Cost who?'

'The people who buy the toys,' B.Z. answered impatiently.

'Oh, nothing,' Patch said blithely. 'We're gonna give it away free.'

B.Z. recoiled against the back of his seat, suddenly strangling. He gasped for breath, clutching at his tie.

Patch stared at him in wonder. 'Oooh, how do you *do* that?' he asked, impressed. 'Turn all red in the face so fast?!'

B.Z. sputtered inarticulately. Spitting out the words that were choking him, he wheezed, '*Give* something away? For *free*??'

128

Patch nodded. 'That's how we do it at the North Pole.'

B.Z. continued to sputter like a wet firework. 'Well,' he screamed, 'that's not how we do it here in a free enterprise society, where –' He broke off, as sudden inspiration struck him. 'Hmmm... On the other hand,' he murmured, as much to himself as to Patch, 'this *would* go a long way to cleaning up my public image...' If he charged money for the things, probably nobody would buy them anyway, the way things were right now.

'Excuse me?' Patch asked, not for the first time not following his new partner's train of thought.

B.Z. rubbed his chin thoughtfully. 'Hmm,' he murmured again, thinking out loud, 'not a bad investment, all that good p.r. –' He looked up at Patch once more. 'I'm intrigued,' he said, his eyes gleaming with heartfelt avarice and his mouth going absent-mindedly slack. This guy might *seem* crazy, but he was crazy like a fox. This could be the answer to his prayers...

Patch leant forward, concern showing on his face. 'Excuse me,' he said politely, 'you're drooling on your tie.'

B.Z. pulled back and snapped his mouth shut. 'I know,' he grated, 'I *said* I was intrigued, didn't I? Now, listen, have you had any experience in toy manufacturing?'

Patch preened confidently. 'I'm entirely elf-taught,' he said, raising his hands, gesturing at his outfit. Surely his background spoke for itself. He looked back at the toymaker. 'What do you say, B.Z.?'

B.Z. took a deep breath, and found the nerve to ask the only question that still filled his mind with uncertain curiosity. Not that it really mattered, but – 'This... this product you say they'll want,' he murmured, with the voracious interest of a hungry shark, 'what is it?'

Patch smiled again. 'It's something that's easy to

make. It's cheap. It's simple. And you can turn them out by the thousands.' It was an idea that never would have occurred to him back home; one that even Santa probably would not have had the vision to approve. 'And . . .' he said tantalisingly, preparing the final, irresistible argument.

'Yes? And?' B.Z. breathed, beginning to salivate again.

'It's got a secret ingredient!' Patch cried triumphantly. He reached into the pocket of his jacket, and pulled something out of his clenched fist. He held out his hand, and opened it. In his palm lay a few precious grains of the magical reindeer fodder, glinting like captive stars.

ELEVEN

It was a balmy if somewhat humid summer's day on Long Island. B.Z. strolled across the grounds of the B.Z. Toy Company towards the one factory building that was not locked up tight and silent as a tomb. Dr Towzer followed faithfully behind him, perspiring, toting a padlocked briefcase. Their footsteps echoed as they entered the one remaining open building, crossing the vast empty space towards an unobtrusive door at its far end.

'Look around you –' B.Z. said, waving his arm. 'No smelly workers, no strikes, no payroll – it's practically Paradise!' He chewed contentedly on his expensive, hand-rolled cigar. This Patch was the best thing that had ever happened to B.Z. Toys, no question.

'Still, giving this toy away for free –' Towzer protested reluctantly, trying to reason with his boss, as he had tried to so often before, but with no more success. Giving away toys for free was the same thing as committing suicide, as far as he could see.

B.Z. glanced at him with disdain. '*That* Dr Towzer, is precisely why *I* am a Captain of Industry and *you* are an insignificant *schlepper*.' He took a deep breath, attempting once again to explain his plan to his overwrought assistant. 'Sure, the first Christmas it's free. But the next one, we say, "You want it? Again? Bigger? Better? Well, this time it's going to cost you." He chuckled, a sound like rubber tearing.

Towzer brightened. 'How much?' he asked, finally beginning to grasp the method behind his boss's apparent madness.

'A hundred bucks?' B.Z. shrugged casually, his eyes glittering. 'Two hundred?'

Towzer's eyes widened. 'Where would they get that kind of money?' he whispered.

'What do I care where they get it,' B.Z. snapped, 'as long as it comes rolling in, eh?' He grinned again, complacently, and linked his fingers together. Arching the bow of his hands, he cracked all his knuckles at once in a volley of sickening *pops*. 'Ahhh,' he breathed, 'wonderful thing, cracking your knuckles. It's the pleasantest sound in the world.' He couldn't remember when he had been happier.

By now they had reached the far door, and he heard the sounds of pounding, hammering and clanging coming through from the mysterious room on the other side.

'What's he building in there?' Towzer asked.

'I'm not sure.' B.Z. shook his head. 'He says it's the "delivery system".' The elf had demanded strict secrecy and security measures for whatever he was building, even extending the secrecy as far as B.Z. himself. B.Z. had given in, reluctantly – being even more reluctant to offend his Golden Goose in elvish clothing. This was the first time in weeks he had even dared to intrude on the elf's work area. But now at last they had the samples he had requested... The door before him was securely locked; a sign posted on it read 'KEEP OUT' in very large letters. He raised his hand to knock, when suddenly the door opened.

Patch stood before them, clairvoyant as always, his eyebrows raised questioningly. He held a brightly-painted wooden soldier in his hand; his sleeves were rolled up and he had the look of somebody who had been interrupted at his work, and was unhappy about it. Behind him, various gaily painted wooden toys were scattered over the floor like pieces of a giant puzzle. B.Z. wondered silently what in the world they could possibly have to do with anything, and what Patch's so-called 'delivery system' could possibly be.   'Yes?' Patch said, a trifle impatiently.

'We've brought the prototypes for . . . *it*,' B.Z. said almost diffidently. He gestured to Towzer, who handed him the briefcase. He opened it. Inside, resting on a velvet cushion, were five lollipops: a round one, a long thin one, a big all-day sucker and a very small one. Their colours and flavours all varied. B.Z. had not the faintest idea what Patch planned to do with the one he chose; but as long as his 'secret ingredient' worked, B.Z. really didn't care.

Patch glanced at them for the briefest fraction of a second. 'That one,' he said, pointing at the small one.

'What colour?' Towzer asked.

Patch shrugged. 'What colour do you like?' he said, as if he couldn't care less.

'I like puce,' Towzer said eagerly.

B.Z. looked at him with disdain. '*You* would,' he said, with heavy sarcasm.

'What's puce?' Patch asked.

'It's like fuschia, but a shade less lavender and a bit more pink,' Towzer gushed, waxing poetic at the very thought of his favourite colour.

B.Z. shook his head. 'Towzer,' he muttered sourly, 'sometimes I wonder about you.'

But Patch nodded. 'Fine, puce then,' he said brusquely. 'As long as it tastes good.' Without another word, he shut the door in their faces.

Towzer stood where he was, flushed with a combination of embarrassment and pride. B.Z. was still staring at him as if he had made a complete jackass of himself. Awkwardly, he said, 'If this catches on, we can come out with a liquid version. Puce juice.' He grinned and giggled inanely.

B.Z. glared at him, utterly unamused. Towzer's giggling laughter died a death by strangulation. B.Z. turned on his heel and stalked away.

Back at the North Pole, light years away from the

B.Z. toy factory in spirit as well as in distance, Santa Claus sat in his rocking chair before the fire, whittling pensively at a block of wood. Anya came in from the kitchen, drying her hands on her apron. She glanced down, and stared in surprise as she saw what her husband was doing.

'Oh, my! An elf portrait,' she said, her voice betraying her amazement. 'You haven't made one of those since...' Her voice trailed off, as a strange feeling, almost of unreality, filled her. Claus had not made a toy with his own hands since they had come here to the North Pole – more time than she could even clearly remember, now. Claus was carving a wooden toy elf, and she saw that he had lost none of his skill in the intervening centuries; in fact, his artistry seemed more remarkable than ever, as if time had only honed it.

'It's for Joe,' Claus said softly, expressing his inner thoughts with hesitant difficulty. 'He makes me think what our son would have been like.' She realised that he was thinking about the boy he had met last Christmas.

Claus looked up at her. 'Nobody's ever given him a present,' he said, his eyes darkening with sadness. 'And he's too proud to ask.' He held the toy elf out to her.

Anya realised then that this toy was very special indeed; that he was making it with his own hands for a very special child. She took the wooden elf from him, looking at it more closely. Her breath caught. 'Why, it's him!' she exclaimed. 'It's Patch!' And indeed, it looked exactly like the one other person that Santa had loved almost like a son.

Claus's face reddened as she looked back at him, her eyebrows raised. 'No, it isn't,' he protested weakly, 'it's just a... well, I suppose it resembles...' He shook his head, sighing in surrender, as he admitted for the first time what his subconscious had led his hands to create. 'My good old Patch,' he murmured. 'I hope he's... all right,' he said inadequately, unable to bear even the thought that

134

his favourite young helper was anything else but all right.

Anya smiled sadly and nodded, her hand resting on his shoulder as she handed the half-finished toy back to him again.

Patch was anything but all right, but he was the last person to admit it, if not possibly the last to suspect it. He had worked diligently in secret all year long, preparing everything for the distribution of the ultimate present for the children of the world; the triumph that would make even Santa Claus admit that he had been wrong, and Patch right, all along. Now the time had come to make the world aware of it ... and Patch was showing uncharacteristic traces of discomfort and uncertainty.

He stood in the middle of a television studio, clad in a *haute couture* version of elf attire which had been personally designed for him: an immaculately cut, styled – and then sequin-covered – travesty of his old clothing, this time made entirely of patchwork squares in vibrant puce and blue. It was far too tight, and even too gaudy for his tastes; but B.Z. had insisted it was vital to present the 'right image' to the public. Tugging at his jacket, Patch looked around him at the setting in which he was about to make his announcement to the children of the world. 'I don't know about this,' he muttered weakly. 'It isn't what the North Pole looks like at all.' He shook his head, but his complaints were too few and too late.

All around him lay a display of almost mind-boggling bad taste and vulgarity, which had been painstakingly constructed and designed to B.Z.'s personal instructions. Gigantic outsized toys – which bore no resemblance to anything the elves had ever made, and were remarkable only for their nauseating, thoroughly calculating over-cuteness – loomed above him, making him feel even more insignificant and out-of-place than he already did. And assembled behind him was something he found even more disconcerting, a line of nubile chorus girls dressed in a spangled, skin-tight puce and blue mockery of elvish clothing, which revealed far more than it concealed. The whole setting reminded him of a bad dream he had had once after eating too much icicle cream for desert. Although he could not find the courage to admit it to himself, in his heart he knew that it was all a distressing perversion of everything elvish, as executed by the heavy hand of his human partner B.Z. But B.Z. claimed that he knew what people wanted...

'Look,' Towzer, B.Z.'s assistant, said reassuringly, 'B.Z. knows what he's doing. He knows how to grab the people.'

'But this isn't real,' Patch insisted, gesturing around him.

'The public doesn't want *reality*,' Towzer snapped nervously. 'They want the *dream*!'

Patch opened his mouth again, and closed it, telling himself for the dozenth time that B.Z. had given him everything he needed until now, and reluctantly admitting that he really didn't know anything about this 'advertising' business himself. Before his doubts could rise up and get his attention again, the floor manager's voice was calling,

'*Places everybody.*'

Patch stood frozen where he was, like a creature caught in the glare of a spotlight, as Towzer and the stagehands melted away from around him, and offstage the announcer's voice began its introductory spiel: 'Live! From New York! Presenting... direct from the North Pole, that perky pixie, that nimble gnome, the elf himself! It's PATCH!'

Patch gasped as the spotlights trained on him for real, and he was irrevocably committed to this bizarre culmination of his plans. Technology compared to magic was what human beings were compared to elves – bizarre, illogical and overly complicated. No longer was it possible simply to wish that the world could hear and see him, and have it happen: he had to remember where to look and what to say while great strange metal monsters trained their glassy eyes upon him with a merciless stare. He took a deep breath and began to recite his greeting to children everywhere.

But the words of merry greeting which he had rehearsed for days now seemed completely unfamiliar to him, as they crawled up out of some hidden depths onto the screen of a teleprompter. Intended to reassure and guide him, he found to his frightened dismay that the printed lines were only leading him astray. First they crawled by so slowly that he had to drag out every word as if he were talking through a mouthful of glue; then they abruptly speeded up until his tongue had to run full tilt to follow; then suddenly they slowed to a crawl again. And at the same moment, he was switched from one camera to another in mid-sentence, leaving him cross-eyed and gibbering.

B.Z.'s venal manipulation had in one stroke reduced the once self-assured Patch, who had been so certain that he was on top of the world figuratively if not literally, to a confused pawn in a game not of his own devising.

As Patch floundered and blew his lines, looking wildly from side to side for the right camera, the studio's harassed floor manager grimaced in silent agony. Where did they find these amateurs, he wondered, and why did he have to be responsible for making them look good – on live TV, to the entire world? No company had ever bought so much advertising at once before. He *had* to make this commercial a success, or he'd never work again. B.Z. would see to that. He paced back and forth, earphones jabbing his head and his clipboard clutched in a deathgrip, trying to outguess Patch's floundering mistakes in time to save the commercial from utter disaster and himself from professional suicide.

As Patch became hopelessly garbled on TV Camera Two, the floor manager hissed desperately into his mike, 'Camera Three! Camera Three!' Patch disappeared abruptly from the monitor screen in front of him, replaced by prancing chorus girls. The manager dashed out onto the stage and hurriedly shoved Patch into the proper position, then darted back into the wings.

Patch heaved a deep sigh of heartfelt relief as he realised that he had miraculously been given a moment in which to collect himself. The chorus 'elves' began to prance and curvette around him, batting their eyelashes at the proper camera as it trained on Patch again. Knowing that he *must* make this a success or all that he had worked so long and hard to prove would come to nothing, he stretched his mouth into his widest and most winning smile. The chorus girls began to sing,

> *'On the first day of Christmas*
> *My true love gave to me –*
> *A Patch present under the tree.'*

They sang and danced gaily to calculatedly 're-vised' Christmas carols, riveting the attention of television viewers everywhere. Across the United States parents and children glanced up from their tree-trimming and present-wrapping to see the odd apparition in the glitzy patchwork suit smile and recite ingratiatingly,

> 'From the Old North Pole,
> Where the elves make toys,
> Here's a Christmas treat
> For you girls and boys!
> Oh, my name is Patch
> And as you can tell,
> I'm an elf myself,
> So let's give a yell!'

'Patch! Natch! Patch! Natch!' the chorus girls cried, flinging their arms into the air.

The bizarre spectacle circled the world, as B.Z. had promised, bouncing from satellite to satellite, emerging in countless languages from television sets wherever they might be...

Even at the North Pole.

In the elves' compound Dooley, Goober and Puffy sat together in the information centre of Dooley's quarters, watching the brightly-painted box that showed them the world outside day by day. (Even Dooley had had to admit that it required modern methods to keep up with the rapid changes in the world and the interests of its children.) The three elves sat gaping as their former companion began to strut his stuff with the singing chorus girls. Their faces turned pale and tight-lipped with shocked dismay as the garish display went on and on, and Patch's obvious Christmas Eve competition with Santa Claus began to take awful shape.

Dooley raised a hand. 'Quick,' he said to Puffy. 'Get him in here right now.'

Puffy leapt from his seat and rushed out of the room to find Santa Claus.

Back in New York City, every one of the half dozen television sets in the window of an electrical shop brayed Patch's message to the passing stream of last-minute shoppers.

Joe stood in front of the shop window, his hands in his pockets, the chill wind forgotten as he stared in wondering disbelief at the sight of Patch reciting,

> 'Well, the patchwork present
> Comes from me.
> You'll find it under
> the Christmas tree
> And best of all, you will agree,
> Is that it's absolutely FREE!'

Skimpily-clad chorus girls sang shrilly, *Deck the halls with Patch's lolly! Fal-la-la-la-la! La-la-la-la!* as Patch held up a small box decorated with a patchwork motif that matched his clothes. The chorus girls waved gigantic lollipops striped like puce-and-white bullseyes around him.

Joe frowned and shook his head. He wandered on down the street, wondering what Santa would think of this brazen competition for the hearts of children everywhere, or if Santa even knew. It occurred to him that in a few more hours he would be able to ask in person. His heart leaped with sudden excitement, and his frowning face began to smile. Only a few more hours... it was Christmas Eve!

In the living room of her townhouse, watching the same thing that Joe had seen, Cornelia frowned too, twisting her hair in silent concern. The strange, garish elf was on every channel of her television, with his brazen challenge to Santa. He was chanting now,

> 'When you look inside,
> Here's what you'll find!'

He held up the box as she watched, and his face suddenly furrowed, as if the next few words were trying to stick in his throat. He coughed, and went on,

> 'A little puce candy
> That'll blow your mind.'

'Patch! Natch! Patch! Natch!' the chorus girls shrilled. 'Snatch the batch from Patch! Natch!' Twining arms and bending their heads, they began to sing in a travesty of reverence,

> *'Silent night, silent night,*
> *In your window, leave a puce light...'*

Managing a shaky grin, as if he had been through an ordeal that was finally coming to an end, Patch waved farewell to Cornelia and all the invisible watchers on the other side of the camera's un-blinking eye.

Cornelia shook her head, the ghastly commercial sitting as uncomfortably in the pit of her stomach as a TV dinner. Just then Miss Tucker entered the living room. Cornelia glanced up at her.

'Cornelia,' Miss Tucker called, 'your step-uncle has stopped by for a minute. Go in and wish him a Merry Christmas.'

140

Cornelia rose distractedly from the sofa and followed her nanny out of the living room, still too worried about what she had seen even to care that she had to face her uncle and pretend to be pleased to see him. She walked down the long, echoing hallway like a sleepwalker to the closed doors of the library. Pulling open one of the heavy doors, she quietly entered the room.

Across the room her uncle was seated in a chair, also watching a television. She could see nothing but the top of his head and a puff of cigar smoke curling above it, as if he were steaming.

'Merry Christmas, Uncle,' Cornelia said politely.

B.Z. swivelled around in his seat, startled, and stared in surprise at his small, waiting step-niece. Then he grinned, flushed with triumph at having just pulled off the greatest promotional gimmick he – or anyone else – had ever dreamed up. '*Merry Christmas*?' he chuckled. 'It certainly should be,' he said cheerfully.

Cornelia, who never remembered seeing her step-uncle even smile at her before, looked at him blankly and thought she hoped he would never smile at her again.

Meanwhile, back at the North Pole, Santa Claus stood grim-faced before Dooley, with Anya and Puffy at his side. The Patch commercial was just ending. He had caught enough of it to realise what his once most highly trusted elf had done; Patch had set himself up in direct competition with the people who had been his family and friends. 'Well, at least he's all right,' Santa murmured at last, when he found the strength to speak again. That was one weight which he was glad to have lifted from his heart, even if it had been replaced by another. Had he really driven Patch to this? Was there some way he might have done things better, and kept Patch from leaving them in such bitterness –? If only he had tried a little harder to talk to Patch. He always had such difficulty discussing

141

things that were painful to him...

'What are you going to do?' Dooley asked Santa Claus at last.

Santa shrugged wearily. 'It's Christmas Eve, isn't it? I'm going to do my job the way I always do.' He sighed. Tonight, for once, it scarcely seemed like the privilege and pleasure it had always been before. He turned and walked out of the room, his face a mask of resignation.

Puffy gestured at the television screen. 'I'll tell you what I think,' he said resentfully, angered at the pain Patch was causing Santa, and still more than a little jealous of Patch in his heart of hearts. 'I think Patch is greedy.'

Dooley sighed, and shook his head. 'Not greedy,' he said sadly. 'Maybe just a little bit elfish.'

TWELVE

Grizzard the chauffeur and Miss Abruzzi stood flanked by a small handful of mystified technicians in the dark, chill silence of the deserted B.Z. Toy Factory. No one spoke as they stood waiting, almost afraid to disturb the silence around them, as if perhaps even here the walls had ears. When you worked for B.Z., you could never be too careful.

Besides the small group of chilly humans, there was only one other sign of any activity, past or present, in the empty warehouse. At the far end of the room a mysterious dais waited, framed by twinkling stars made of dozens of tiny lights, and completely shrouded by a tinsel curtain glittering with patriotic red, white and blue. There was no sound or sign of life from within, and the waiting group glanced at it nervously as often as they glanced nervously at the lift doors behind them. It was Christmas Eve and they had all been summoned here for the unveiling of Patch's big surprise. They were waiting now for B.Z. to arrive... and beginning to wonder seriously about what they were waiting for, since Patch seemed to be nowhere in evidence.

The clunk and whine of an arriving lift echoed loudly at last in the expectant silence. The doors slammed open and B.Z. stepped out, rubbing his hands together in eager anticipation. The small, waiting group clustered around him like flies around spoiled meat, all trying to be the first to greet him.

But B.Z. looked past and through them, peering towards the two immense, closed doors at the far end of the building, doors large enough to let a fairly large aeroplane pass through. A great blinking ramp had been constructed, leading towards them from the hidden dais. But the doors were firmly closed, and nothing stirred at the far end of the building, where the dais still awaited like an unopened present. 'Well? Where is he?' B.Z. said impatiently.

The others turned with him, following his gaze, all wondering the same thing and surprised that even he didn't know. The elf had been mysterious all along, but...

Abruptly the glittering curtain of tinsel began to part. As one, the watchers drew in a deep breath of wonder, their eyes wide as they took in the sight it revealed.

The first thing they saw was a remarkably lifelike reindeer... but this one was only inches high, and shone with chrome plate. It perched, as if ready to launch off into the air, on the bonnet of a car. A car like none of them had ever seen before. Before them lay... the Patchmobile. It was blindingly yellow in colour, and its radiator grill was bright red. Its bonnet looked like a jigsaw puzzle; the headlights were the drum heads of four toy soldiers who stood on the front bumper, ready to play; the pistons had toy mushroom caps; the tyres were over-inflated beach balls with gay red and green stripes. Its two antennae protruded from turrets of two red castles, and had giant pinwheels at their tips; several large tops, ready to spin, balanced over its motor. Two outsized Roman candles were mounted on its outsized rear bumper – exhaust pipes, poised and waiting for its driver to fire up its engines. The back of the car was an open rumble seat of unusual size, which was now filled with an enormous pile of patchwork-wrapped lollipop presents. Seated behind its wheel, almost invisible inside the splendour of his new 'delivery system', was Patch, dressed in his own comfortable elf garb, with a pair of goggles pushed up on his forehead.

This was Patch's answer to Santa's sleigh and reindeer, and although it looked deceptively like a toy, in spirit it was the ultimate in modern rocket technology, the very antithesis of everything Santa Claus held dear.

Beside the car sat a red, white and blue petrol pump shaped like a robot, with a clear plastic dome for a head and long, silvery hose-arms. Within the clear tank attached to its side were gallons and gallons of fuel, sparkling and glittering with a high-test mixture of magic sawdust. At Patch's gesture, the waiting technicians ran forward to the pump, and began to fill the Patchmobile's tank with fuel.

When the fuel gauge measured full, Patch turned on the ignition and his car sprang to life like an enchanted toyshop window. The tin soldiers played a drum roll; their drums spun around and forward to become bright headlamps. The tops spun; the beach ball tyres began to turn, their colours spiralling hypnotically. The entire car seemed almost to take on a life of its own, quivering with excitement. Patch pressed the horn, grinning, and it played the eight familiar notes of the musical jingle that had filled his television commercial.

B.Z. grinned too, puffing madly on his cigar as he gazed on the magnificent culmination of all Patch's work... and his plans. This was the greatest moment of his megalomaniacal life. 'Knock 'em dead, kid!' he shouted triumphantly. 'Knock 'em dead!'

Towzer swallowed the large lump of maudlin sentiment that choked his throat and mumbled, 'It's moments like this that make me proud to be an American. Free Enterprise, by God! This could never happen in Russia.'

Even Miss Abruzzi, carried away by the magnificence of the moment and her participation in it, began to jump up and down, clapping her hands. 'All the way, Patch! Go for it, baby!' In that moment even B.Z. could have believed that once she had been head cheerleader, and the most popular girl in her class.

At last, with its engines revving up to full power, the Patchmobile began to roll forward off the display turntable. The motor's soft thrumming became an ear-numbing roar as the rockets fired up. The Roman candle exhaust pipes flared with a shower of sparks, and great clouds of puce smoke spewed from their mouths.

Patch shifted gears, grinning with the unbelievable thrill of it all, and stamped his foot down hard on the accelerator.

The patchmobile roared forward with a burst of speed that thrust him back into the cushioned seat. Up ahead, the hangar doors opened automatically, as if on cue, revealing the black velvet sky sprinkled with diamonds and a moon like a vast pearl. Below – three or four storeys below – lay the silhouetted trees and houses of Long Island, and far off in the distance, the night-time skyline of Manhattan, rivalling the moon and stars with its lights.

The Patchmobile roared forward up the lighted ramp, crossing the distance to the open doorway in a matter of heartbeats – and plunged over the edge into the open air. But instead of roaring off the brink to crash several storeys below, it launched upwards into the night.

In a dazzling burst of stardust, the flying car zoomed straight out of the warehouse doors like a rocket, its already remarkable speed still increasing. With a trail of puce smoke pouring from its exhaust pipes, it thundered away into the night in a flashy imitation of another Christmas flight, one which was taking place at just exactly the same time.

Far away at the North Pole, the elves gave their customary cheer as Santa Claus, with his sleigh and reindeer, took off into the sky for his annual midnight journey. But in the hearts of some of the watchers there was not the same joy there had always been before. Dooley and Anya thought of their strayed sheep Patch, and what he was doing tonight, and their cheers rang hollowly in their ears.

But back in the empty hangar, B.Z. and his gaping-mouthed cronies let out a cheer of their own that was entirely heartfelt as they watched Patch disappear into the night.

'He did it!' B.Z. shouted exultantly, shouting with something besides anger for the first time in years, as he realised that all his trouble and expense had actually paid off after all. 'That little son-of-a-gun! He said he'd do it and he did it!' The Patchmobile was more unbelievable than anything he had ever dreamed of. If Patch's puce pops were even half as remarkable, he was set for life... His hands clenched, clutching fistfuls of imaginary paper money.

Santa Claus journeyed fast and far that night, bringing his gifts to the children of the world as he had always done. But tonight Patch, in his rocket car, was always faster, always one or two or even three stops ahead. His Patchmobile would roar off again into the night in a cloud of puce smoke even as Santa's slower, old-fashioned sleigh was just silhouetted against the moon, spiralling down to a landing...

Santa Claus entered the familiar surroundings of one more home, this one a home that he remembered quite vividly from last Christmas – the home of the boy who had wanted a fishing rod. It was also the first home he had visited with Joe at his side. But tonight his memory of that happy moment was marred by the knowledge of what had followed that last Christmas Eve... culminating in what had happened to him in home after home tonight.

He moved slowly, even his sack seeming to weigh too much as he crossed the room from the chimney. He did not glance around him to admire the cheerful decorations, did not touch a single one of the biscuits that had been left out for him... or

147

someone. He pulled a gift out of his sack almost absently and carried it to place beneath the tree. But as he reached to set it down, he froze, as his gaze fell on something already waiting there. It was yet another tiny present wrapped in patchwork paper, narrow and thin and only about four inches long.

Santa stared at it, moving closer, mesmerised by the sight, like someone hypnotised by a snake. It certainly didn't look like much. Could it really be so wonderful...? He put out his hand, reaching tentatively for the patchwork box; pulled it back again, somehow unwilling to actually touch his rival's tiny present, even though his curiosity about what lay inside was almost unbearable. Hurriedly picking up his sack again, he disappeared up the chimney once more.

And high above in the night Patch flew on, leaving a trail of puce smoke to mark his passage, and mar the sky. Leaning on his horn exultantly, Patch laughed in giddy glee as he roared between the starry towers of Manhattan to the strains of his very own Christmas theme.

Santa climbed into his sleigh and started his reindeer away once more into the night, again at a much slower speed. Struggling to keep his flagging spirits up, he shouted to the reindeer the words he desperately needed to hear himself: 'Well, don't let it get you down, boys,' he called with false heartiness. 'It's still our night, all right.' He looked down across the night-time landscape, which had always filled him with such pleasure. 'There are still all the beautiful trees and the windows welcoming us with their red and green –' He broke off suddenly. 'Oh.'

Down below, coloured lights winked and flickered as they always had ... but tonight they were all one colour. *Puce*. Looking up and away to the south, he saw that even the Empire State Building was not wearing its traditional holiday crown of red and green, but shone with the same lurid pinkish-purple glow. B.Z.'s mercenary machinations had succeeded in reaching new heights of crass exploitation.

Santa looked back again at the reindeer surging ahead of him through the sky, the only sight he was sure he could still trust. 'Well...' he murmured, his heart sinking, 'seems as if the public is a little more fickle than I –' He glanced down, as a motion his subconscious had been searching for all along registered in his thoughts. Abruptly his smile came back, as wide as ever, 'Ah,' he sighed. 'At least somebody down there likes me.'

Far below him stood the small form of the boy Joe, waving wildly at him from the roof of a building.

Santa shifted the reins, and the eight reindeer began to circle downward as one, to come in for a perfect landing on the rooftop below.

Joe stood watching in silent wonder as Santa's sleigh landed with perfect grace before him, some fifteen feet away across the roof.

Santa Claus sat in his sleigh for a long moment, caught in the same awkward moment of self-conscious silence as the boy, both of them so filled with emotion that they were suddenly afraid any movement or word would make it overflow in embarrassing tears.

At last Santa roused himself and climbed down from the sleigh. Tonight he did not move with his usual youthful energy, but instead seemed to move as if all the long years had caught up with him at once. 'Joe,' he murmured, suddenly unsure of how to begin. 'Hello.'

Joe twitched his shoulders, equally uncertain, hiding behind the too-familiar cool manner that protected his real and very vulnerable feelings from hurt and disappointment. 'Hey, how's it goin'?' he said casually, his hands in his jacket.

Santa nodded, equally restrained, sensing Joe's uncertainty; trying to feel his way past it without saying the wrong thing. 'Pretty well. Yourself?'

'Oh, me, I'm... er...' Joe's voice suddenly fell apart as his emotions surged upward so strongly that they shattered his cool pose and burst out of him in a rush. 'I was afraid you'd forget about me,' he blurted, his eyes suddenly too full, like his heart. He ran to Santa Claus and threw his arms around him, hugging him tightly. It had been such a long, cold night; every minute had seemed to last for hours... But it had all been worth it; because he had finally found someone who didn't let him down, someone worthy of his trust and love.

'Well,' Santa murmured, hugging the boy to his heart; more deeply and profoundly moved by this moment than he had been by anything in a long time. 'It seems I've still got *one* friend left.' And heaven knew, he felt as if he had never needed one more than tonight.

Joe pulled back, gazing up at him with wide brown eyes. 'Oh hey, are you kiddin'? I'm your pal for life, honest.' A frown of concern suddenly wrinkled his smooth young forehead. 'Oh hey, listen –' he said, suddenly remembering. 'There was this weird guy on television, this patch-natch-scratch guy, and he said –'

'I know, I know,' Santa said hastily. He patted Joe's shoulder. 'Don't worry about it.'

Joe relaxed smiling again, glad to believe in Santa's reassurance. If Santa wasn't worried about competition, then he certainly wouldn't be. After all, Santa was one of a kind. Who could compete with him? 'Oh, that's all right then.' He nodded, content, and looked away towards the waiting sleigh. 'Hiya Blitzen!' he called. 'Donner, how's it going'? Hey, Comet, awright!'

His three favourite reindeer looked towards him, shaking their heads in acknowledgement and smiling at his irrepressible grin.

Santa stood watching Joe's grinning face for a long moment, his own contentment and the confidence that had been beginning to fail him coming back to him in a rush as he watched. He *could* still bring joy and happiness into the lives of children, which was all he had ever wanted to do... He started back to the sleigh and climbed aboard. 'Coming?' he called to the breathlessly waiting boy.

'Yes!' Joe cried. He ran forward, not needing to be asked twice this year. He had spent a whole year dreaming about waiting for this moment. He scrambled up into the sleigh beside Santa and settled himself comfortably in the seat.

As he leaned back, Santa reached down beneath the seat and pulled something out. 'Oh, I almost forgot,' he said, as if he were speaking of the weather. 'This is for you.'

He handed Joe the special handmade present he had put there especially for him.

Joe took the present uncertainly, his face stunned with disbelief. 'For me?' he whispered. 'A present?'

'Yup,' Santa said, smiling gently.

Joe unwrapped the red-and-green paper with clumsy haste, revealing the carved figure of an elf. He stared at it in fascination, turning it around and around in his hands. He had never seen anything like it before. There was something so real about the small wooden figure that he almost expected to hear it speak to him. And what made it most wonderful of all was that it was the first Christmas present he had received since running away from the orphanage.

'Excellent!' he said with a grin, unconsciously echoing Cornelia's favourite expression. 'Thanks.' He held Santa's gaze for a long moment. Then, suddenly reminded of the little girl, and feeling the need to say something more, he asked, 'Did Corny get something? That... um... that girl,' he added, suddenly turning shy at Santa's raised eyebrows and smile.

'Do you see much of her?' Santa asked, with careful casualness.

Joe's face reddened and he gulped visibly. 'Actually,' he murmured, finding his voice again, 'yes, actually.' He had in fact seen her nearly every week during the entire past year. She had given him food and extra clothing, becoming more expertly streetwise at sneaking leftovers from the table than he had ever been at feeding himself. But even more important than the food, she had given him her friendship – the knowledge that there was someone in the world who liked him and valued his company. The two lonely children had become friends through their shared moment with one extraordinary person named Santa Claus. And, as they had discovered the many other surprising things that they had in common, they had forged a bond of friendship that was strong and true enough to overcome almost any difficulty.

Santa grinned, touched and gently amused by Joe's sudden happy embarrassment. It reminded him of his own far-away youth. Anya had been *his* childhood sweetheart . . . 'Of course I've brought her something,' he said, remembering to answer Joe's question. 'Writes a lovely letter, that girl.' He thought fondly of her thoughtful and gracious thanks for his last visit to her house; so unlike so many letters, that never said thank you at all. 'Asked for a toy piano.' He glanced back at Joe again. 'Well? Come on?' he urged good-naturedly.

'Huh?' Joe said, looking blank.

'Where's the "Yo"?' Santa gestured at the reindeer.

'Oh, right!' Joe nodded, suddenly remembering. His heart leapt. He was going to drive the sleigh again! Taking a deep breath, he called out, loud and clear, 'YO!'

The reindeer reared up and sprang away at his command, taking off into the sky. For both Joe and Santa, Christmas Eve had truly arrived at last.

THIRTEEN

The next morning dawned clear and crisp over New York and its sprawling suburbs. In homes and apartments all around the city – and all across the country, and all around the world, as morning came – children awoke and came running to discover what surprises had been left for them on tables, beside hearths and beneath Christmas trees.

In one sunny home, a blond tousle-headed little boy thumped down the steps into his living room, still in his pyjamas, his eyes wide with excitement. He ran to the Christmas tree and, plopping down, seized the small patchwork present that waited there, ignoring everything else. He had seen the elf on television last night and Patch had dazzled his five-year-old mind so utterly that he had not even thought of Santa Claus since then.

Tearing the paper from the box, he opened it and looked inside. A small puce coloured lollipop waited there, as promised. It was the most wonderful lollipop he had ever seen, for it seemed to glow all by itself, like the lights on the tree. At its centre was a single tiny grain of stardust – the magical dust that was meant to enchant the feed of Santa's own reindeer.

The excited child put the lollipop into his mouth and began to suck on it. It had a bland, sweet flavour that tasted vaguely like bubble gum, and vaguely like cherry, but not exactly like anything at all – a taste designed to appeal to children everywhere.

The little boy took one step and then another as he licked the sweet, beginning to wander towards other packages under the tree. But as he took another step, something remarkable began to happen to him: he began to rise up into the air. He rose halfway to the ceiling with his next step and hovered there, his mouth and eyes open wide in astonishment. And then his mouth stretched into a smile of pure delight. The Patch present *was* the most wonderful thing he had ever been given – it let him walk on air!

He settled gently to the floor again, his face still filled with awe. Moving very cautiously, so that he did not float upwards again, he went into the kitchen.

His mother stood in the pantry, choosing ingredients for the special breakfast she always cooked on Christmas Day as a treat for her son and her still-sleeping husband. She heard the soft sound of her little boy's feet come up behind her, and smiled.

'Mummy, can I have a biscuit?'

She glanced down at him and up at the biscuit tin on the shelf above her, purposely well out of reach. 'Before breakfast?' she said, surprised at him. 'Absolutely not!'

And then she jerked back with a gasp of astonishment, as the two small, pudgy hands she knew so well suddenly reached past her shoulder *from up above* and snatched the biscuit tin from the shelf.

A few hours later, somewhere else in the city, a boy and girl of twelve strolled down the snow-piled street together, walking side by side along a high wooden fence. Their heads bobbed in unison, at just equal heights above the fence top.

'Gosh,' the girl said, tossing her dark hair flirtatiously, 'I never noticed you in the neighbour-hood before.' She was tall for her age and she was surprised and very flattered by the sudden attention of a boy as tall as she was – there weren't very many of them, yet.

'Oh, yeah,' her new suitor said, swaggering a bit. 'I've been here quite a while. I've noticed *you*.'

The girl giggled. 'You're really nice,' she said, because he was. She wondered why in the world she'd never noticed him before.

They reached the end of the fence and turned the corner, crossing the street to the row of neat houses where she lived. She stole another shy glance at her new boyfriend's handsome face, never thinking to look down at his feet . . . which she would have found hovering more than a foot off the ground. He was quite literally walking on air at her side, Patch's lollipop magic letting him match her height as they walked. It was certainly the best Christmas present *he'd* ever had.

In another corner of the city, two six-foot-plus future basketball stars were playing a fast and furious game on an empty court at the local school. An envious eight-year-old, barely half their height, stood behind the chain link fence watching them and dreaming, as he had done so often.

But today he had found a special package under his Christmas tree, and it had the power to make his dreams come true. Suddenly he darted out from behind the fence like quicksilver. Crossing the court, he stole the ball from the older boys and began to dribble it frantically towards the hoop.

'Hey, kid,' one of the boys shouted angrily, 'give me that ball!' He loomed over the eight-year-old, reaching out to block his shot – when suddenly the little pipsqueak soared past him and sprang five feet into the air to score a goal that would have made anyone proud. The ball shot through the net and landed on the ground, bouncing away from him as the two older boys stood frozen, still staring. Because the kid was already disappearing across the empty playground . . . and he still hadn't come down.

Out in the suburbs, a middle-aged matron heard her small and particularly bad-tempered dog yapping and barking hysterically in her front garden. He was notorious for his barking, and for nipping the neighbourhood children, whom she disliked; so she did not rush to the door to see what he was barking so furiously about.

If she had, she would have seen the next door neighbours' son floating five feet above the dog's head, driving her beloved Nipper into a frenzy of frustrations as he enjoyed his revenge on her much-hated nuisance of a pet. Patch's gift was the Great Equaliser, the realisation of every child's fantasies.

In only one home in all of New York City did the patchwork present lie unopened beneath the tree. Cornelia sat on the thick rug in the study, picking out the tune to 'Jingle Bells' on her new toy piano, letting the melody conjure up for her the image of Santa's merry, smiling face. She had slept soundly all through the night, in spite of her resolution to wake at the slightest sound and see him again. But in the morning his brightly-wrapped present had been waiting for her – the new piano, just as she had requested. (The thing Miss Tucker had steadfastly refused to buy for her, calling it a 'noisy nuisance').

Also waiting for her had been the patchwork gift promised in last night's repulsive commercial, and she had refused with stubborn loyalty to even touch it.

Miss Tucker stood on the other side of the tinsel bedecked Christmas tree, holding Patch's gift out to her with impatient curiosity. 'But don't you even want to try it?' she insisted.

'I certainly do *not*,' Cornelia said adamantly.

Miss Tucker looked at the present with longing. She never got any presents, (except the very large brandy-soaked fruitcake she bought for herself). 'Well...' she said hesitantly, 'it seems a shame to let it go to waste...' She looked at Cornelia again. 'Do you mind if I take it?' she asked at last.

Cornelia didn't even bother to look up. 'I don't care,' she said, still picking out the tune to 'Jingle Bells' with single-minded care.

Miss Tucker unwrapped the present with eager fingers, revealing the glittering puce lollipop within. Never a delicate eater – as her size and girth amply demonstrated – she pulled the whole lollipop from the stick in one bite, and crunched it up with her strong horselike teeth, licking her lips.

And then the magic began to happen with a vengeance. Like a hot-air balloon, Miss Tucker began to drift up from the floor. '*Whooo*!' she gasped, clutching her head in astonishment.

She hovered in the middle of the room, halfway between the floor and the high ornamental ceiling.

Cornelia stared in open disbelief as Miss Tucker began to flap her arms like wings, scooting across the room like a ponderous hen trying to stay airborne. 'Ooooh!' she shrilled, laughing giddily for the first time either she or Cornelia could remember. 'Look at me! I feel just like Mary Poppins.' In her own secret dreams she had always imagined being that ultimate nanny – so perfect in every way that she could even perform magic. The waking Miss Tucker had never had a magical moment, or even a magical thought, in her life until now.

Cornelia sat speechless on the floor. Her heart filled with sorrow for Santa... and although she would never admit it even to herself, a touch of envy as she watched Miss Tucker. How could anyone compete with a present that let you walk on air?

Santa walked down the street of a small town, moving through the real world by daylight for the first time in centuries. After he had said good-bye to Joe and gone on with his Christmas Eve journey, he had found a Patch present waiting for him – and for every child – in every home in the world. His feelings of depression and sorrow had come back with a vengeance, until at last he had decided not to return to the North Pole at dawn, as he had always done before. He had to wait until Christmas Day arrived, and see for himself what was in Patch's present. Was it truly so wonderful that it would make children everywhere turn their backs on the man who had loved them so unselfishly for longer than they could imagine?

It was a strange and uncanny feeling to walk down a small town street in the flesh, as a real person rather than a phantom out of legend. He looked right and left at the modern homes and office buildings, at the television aerials – his bane by night – sprouting everywhere, and the cars lying patiently under blankets of fresh snow. But even the marvellous strangeness of all he saw could not lift the heaviness of his heart. He turned a corner, following the pavement aimlessly, and came face to face with a large metal dustbin. Lying helter-skelter on top of the rubbish inside, just as they had landed when they were tossed there, were half a dozen of the distinctively wrapped red-and-green presents that he had so patiently and lovingly left for children in their own homes the night before. And now they were being thrown out, callously rejected by uncaring children who had not even bothered to open them to see what was inside, before throwing them away.

He stood motionless for a long moment, shaking his head despondently. And as he stood there without the strength or spirit even to move, two boys rounded the corner at a run and crashed into him.

They stopped, recovering their own balance, glaring down at him as if the collision had been his fault instead of their own. 'Watch it, mister!' the first boy snapped.

'Look where you're going,' his companion said sullenly. Neither one of them made any move to help the elderly man get to his feet.

The first boy looked Santa up and down, seeing his classic red suit and white beard, and his face twisted. 'Hey, mister,' he sneered, 'you oughta get yourself another outfit.' He waved his hand. 'What do you want to dress up like that loser for?' The two boys started to move past him.

Catching his breath, Santa Claus called out, 'Hey, boys –'

They stopped, turning back with impatient faces. 'Yeah?' the first boy asked.

'May I ask you something?' Santa said, as pleasantly as he could manage. 'What did you get this Christmas?'

'The puce lollipop!' the boy answered, his face lighting up. 'The greatest!'

'I thought I'd *never* come down!' his friend shouted, balancing on one foot as he remembered walking on air.

Santa Claus searched their faces, seeing nothing but selfish satisfaction. Remembering what had made him begin giving his gifts on this special day, so long ago, he asked softly, 'And what did you *give* this Christmas?'

The boys stared at him uncomprehendingly.

'What did we *what*?' the second boy asked.

'Give,' Santa said again.

'"Give"?' The first boy turned to his pal, equally blank-faced. 'What's he talking about?'

The second boy waved his hand, wiping away the question and the sight of the strange old man in the Santa suit along with it. 'Who cares?' he said sourly.

They turned away and walked on again, leaving the formerly merriest man in the world looking the saddest, and feeling the loneliest.

Santa's sleigh returned to its welcome berth at the North Pole at last, much to the relief of the worried elves, and Santa's worried wife. As Anya and Dooley stood together, watching the sleigh draw near through the twinkling darkness, they both noted silently how much more slowly it flew than it had ever flown in the past... as if the weary, disheartened reindeer were pulling the weight of the world behind them.

At last they came in for their tunnel landing, stumbling ungracefully with fatigue as they slid to a stop. Santa Claus climbed down from his seat, and Anya's smile of relief faded; her heart pinched with pain as she saw his face. Plainly this night had gone even worse than he or they had feared. She wondered what could possibly have happened to make her cheerful, beaming Claus look as haggard and depressed as though he had aged a hundred years in a night.

She hurried to his side, with Dooley following, as Honka, Boog and Vout rushed to tend the drooping reindeer. 'Where were you?' she asked, her voice tremulous with concern.

'Out,' he answered flatly, his voice as dull as his gaze. He began to walk back towards their house without another word, forcing her to follow.

She caught at his arm. 'What's the matter?' she asked, trying to make him stop and look at her.

But his only answer was to wave his hand at her, in a hopeless, despairing gesture that told her he did not want to talk about it. He went on alone, leaving her to stand rooted where she was, the elves standing beside her, equally perplexed. She glanced at Dooley, who could only meet her alarmed stare with his own.

FOURTEEN

B.Z. leaned easily against his raised desk, glancing
around his crowded office at the B.Z. Toy Company.
The large room was packed wall-to-wall with
reporters, photographers and television camera
crews, all eager to get the story on the elf who had
scooped Santa Claus – and his magnanimous
sponsor. Patch stood uncomfortably beside B.Z.,
ready, he hoped, to meet his public face-to-face at
last.

'Ask him anything, boys,' B.Z. said grandly,
gesturing at Patch. He straightened his tie, worn
with his usual conservative white shirt and grey
suit to honour this momentous occasion.

The reporters crowded forward, their voices rising
in a clamour, vying for attention. 'Where do you
come from?' someone shouted at Patch.

'Top of the world,' he said matter-of-factly, with
an elf-conscious smile.

'That's how we all feel today!' B.Z. cried expansively, flinging his arms wide. His Christmas
campaign had been a greater success than even his
greediest dreams. Lollipops that let kids walk on
air! What a gimmick. It was sure-fire, if he did say so
himself. The B.Z. Toy Company was hot again, and
no longer in hot water. He had never felt more
brilliant, or more self-satisfied. Just wait till *next*
year . . .

'Do you work for the company?' another reporter
asked Patch. The nature of their relationship was of
the greatest interest to everyone in the room today.

'Currently, I'm elf-employed,' Patch said, with a

modest shrug. B.Z. glanced at him and opened his mouth.

'What's in those lollipops?' the reporter demanded, like a hound on the trail of a suspicious scent.

'Only natural ingredients,' B.Z. snapped, hastily and defensively, before Patch could even begin an explanation. 'No additives.' Even he didn't know what the secret was; and he was damned if he was going to let anybody else find out. Patch had assured him that it was perfectly harmless, and it must have been, because he hadn't heard anything to the contrary.

A third reporter said, grinning, 'Mr Patch, has the National Space Agency contacted you yet?' Everyone in the room chuckled in amusement.

Everyone but Patch. 'Who?' he asked blankly.

'The astronauts,' the reporter said.

Patch shook his head, the blank expression still on his face. 'They'll have to write to Santa Claus just like all the other boys and girls.'

B.Z. glanced over at Patch again, then back at the crowd of nonplussed reporters, with a fleeting frown. He realised suddenly that he should have known better than to let the elf speak for himself. Before anyone had the chance to probe Patch's mystifying response further, or decide he was a nut case, B.Z. threw a paternal arm around Patch's shoulders, smiling broadly and looking as much like Mr Nice Guy as he could manage. The reporters took quick advantage of the photo opportunity. Smiling voraciously, B.Z. intoned, 'All we want to do is bring joy and happiness to the children of the world. And that's why I'm proud to announce that, beginning today, my pal Patch here is exclusive with B.Z. Toys.'

Gasps and murmurs and excited whispering filled the room, as reporters scribbled hastily in pads. Cameras whirred and flashed as B.Z. and Patch posed arm-in-arm, with big matching grins on their faces. No one seemed to notice that Patch's

162

grin had a certain stiffness about it, which seemed to hide some other expression.

Overcome with the splendour of the moment, B.Z. said grandly, 'Boys, let me tell you – I owe all this good fortune to me, my elf and I!'

But not everyone in the room smiled; not everyone there had as short a memory as B.Z. liked to hope the public did.

'What about the fact that the Senate Sub-committee on Toy Safety cited this company for fifteen separate violations of –'

B.Z.'s mouth snapped shut, his toothy grin disappearing. He glared out over the crowd of reporters, trying to see who had dared to bring that piece of old news up again. The grin came back hastily and he interrupted the rising flood of questions with false affability, 'Okay, ladies and gentlemen, that's it for now.' He wasn't going to let some hotshot ruin his afternoon by making anybody start to think. Nipping the whole unpleasant matter swiftly in the bud, he said, 'Thank you for coming,' and started forward, gesturing the reporters towards the doors.

At his cue, Towzer and Miss Abruzzi, and most importantly his brutish chauffeur Grizzard, moved forward from their unobtrusive places along the wall to flank him, herding the press from the room.

As the last reporter was pushed rather unceremoniously out of the doors, B.Z. remained behind with only Patch beside him. He locked the doors.

Patch looked up at the toy manufacturer, his face troubled. 'What was that he said about a Senate Sub-committee?' He wasn't quite certain what that was, but he understood 'toy safety' and 'violations' well enough.

B.Z. waved a heavy hand, sweeping the implications aside. 'That's just typical newspaper garbage. Silly stuff. Don't take it seriously.' He snorted contemptuously.

But the frown did not fade from the elf's face.

163

'What was that business about our future plans?' Patch asked, still worried. In the very few minutes the Big Interview had lasted, he had heard a disquieting number of things he wasn't sure he liked, let alone understood.

'The future is ours, Patch!' B.Z. said heartily, putting an arm around the elf's narrow shoulders as if he could physically squeeze their wills into one.

'But I'm going back to the North Pole,' Patch protested.

B.Z. drew back, staring at him in disbelief. 'Says who?' he demanded. This was the first time he'd ever heard about that. His eyes narrowed. Was Patch trying to hold him up for something?

But Patch only looked away towards the room's wide window, which faced north. 'Well... nobody, yet,' he said, a little wistfully. 'But now that I've shown Santa Claus what I can do, it's for sure he'll send for me to come home.' His heart squeezed with longing inside him. The more time he had spent in the real world, the more he had realised how much he had left behind at the North Pole. The real world was no place for an elf – he found it far too complicated, contradictory and confusing. He belonged back in his own enchanted village. He only wanted to be *appreciated* there, that was all. He had his pride, and it would not let him return until he had proved to Santa and all the rest of them how much they really needed him. All year long he had hoped for some message calling him home... but nothing had come, and so he had buried himself in his work, telling himself that his triumph would be the thing that made them admit how much they missed him...

'Why would you want to do that?' B.Z. said irritably, not hearing the longing in Patch's voice; not wanting to know about it. 'What does the North Pole have that New York doesn't? Ice and polar bears.'

Patch looked back at him. 'And Santa Claus. And my friends,' he said simply.

164

B.Z. shook his head in exasperation. The ungrateful little creep really seemed to mean it. He rubbed his chin, thinking furiously. He didn't really need the elf anymore – just that secret ingredient. Patch could leave if he wanted to; but there had to be a way to make him leave that secret stuff behind.

Trying a new tack, B.Z. said with seeming reasonableness, 'Awright, awright, I'll tell you what. Just do me one favour before you go.' He watched Patch through narrowed eyes, his face a mask of friendly concern; seeing the elf's hesitation, playing on his obvious vulnerability and need to be liked. Guilt could move more mountains than faith ever did. 'Hey, sweetheart, c'mon ... you owe me.' *No, no, that wasn't exactly it* – 'You owe those marvellous kids who put their faith in you, right? Am I right? C'mon, this is for them, for the kids of this miserable old world –' His voice took on a wheedling whine; he spread his arms like a preacher, let them drop again, looking Patch in the eye. 'So will you do it?' he asked.

'What is it?' Patch asked hesitantly, his face brightening with the thought of the children, his determination wavering.

B.Z. smiled, like a barracuda about to swallow a minnow. He had him now ... 'This magic stuff, these reindeer cornflakes, whatever it is that made the kids float on air – what would happen if you er, juiced up the formula? Made it stronger.'

Patch shrugged, surprised at the simpleness of the question. 'Why it's elf-explanatory,' he said. 'It would make them fly.'

B.Z.'s jaw fell open, and flopped. 'You mean *fly*??? Like fly –' he gasped, waving his arms again.

'Like fly high in the sky.' Patch gestured at the ceiling. 'Ten times the stardust gives you ten times the height, ten times the power. Twenty times the stardust –'

'Could you do that?' B.Z. burst out, unable to

165

contain himself any longer. '*Before* you go. It won't take long.'

'Lollipops?' Patch asked. His quick mind had already begun to work on the new challenge before he quite realised it; and, as usual, failed to consider the consequences while it analysed the technical aspects.

B.Z. shook his head emphatically. 'No, we've already done those. That's yesterday's news. The consumer always wants a new model.'

Patch frowned in thought, searching for inspiration. He looked up again after a moment. 'Candy canes?'

B.Z.'s mouth stretched into a broad smile again. 'Candy canes! They're cute, they're simple – Patch, you are some terrific elf!' he said, for once completely sincere.

Patch looked down, blushing, drinking in the sort of praise he had not heard in far too long. 'Well ... I could convert the machines to do candy canes – that would only take a week or two – and then, I suppose ...' His voice trailed off; he was lost again in thought. It wouldn't take *too* long. Then he could return to the North Pole feeling as if he had done right by the other noble toymaker who had helped him so much.

'Let's see,' B.Z. interrupted, filling the void with his own thoughts, already planning his new selling strategy. 'Let's see, we'll launch the ad campaign tomorrow – strike while the iron is hot, see –' he glanced up eagerly. 'And can I promise delivery in three months?'

'Three months!' Patch protested. 'But Christmas is a year away!'

B.Z. shook his head at his partner's continuing naivety. Some people never learned. 'When you've got a hit like we have, the public doesn't want to wait for a whole year,' he explained patiently. 'They're dying for a sequel.' His eyes filled with the vision of other sequels that the public had gulped down, in ever greater numbers, by conditioned response... 'A sequel! Yeah, that's it!' he shouted, as his most brilliant merchandising scheme yet struck him like a meteor. 'We'll bring it out on March the twenty-fifth and we'll call it *Christmas Two*!!!'

'Maybe the whole idea's no good any more,' Santa Claus murmured unhappily. He sat at the table, his dinner lying before him untouched. Anya brought a hot apple pie to the table and set it down, still steaming from the oven, the smell of it as sweet as ambrosia. It had been Claus's favourite for the past century, but tonight he didn't even notice it sitting before him.

'What are you talking about?' Anya said, her forehead wrinkling with concern. 'What idea?'

Claus struggled for a moment to form the word. '...Christmas...' he said softly. Perhaps it had just gone on for too many years...

'Claus!' Anya exclaimed, her face filling with shock and disbelief. Christmas had a meaning far larger and more significant than simply the day Santa Claus delivered gifts. It had always been a day that existed to remind people of the goodness and belief, the sharing and generosity, that lay inside them waiting to be set free; it was a day that had been meant to remind them of how much unselfish love human beings were truly capable of. Christmas was not a fad, a thing so shallow that it lost its meaning because someone had finally grown tired of it.

But Claus only sighed. 'The world's a different place now, Anya,' he said morosely. 'You don't get to see it. Count yourself lucky.' He shook his head. 'The people, they just don't seem to care about giving a gift to see the light of happiness in a friend's eyes. It...' he broke off, struggling to find the words to give shape to the formless sorrow that was weighing so heavily on his soul. 'It... just doesn't feel like Christmas any more. Maybe... maybe I'm just an old fool.'

Anya moved quickly to his side and hugged him.

167

Holding him tightly against her heart; trying not to cry as sudden tears filled her eyes. 'Old-fashioned, maybe,' she murmured fiercely. 'But not a fool. *Never* a fool.'

But her husband only shook his head and didn't answer.

FIFTEEN

Patch sat behind the controls of his state-of-the-art control panel, overseeing the endless metal forest of robotic arms and automated machinery which produced more candy canes in an hour than he could have imagined producing in his wildest dreams. No need for awkward cobbled together assembly lines made of assorted bits and pieces here. B.Z. did everything first class if there was money in it for him.

Patch watched the candy canes flow past him on the conveyor belt in an endless river of glowing puce. They shone so very brightly from the extra pinch of stardust inside every one that their glare made him squint. The machines droned on, *chunk-chunk-chunk*, a far drearier and more depressing sound than the music he had made for the elves to work to... but then, there were no elves, or even human beings, working here. He had made everything brightly-coloured, as it had been at the North Pole, and he had even put up his own private sign which read: THE PATCH TOY CO. But in spite of his efforts to make it feel like home, this production line was heartless as the human vulture who had provided it, a face which Patch, with his innate belief in the good-heartedness of others, did not really understand.

He only knew that he was very unhappy – that he missed Santa and his friends more than he had ever dreamed possible, that he had never appreciated any of them, or the wonderful village in which they existed, nearly enough. He *had* been elfish, he realised, thinking only of himself and his personal glory, not thinking enough about the real reason they were all there – to work together to make the best toys possible, unselfishly and lovingly, in order to bring happiness to others.

He let his mind drift out of his joyless surroundings, into another fond daydream of Season's Greetings at the North Pole – the happy bustle of activity, the smiling faces, the large, jolly figure of Santa moving among the hard-working elves, making certain that everything was just as it ought to be and everyone was content.

If he had realised what a changed and disillusioned person Santa Claus had become, if he had known one tenth of the real grief he had caused Santa and his friends, Patch would have been prostrate with grief himself. He had never meant to hurt anybody; he was just too elf-centred to consider the consequences of his actions. He only saw things from the perspective of his own wounded pride... and he only wanted, achingly, to go home.

Abruptly, the sound of a loud alarm buzzer echoed through the factory, jarring Patch back into the present. The robot machines ground to a halt before him as the monitor on a critical gauge measured *Empty*.

Patch peered at the board before him. 'Whoops,' he murmured. 'Time to put more stuff in the hopper.' The sooner he finished this project, the sooner he could start homeward. He got up from the control board and hurried to a nearby door; glad for even an excuse to stretch his legs. He opened the door and started down a long, dark flight of echoing metal stairs into the factory sub-basement.

At last he reached a dank, black, empty room littered with old machine parts and junk – a room he was sure no one besides himself had visited for years. Looking cautiously over his shoulder, he entered the room and walked to a battered metal filing cabinet. He peered around him one more time to make certain that he was alone; not sure why he had become so suspicious since living among

170

humans, but very certain somehow that it was the right way to act. At last he pulled open a squeaking drawer.

The night-dark room was suddenly suffused with a sunlight glow, as the open drawer revealed the sack of magic grain lying inside it. Carefully Patch climbed up onto a box and scooped out a handful of stardust – which instantly, magically replaced itself, leaving the bag as full as ever. Patch climbed down again, closing the drawer securely, until there was not the faintest sparkle showing. Then he started back up the stairs with his precious handful of magic.

Beyond the factory walls a cold, hard winter rain was drenching New York. Joe scurried along the darkened street towards his alleyway, soaked to the skin in spite of his best efforts at keeping dry.

He stopped beneath the light at the alley entrance and glanced across the street towards Cornelia's townhouse, wiping his runny nose on his sodden sleeve. He looked back into the dark, icy alley he had planned to spend the night, and then across the street at Cornelia's townhouse again. He was shivering so hard that his teeth rattled. He bit his lip, then started out across the street, to disappear behind the tall, white stone house.

Joe squeezed between the bars of the high, padlocked wrought-iron gate in the back fence, a trick that had become more difficult since he had been getting fed more regularly. He crept across the back garden and around to the side of the building. Picking up a pebble, he took careful aim and tossed it against an upper window.

A moment later a lamp came on inside the room, which was Cornelia's bedroom. Cornelia came to the window and pushed it open, leaning out, her flannel pyjama sleeve whipping in the cold wind.

'Hi,' Joe said, his nonchalant pose ruined by a loud, sudden sneeze.

'Hi!' Cornelia said happily. 'Oh! You're soaked to

171

the skin!' Her face filled with concern as she saw him shivering and sneezing.

'It's rainin',' Joe said, pointing out the obvious. He sneezed again.

'Come up, quick,' Cornelia whispered loudly, beckoning with an outstretched hand.

Startled by the invitation, but hoping for it all along, Joe didn't wait to be asked twice. Taking in the lay of the building's wall, he ran to the corner of the house and shinnied up the drainpipe, then darted across a ledge as sure-footedly as a cat to Cornelia's window. He climbed in over the sill, to stand wonderingly in the actual room, like a very young Romeo inside Juliet's house at last.

Cornelia grinned broadly, thrilled to the core by their daring conspiracy and the excitement of the moment. 'Don't worry about Miss Tucker,' she said. 'She's asleep in her room and nothing wakes her.' She lowered her voice, whispering confidentially, 'I think she likes brandy.'

Joe sneezed again. Cornelia broke off, her excitement changing back suddenly to worry. 'You've caught a cold!' She moved to Joe's side and felt his forehead with her hand, as she remembered her mother doing for her, so long ago. 'You're burning up!' she said. She looked at him with fresh concern shining in her eyes, feeling a sudden fierce desire to protect and care for this boy who had no one at all to take care of him.

'I'll be awright,' Joe said, with unconvincing bravado. He coughed loudly, to cover his embarrassment; but happiness filled him as the look of concern deepened in her large brown eyes. Secretly he craved the warmth and tenderness that had been missing from his life for so long, although he would never bring himself to admit it.

'You stay out there and you'll be *dead*, that's what you'll be,' Cornelia said adamantly. She gestured at the cold, rainy night beyond her window. 'You're staying here.'

'I'm what?' Joe said in disbelief.

Cornelia's eyes shone with fresh excitement and sudden inspiration. The words burst out of her in a rush. 'There's an empty room in the basement near the furnace room. Nobody ever goes down there. I'll fix you a place to sleep on my old inflatable rubber boat from the summer and this house has tons of blankets and pillows –' She broke off, breathless, searching his uncertain face. 'Oh, please, Joe, just till you get better.'

Joe did not answer for a moment, a little daunted by the prospect of hiding in someone's home, and so touched by Cornelia's concern that he was afraid to speak, afraid of giving too much away. But to be warm and dry and cared for would be so nice... At last, looking down at his worn-out sneakers, he mumbled, 'Well, okay, but just till I shake this –' Another huge sneeze interrupted him.

Cornelia turned away to her bureau drawers, beaming and efficient. She began to rummage through them, pulling out and rejecting pieces of clothing as she said, 'I'm going to go down and sort out your room, and I'll bring you a glass of orange juice and an aspirin –' She tossed two pieces of clothing at him. 'Here. Get out of those wet clothes and put these on.'

Joe caught the clothes by reflex, looking down at them with a scowl. '*Girl's* clothes???' he said, indignant and mortally offended.

'They're unisex,' Cornelia said firmly, ignoring his display of peevish male chauvinism. 'Now hurry up.'

She bustled out of the room with an armful of blankets, leaving him privacy in which to change. Joe held the clothes she had given him at arm's length, eyeing them suspiciously. One garment was a pair of grey tracksuit bottoms, and the other a T-shirt with *Miss Briley's School for Girls* stencilled across its chest. *Unisex, huh?* Joe frowned again and turned the shirt inside out.

As the weeks had passed, Santa Claus's depression

seemed to have grown worse with every passing day. Day after day he sat unmoving in his chair before the fire, staring into space. He had not set foot outside his house to monitor the progress of the toy-making, a duty and a pleasure that had formerly kept him happily occupied for most of every day.

Anya and the elves tried every imaginable thing that they could think of to rouse and interest him, but nothing succeeded. Anya cooked his favourite foods for him at each meal, only to see them left nearly untouched on the table. She and Dooley told him stories, jokes, news of the outside world (carefully excluding anything they heard about B.Z.Toys), trying to catch his interest, to no avail.

Puffy faithfully brought him the blueprints and mock-ups for every new toy, only to receive the same listless response that Anya and Dooley did.

'It's ... it's a ... new doll,' Puffy said hesitantly, holding out his latest design – the cuddliest, most irresistible baby doll he had ever created. Anya and the others watched silently from the doorway, waiting anxiously to see if *this* time they had found the thing that could raise Santa's spirits.

'A doll,' Santa said dully, with hardly even a glance at the new toy.

'Children ought to like it,' Puffy suggested, his voice hopeful and bright.

'Does it fly?' Santa asked sourly.

'It ... er ... wets,' Puffy answered, glancing away in sudden embarrassment.

Santa pushed his outstretched hands, and the proffered toy, away in silent dejection. Anya and Dooley looked at each other, defeated, as Puffy started back to the door again, his face forlorn. It would take a miracle, they thought, to undo the harm that Patch had wrought so unwittingly.

SIXTEEN

On another frigid, rainy night, a surreptitious figure made its way up the street to B.Z.'s townhouse and knocked on his door. The only light in the silent house shone out into the street from B.Z.'s study, where he had stayed up late to gloat over the figures of his fantastic profits one more time. He rose from the desk in his study as he heard someone knock, and went cautiously to the door.

Dr Towzer stood on his doorstep, looking like a drowned spaniel. B.Z. stared at him in astonishment, and then remembered to let him step inside.

'Good Lord, man!' B.Z. said, keeping his voice low but not bothering to whisper, certain that everyone else was long since soundly asleep. 'Haven't you ever heard of the telephone?'

'I couldn't use the phone,' Towzer mumbled, looking distraught and furtive.

'It's really quite simple, Towzer,' B.Z. said, his voice dripping sarcasm. These scientific types should never be let out of their ivory towers alone. 'You pick up the receiver and then you dial those funny little numbers –'

Towzer shook his head insistently, his face tense and his eyes white with fear. 'I didn't *dare* use the phone, B.Z.! I couldn't take the chance of anyone hearing.'

'Hearing what???' B.Z. bellowed, forgetting himself in his exasperation and sudden worry. Lowering his voice, he asked more calmly, 'Hearing what?'

Towzer glanced from side to side nervously. 'Are we alone?'

'My niece and her nanny are fast asleep,' B.Z. said patiently, quite confident that they were.

He was half right. Miss Tucker was snoring loudly in her bed, but down in the basement Cornelia was sitting on the floor in her dressing-gown next to Joe's makeshift rubber-boat bed. She was wide awake and having a wonderful time playing Florence Nightingale. She removed the thermometer gently from Joe's mouth and read his temperature.

'Ninety-nine,' she said. 'You still have a temperature.'

'Four dopey points, big deal.' Joe shrugged, secretly glad that he still had one. He was enjoying their secret – this warm place to sleep, plenty of food and Cornelia's fond attention – at least as much as she was.

'More liquids, that's what you need,' Cornelia said, in her best efficient nurse's tone. 'Vitamin C. Come on, let's get some orange juice.' She beckoned him up. There was also a little ice cream left in the freezer...

They started up the cellar steps, moving as quietly as possible because her uncle was still awake. It was inconvenient that he stayed up so late, but at least his study was at the front of the house... As they reached the top of the stairs, Cornelia froze, motioning for Joe to stop too, hearing men's voices coming through the door. The two children looked at each other with wide, warning eyes as they stood perfectly still, listening.

In the kitchen B.Z. poured himself a beer and filled a glass for Towzer with cloudy-looking water from the faucet in the sink. It was just like that fool Towzer to ask for water when he was already soaking wet. B.Z. glanced at him with disgruntled disgust. He held out the glass, muttering, 'Towzer, Towzer, with you it's always some new melodrama. Well, let me tell you, my friend, today nothing can upset me.' He took a hearty swig of his beer, mellowing again. 'Towzer, the money is coming in

176

so fast you'd think we were printing our own! Do you realise what this means, man?' He smiled, a smile that Attila the Hun would have appreciated. '*Santa Claus is finished!*'

In the stairwell, Joe and Cornelia turned to each other, their eyes wide with silent horror.

B.Z. held up his beer mug to toast himself. 'I'm taking over Christmas!' he cried. Ever since he had got into the toy business, he had hated the very idea of Santa Claus, a man who *gave away* countless gifts every year at the most profitable season of all. And after he had met Patch, and realised that Santa Claus was real, not some phony do-gooder's tall tale, the thought of that fat man in red cutting into his market had galled him even more. But now, thanks to Patch, he had found the way to get rid of his biggest competition once and for all. 'By next December they'll be writing to ME!' he gloated. 'B.Z.!'

Joe and Cornelia stood motionless, holding their breath, their minds racing as they listened to her step-uncle's appalling plans. And then suddenly Cornelia saw a new kind of horror fill Joe's face. His nose twitched and his mouth popped open as he inhaled sharply. He was about to sneeze. He grimaced desperately, struggling against the irresistible urge. Frantically Cornelia pressed her finger against his upper lip just below his nose – a sure-fire sneeze stopper – but it was too late.

'*Ah-choo!*' Joe sneezed resoundingly. The sneeze echoed back down the stairs and carried very clearly through the closed basement door into the kitchen. The two children turned as one and started to run pell-mell back down the stairs.

B.Z. who had settled comfortably into a chair at the kitchen table, leapt to his feet. 'What on earth –' he cried in sudden fury.

Joe pushed Cornelia ahead of him as they reached the bottom of the stairs, shoving her into the only hiding place he could immediately spot, behind the wine racks. He looked around desperately, search-

177

ing for another place for himself. But before he could even duck out of sight the basement door was flung open, pinning him like a frightened animal in a shaft of blinding light, and B.Z.'s silhouette loomed above him. B.Z. roared down the stairs and was on top of the petrified boy before he could move, grabbing him by the collar and dragging him back up the steps into the kitchen. Shaking Joe like a dog with a rag doll, B.Z. shouted, '*Who are you? How'd you get in here*?!'

Joe, recovering from his initial fright at being captured began to kick and struggle, lashing out at his captor with all the streetwise moves he knew.

Frantic at their discovery, Towzer rushed to the backdoor and whistled loudly. A moment later Grizzard, B.Z.'s massive chauffeur, appeared in the doorway in answer to his summons.

Joe took one look at the huge driver and knew any chance of escape he still had would disappear the minute Grizzard laid hands on him. He twisted desperately in B.Z.'s grasp, making a final, frantic effort to break free. He found the toy mogul's hand on his shoulder and bit down on it as hard as he could.

B.Z. howled with pain. 'Little menace!'

Joe wriggled free as B.Z. lost his grip, and tried to run; but Grizzard leapt for him, grabbing him with ham-sized fists as Towzer slammed the open door shut again. Grizzard caught the boy in a painful, vicelike grip while Joe squirmed and struggled like a wild animal, making even the human gorilla who held him grunt with effort. 'Who is this kid?' he gasped.

'Some damn little sneak thief –' B.Z. snarled, sucking on his wounded hand.

'I heard what you said!' Joe cried defiantly. 'You ain't never gonna beat Santa Claus! *Never*!! I'll tell him and he'll beat you, he'll get his guys –'

B.Z.'s eyes narrowed ominously; he glared at Joe with sudden suspicion. Was this kid more than he seemed? Could this Santa Claus actually have planted a kid in his house as a spy? He couldn't afford to take any chances, either by letting the brat go or calling the police... 'Put this kid on ice,' he said, his voice suddenly deadly. No little punk was going to ruin his scheme. 'I'll deal with him later.'

Joe's heart squeezed with terror as he saw the expression on B.Z.'s face. He knew what a look like that meant, far too well. But he was helpless in Grizzard's grasp, no matter how he struggled. Grizzard lifted him completely off his feet, tucking him under one arm like a sack of flour. The chauffeur's other beefy paw clamped firmly over his mouth, keeping him from crying out as Towzer opened the back door again. Grizzard carried the helplessly struggling boy out to B.Z.'s waiting limousine, and locked him in its boot. B.Z. watched in satisfaction as the long black car drove off into the night, heading for his factory.

Down in the basement, Cornelia, still hidden behind the wine rack, listened to the commotion up above with tears of anger and fright in her eyes. What was happening to Joe? What could she do, what *should* she do now -? She looked around her frantically, searching for a safer hiding place, or a way to escape from the cellar unnoticed.

Suddenly the cellar door slammed open at the top of the stairs. She heard her step-uncle snarl, 'See if there are any more of 'em down there! For all I know I could have a whole *nest* of brats in the basement.'

Towzer rushed obediently to the stairway and started down. He searched the poorly-lit corners of the basement room with the exquisite care of a confirmed paranoid. He searched behind the wine rack twice, because it looked so much like somewhere where someone *must* be hiding. But he found no trace of anyone, large or small. Heaving a long sigh of relief, he stumped back up the stairs at last to make his report, shutting the door firmly on the empty room below.

SEVENTEEN

B.Z. shook his head, taking a long swig of his beer to calm his frayed nerves. 'Boy! Have you ever had one of those days where you just want to drop a bomb on the world?' he snarled feelingly. 'First some wretched kid in my basement and then you come waltzing into my house in the middle of the night and –' He broke off, staring at Towzer as if he had only just noticed him. 'Hey, yeah, Towzer, what *do* you want anyway?' he snapped.

Towzer took a deep breath, rubbing his hands together in a curious washing motion, his own nerves completely unravelled. He looked down, lips trembling as he forced the bad news out between them, 'It's the candy canes.'

'What about them?' B.Z. took another gulp of beer.

Towzer glanced up at him, squirming. 'This Patch guy...'

'Uh-huh,' B.Z. said, going restlessly to the refrigerator for another beer. It always took Towzer forever to get to the point; especially when the point was an unpleasant one.

'He told me he keeps that secret ingredient of his in cold storage because it comes from the North Pole.'

'Uh-huh.' B.Z. moved back to the table with his new can of beer.

'So when he started manufacturing the candy canes –' Towzer stared at the ceiling as a change from his feet, '– it's a very powerful mixture, you know –'

'Uh-huh,' B.Z. grunted again.

'So I just assumed I should refrigerate them too.'

180

B.Z. glanced up at him, his strained patience snapping. 'Come on, man, tell your story! Don't keep giving me these short sentences and making me go "uh-huh, uh-huh, uh-huh" like some kind of a moron.' He sat back, glaring at Towzer, waiting expectantly.

And in her hiding place, crouched behind the closed doors of the dumbwaiter, Cornelia waited too, straining to make out Towzer's next few crucial words. Picking up Joe's empty orange juice glass, which she had somehow managed to hold onto in spite of everything, she pressed it against the wall to let her hear better.

'I had to move one of the batches of candy canes to another part of the factory,' Towzer went on at last, still wringing his hands. 'I left one box next to a radiator in the lab.'

'*And*???' B.Z. bellowed.

Towzer grimaced. 'There's no more lab!'

B.Z. choked on his beer, sputtering and coughing as if a noose had suddenly tightened around his neck. And on the far side of the kitchen, Cornelia swallowed her own gasp of horror as she peered out through the crack she had opened between the dumbwaiter doors, silently witnessing everything that happened.

'The candy canes exploded!' Towzer cried, waving his hands, verging on hysteria as the horrible secret he had been holding inside him for hours burst out of him at last. 'They react to extreme heat and turn volatile!' He thought of the innocent children who could be hurt or even killed by overheated candy canes ... he thought of their outraged parents and law cases, and spending the rest of his life in prison. 'We've got to stop this!'

B.Z. glared at him with just the expression Towzer had feared – and expected – to see. 'Stop? Are you insane?' B.Z. growled. 'Millions of dollars are pouring in every day, most of them in cash. *Cash* man! Small, unmarked notes!' He rubbed the invisible money between his thumb and forefinger.

Towzer held up his hands in useless protest. 'B.Z., this stuff can kill people!' he murmured.

B.Z. sneered. 'Are you going soft on me?'

Towzer stared speechlessly at B.Z.'s face, which seemed to his distracted mind to expand until it filled the room, the way B.Z. himself dominated Towzer, body and soul.

'Look, you idiot,' B.Z. went on, thinking furiously, 'who else knows about this?' There had to be some way to get around this nasty little complication...

'Nobody,' Towzer answered, 'but –'

'What about Patch?' B.Z. snapped, looking up at him again.

'He was asleep in the other side of the building,' Towzer said hastily. 'He didn't hear anything.'

B.Z. nodded in satisfaction. That was one problem he didn't have to worry about, at least. 'Good. *Don't tell him.* Don't tell anybody!'

Cornelia cracked open the dumbwaiter doors another inch, biting her lip.

'But B.Z.,' Towzer whined, sweating profusely now, 'these are *children* we're talking about.'

B.Z. leered at him, his voice a parody of pious appreciation as he said, 'Yes, and who appreciates them better than I?' He raised his own hands to his chest. 'These industrious little boys and girls saving up their pocket money to get the magic candy cane I promised.' His mocking facade fell away and he snarled, 'They'll get what they paid for. If these people are so reckless as to have radiators in their homes –'

'Reckless!' Towzer exclaimed, in honest disbelief.

B.Z. grinned at him, now, the smile stretching his face until he resembled Jaws. 'Towzer, how does Brazil sound to you?'

Towzer looked at him blankly.

B.Z. popped open his new can of beer and began to stroll out of the kitchen, heading back to his study as unconcernedly as if there were suddenly no problem at all. Towzer followed after him, as

182

nonplussed and uncomprehending as a loyal family
dog.

Cornelia pushed open the dumbwaiter doors as
they disappeared from the room and crept out into
the kitchen, listening to their voices trail away
down the passage.

'Sandy beaches,' B.Z. said expansively, 'tropical
breezes, big rum drinks with pineapple in 'em,
senoritas in string bikinis,' he glanced back at
Towzer, 'and, oh yes, no *extradition proceedings.*'

'You mean -?' Towzer gasped, comprehending
B.Z.'s plan, and the fact that he was included in it,
in the same astonished moment. Tears of pathetic
gratitude welled in his eyes.

'You and me, Eric.' B.Z. put a hand around his
chief designer's shoulders, filled with good fellow-
ship as he realised how simple the solution to all
their problems really was. 'We'll take the cash and
let the elf face the music.' He chuckled as the two
men drifted companionably into his study, not quite
bothering to close the door.

Cornelia, seizing her opportunity, tiptoed down
the passage past the half-open door and crept
silently back up the stairs to her bedroom.

Patch lay in his bed in the empty B.Z. Toy Factory,
enjoying the peace and quiet of the silent night,
totally unaware that it was only the calm before the
terrible storm. He had converted the rumble seat of
the retired Patchmobile into a cosy elf-sized mini-
bed, complete with a down mattress and quilt like
the ones he so fondly remembered from his old home
in the stable.

His eyes began to grow heavy with the com-
plexities of the computer-robotics manual he had
been studying (while he still had easy access to such
things); yawning, he reached up at last to switch off
his reading lamp. Then he pulled the rumble seat
cover over his head and settled down for the night in
the cosy shell of darkness.

As Patch drifted down into dreamland, B.Z.'s long black limousine pulled up before the factory like a cruising shark. Grizzard hauled Joe, battered, dazed and half-frozen, out of its boot and stuffed a gag into his mouth, tying it firmly in place. Then he dragged the shivering boy into the cavernous darkness of the factory building. As he passed the Patchmobile, his utterly helpless captive firmly in his grasp, he heard what sounded like faint snoring; he glanced at the car in vague curiosity. Patch, sound asleep within it, heard nothing at all.

Grizzard dragged Joe down the black, echoing stairwell into the sub-basement where, unknown to him, Patch had his secret store of magic dust hidden. Unconcerned, Grizzard dropped Joe's limp body roughly onto the floor. Joe lay without struggling on the cold, dank concrete while Grizzard bound his feet together. Joe whimpered silently, completely overwhelmed by his captor's brutal strength and the terrifying helplessness of his situation. The armour of his tough streetwise manner had been torn away and he was only a ten-year-old boy again, a ten-year-old boy who knew with horrifying certainty that he was not going to get much older. Glistening unshed tears rose in his eyes, filling them until he could barely see.

Grizzard pulled out another length of rope and bound Joe's hands to a water pipe, completing his imprisonment. 'Listen, kid,' he rasped, 'if you wanna die on me while I'm gone, be my guest.' He laughed hoarsely and started up the stairs again without a backward glance. The tears in Joe's eyes overflowed as he watched Grizzard abandon him in this freezing, empty cellar. He slumped against the clammy wall, sobbing brokenly, as Grizzard's footsteps faded into silence, utter silence.

Waking to a new day, Cornelia leapt from her bed. She had lain awake for hours last night, thinking about all she had heard downstairs, worrying about Joe. At last, knowing that she could do nothing more until morning without her uncle growing suspicious, she had fallen into an exhausted slumber. Now, with the new day's sunlight bright beyond her window, she knew exactly what she must do. She ran across the bedroom to her writing desk and took out pen and paper. She sat down and began to scribble the words she had composed last night as quickly as her hand would form letters:

To: Santa Claus
North Pole
EMERGENCY! OPEN IMMEDIATELY!

She pushed aside the finished envelope and reached for her notepaper, whispering each word to herself as she began the most important letter she had ever written; making certain every word was clear:

Dear Santa, You've got to help right away. Joe has been taken prisoner by a very bad man. I'm sorry to say he's a relation of mine, sort of. I'm scared he will hurt Joe, and –'

Her head came up in sudden fright as her bedroom door was flung open. Miss Tucker stood there, with her step-uncle glowering in the background. Cornelia stared guiltily, covering her letter with her hands; but fortunately Miss Tucker did not seem to notice.

'Cornelia!' Miss Tucker said sharply. 'What are you doing? You're ten minutes late for breakfast.'

Cornelia nodded mutely and turned away from them, hiding her actions as she crammed the half-finished letter into its envelope. 'I'm coming, I'm coming,' she murmured, getting up from her chair. She ran to the door and out into the landing with seeming eagerness, before anyone could become curious enough to check on what she had been doing; making certain as she went to close her bedroom door tightly behind her.

The letter lay where she had left it on the desk in

the quiet room, and for several moments nothing more happened. But then, as if the room itself were sighing, a gentle breeze began to stir the air. The breeze cupped the letter in its invisible hands, lifting it gently from the tabletop and carrying it towards the fireplace. In an eyeblink the letter had disappeared up the chimney.

EIGHTEEN

In the stables of the elves' village, in what had once been Patch's home and was still home to the reindeer, Boog and Honka waited with worried faces. Vout removed two large, gracefully curling reindeer thermometers from the mouths of Comet and Cupid and read them; he began to frown. 'Just what I thought,' he murmured. He looked up again, his frown of concern turning to sympathy as the two miserable-looking, red-eyed animals sneezed loudly, almost in unison, where they lay. They had come down with the flu. *What next?* he thought. It almost seemed as if the general air of unhappiness around the village was becoming physical. The reindeer had never had a sick day in their lives while Patch had been here to tend them. He sighed, shaking his head, and gave the other elves instructions for administering medicine and making sure the sick reindeer got enough fluids. Then he went to tell Santa. Even though Santa Claus was not himself these days, Vout was sure he would want to come and visit the sick animals.

Meanwhile Santa Claus was wandering alone through the now-empty toy tunnel, his footsteps echoing, his lantern casting eerie, lonely shadows on the bare shelves and walls. Standing alone in the scene of his former happiness, the place that had always symbolised everything he believed in, he found it sadly fitting to find the hall so empty. Sighing heavily, he turned and trudged back towards the high doors at the tunnel entrance. He still had to see Dooley today; his responsibilities refused to go away, no matter how much he wished they would.

He reached Dooley's office at last. The chief elf tactfully made no comment about his lateness. Santa sat down and began to thumb half-heartedly through the ledgers that Dooley set before him. A small fire burned in the fireplace at his back, the hearth being as empty of letters at this time of year as the toy tunnel was empty of toys.

'I think we ought to provide the first shipments of pinewood as early as April this time so we don't run short,' Dooley said. 'Don't you, Santa?'

Santa nodded mechanically, giving the question none of his former quick attention or careful thought.

Dooley glanced away again as a sound like bird wings fluttering caught his attention. He looked instinctively towards the fireplace, started in surprise as he actually saw a letter drop down the chimney and sweep past the flames to land on the hearth all alone.

'What's this?' Dooley murmured curiously.

Santa Claus followed his glance. 'Looks like a letter,' he said, without much interest.

'In January?' Dooley raised his bushy eyebrows. 'A bit early for next Christmas, isn't it?'

Santa sighed at this new complication. 'Maybe it got lost in the mail. You know the Post Office these days...' All he could think of was yet another child who would be disappointed in him. He got slowly to his feet and went to the hearth to pick it up. He stared at the curious message written on the envelope: EMERGENCY! OPEN IMMEDIATELY! 'Familiar handwriting,' he murmured.

Sitting down again, he tore the envelope open with practised efficiency and pulled out the letter. He read it. His eyes widened and he leapt to his feet. Dooley stared at him in astonishment. Santa strode across the room, galvanised with energy. 'It's Joe!' he cried. 'Saddle up the reindeer!'

Dooley's mouth flapped; for once he was quite

speechless. He had no idea of who 'Joe' was, not to mention what was going on. 'But it's only two weeks since they've been out,' he gasped at last.

'Sir –' Boog, Honka and Vout burst into the office before Santa could reply, adding to Dooley's already considerable confusion.

Santa Claus grinned at them. 'Just the elves I wanted to see,' he said briskly. 'Hitch up the team. We're flying out at 0900 hours.'

The elves gaped at him, as Dooley was still doing. 'But that's what we came to tell you,' Boog protested. 'It's Comet and Cupid –'

Santa hesitated, seeing their worried expressions. 'What about them?' he asked.

'They've got flu,' Honka said.

Santa frowned, stroking his beard and pondering. 'Hmm, that's unfortunate,' he muttered, deeply distressed. He couldn't take them out on a winter night in that condition; they'd have pneumonia in no time... But Joe needed his help; Joe was in serious danger. Joe *needed* him. He looked up again, his decision made. 'Well, I'll have to make do with six of 'em, then,' he said. 'Feed them! Hitch them up! Joe needs me!' He strode out of the room like a general heading out to rouse his troops, his eyes bright and alive, his soul-deep lethargy gone as if it had never existed.

Everything was made ready in record time, as both man and reindeer prepared for unexpected action. Anya, still wearing her yellow-striped nightshirt and cap (when Claus couldn't sleep, neither could she), was stunned by the transformation that had come over her husband. It sent her own spirits soaring to see her beloved Claus acting like himself again. In fact, she had not seen him so bold and determined, his eyes flashing so brightly, for centuries. She had almost forgotten that look in all these long years of peace and happiness. And as she watched him hurry away towards the tunnel and his waiting reindeer, she suddenly thought of something else she had forgotten for years. Rushing into their bedroom, she rummaged through a trunk for the one thing she had kept from their former life, through all these countless years. Finding it at last, she hurried after him, catching up with him as he reached the toy tunnel, which was empty now except for his ready sleigh. 'Wait!' she cried.

Claus looked back at her; he had already reached his sleigh, which had only six reindeer hitched to its traces this time. 'I can't wait!' he shouted, waiting. 'What is it?'

She ran up to his side, breathless, and thrust out the thing she carried. 'Here,' she said, 'you'll need this.'

He took the offered item from her hand, and stared at it. It was a tiny, ancient, bottle of *schnapps*. He blinked in disbelief. 'How long have you had this?' he asked wonderingly, looking up at her.

'Since the tenth century.' Anya smiled, suddenly looking a little embarrassed. 'I was saving it for a special occasion.'

Claus grinned and tucked the bottle into his pocket. They kissed briefly but fondly, as Claus embraced her with the passionate urgency of a soldier leaving his family to fight the battle of his life. Then she turned with a last smile, one that begged him to come back home safely, and hurried away to find Dooley and his telescope.

Santa Claus strode forward along the length of the ancient but perfectly-preserved sleigh to face his reindeer. Putting his hands on his hips like a coach before the kick-off, like a general exhorting his troops, he began to speak to the waiting animals. 'Boys,' he said, with quiet intensity, 'I know it's only a few weeks since Christmas. I know you're still beat to your hooves. I know you're looking forward to a year's rest and relaxation, and believe me, *nobody deserves it more*. Nobody!' He leaned forward, clenching his mittened fists, meeting one pair of weary reindeer eyes and then another as he cried with heartfelt concern, 'But boys, we've got ourselves one heck of a problem here. Our little friend Joe is in trouble. *Big* trouble.' He swept his hand across the dark, frigid sky, pointing south. 'If we don't help him...' His face turned grim and his eyes darkened as he imagined what might happen. The reindeer pricked their ears in sudden interest and concern at his expression. 'I don't even like to think of what could happen,' he murmured.

Santa shook his head; he took a deep breath, and his voice rose again, filling the echoing toy tunnel with the sweeping irresistible power of a rising tide. 'Now I know we're two men short today, but this time you've got to fly like the wind!' He lifted his hand. 'Can you do it for me? *Can you do it for little Joe*??? OF COURSE YOU CAN!!!'

The reindeer's heads swivelled to follow him as he bounded back to the sleigh and leapt into its seat, grabbing up the reins. The twins Dasher and Dancer looked back at each other, then straightened in unison, ready for action. Blitzen stretched his neck, snorting at the stars, his passive indifference to the world gone for once, as beside him Donner put aside his fright with equal valour, gritting his teeth as he stood poised and ready for their impending flight.

'So give me that extra effort,' Santa Claus cried. 'I'm counting on you!' He tugged on the reins, giving the signal for lift-off. 'YO!'

The six reindeer leapt forward and galloped down the tunnel, launching away into the sky with all the speed and energy of eight.

In Dooley's study, Anya watched the sleigh's departure through the telescope, a thing she always did, because she believed it brought him luck and brought him safely back to her. This was one time that she did not want to miss his departure. Her heart beat with a confusion of emotions as she watched her husband of centuries fly off on what might be his final mission: pride, courage, loyalty, fear... but most of all love, a love that over the

191

centuries had only grown stronger. She was afraid for him, and yet she understood perfectly what made him so determined to go – the knowledge that he alone held the fate of a lost little boy in his hands. He was her Claus and he could do nothing less than what he had chosen to do tonight. She lifted her hand in a wave of farewell that was also a salute, as the sleigh and its lone occupant disappeared into the night.

NINETEEN

Cornelia paced restlessly about her bedroom, ready for action in a warm coat and blue jeans, but unable to sit down or to stop worrying. When she had returned to her room after breakfast, she had found the letter she had written missing from her desk. Since no one had come into her room to drag her away as they had done with Joe, she thought that it must by some magic have found its way to Santa Claus. But if he had got her letter, where was he? What would she do it he didn't come? What if –

Suddenly a great *whoosh* filled the hearth of her fireplace with a cloud of ashes, and the man she had been longing to see appeared abruptly on the flagstones before her. Santa Claus stood smiling before her, answering her own joyful smile of relief; but then his face turned sober with concern.

'It's you,' Cornelia burst out, overwhelmed with relief. 'Thank heavens!'

'How is he?' Santa asked urgently, glancing around the room as if he were searching for Joe.

'I don't know!' Cornelia cried, her desperation abruptly returning as she remembered why Santa was here.

'*Where* is he?' Santa asked.

Cornelia's hands made fists. 'My step-uncle's got him. Listen –' She broke off, suddenly embarrassed to hear herself speaking so abruptly to Santa Claus. Struggling to recapture her good manners, she said, 'I mean, excuse me, but I've got to tell you something else. Those candy canes –'

But Santa was already gesturing her towards the chimney. 'Tell me on the way.' He swept her into the

193

circle of his magic spell, and, touching the side of his nose, transported them to the roof and his waiting sleigh. The reindeer launched off into the sky at his command, flying over the city and the surrounding countryside by daylight for only the second time in all their lives. The sleigh banked and headed eastward at Cornelia's instruction, heading for the B.Z. Toy Factory. As they flew, Cornelia breathlessly explained to Santa all that had happened, trying very hard to concentrate on her story and not on the fact that she was really flying over the city in Santa's own sleigh.

'They *exploded*?' Santa asked, aghast, as she finished describing the problem with Patch's candy canes.

She nodded. 'That's what he said. When they got hot. I called the police but I don't think they believed me.' She was old enough to realise that people in authority thought she was still too young to trust.

Santa's face grew even grimmer. 'We haven't a second to lose –' he said, and shouted to his reindeer, 'On Donner! On Blitzen! On Dasher! On Vixen! On Cup –' He broke off, remembering, as his eyes found only empty space. 'Oh, I forgot. We've only got six.'

'Times are tough, huh?' Cornelia said soberly, and suddenly thought of Joe; the more time they spent together, the more they sounded alike. She met Santa's questioning, worried glance with her own, and they flew on in silence.

Patch sat at his control board, lost in a daydream as usual as the robot machines made their endless candy canes with mindless efficiency. But once again, as it did two or three times a day, the buzzer sounded as the stardust hopper's gauge registered empty. Patch roused himself from his seat and started for the door to the cellar. He clattered down the metal staircase, and, with a quick glance over his shoulder, entered the dark, dank room.

Striding sure-footedly towards the metal filing cabinet, Patch suddenly stopped short as a small,

194

muted sound registered in his ears. He turned, peering around in the darkness as his eyes adjusted. It sounded like... someone crying? He began to search the supposedly empty room, tracking the sound with his sensitive ears. At last, rounding a large rusty dust-bin, he found its source: a young boy, bound and gagged, tied to a pipe.

'What -?' Patch breathed, for a moment not believing his eyes. 'Oh my gosh -' He kneeled down and with fumbling hands started to untie Joe's hands and feet, stopping only to remove the gag from the boy's mouth. 'What are you doing down here?' Patch asked, his voice shaky with surprise.

'As if you didn't know, creep,' the boy said bitterly, his reddened eyes blazing.

Patch sat back, his astonishment complete. 'Me????' he asked.

'You're the one,' the boy said furiously, tears of helpless anger still running down his cheeks. 'You ruined Christmas.'

'I never did!' Patch said indignantly, not having the slightest idea what the boy was talking about, but feeling a strange, painful twinge of guilt anyway. He stood up, his own anger rising as he remembered why he had left the North Pole, and that Santa never had called him back. How dare this kid tell him that *he* had ruined Christmas!

The boy scrambled to his feet and stood before him with clenched fists, looking ready to start a fight at the least provocation. 'He told me!' the boy insisted, his own voice shaking with anger. 'He said the kids didn't like him no more on account of you!'

Him -? The boy could only mean Santa Claus. 'You don't even know Santa Claus,' Patch said, all his sympathy for the boy's plight forgotten and his own temper flaring. No wonder someone had dumped the nasty little brat here.

'Do so!' Joe cried.

'Do not!' Patch shouted back, sinking rapidly to the boy's level.

'He said I was his only friend left, ya dumb punk!'

the boy said shrilly. He began to cry again.

Patch froze, his anger draining away as suddenly as it had come, as he realised that the weeping boy was really serious. His heart sank. Was it true? Had he really ruined Christmas? Had his plan to win back Santa's love and respect truly backfired so completely? Was that why Santa had never sent for him? He thought of B.Z., and suddenly all the vague and formless doubts that had been floating free in his subconscious mind formed one awful image. B.Z. had taken advantage of him in ways he had never even dreamed of, and he had only himself to blame. He had *never* meant anything like this to happen... He stood without speaking, no longer even looking at the boy; caught inside his sudden revelation.

All the wild fury that had been trapped inside Joe during his ordeal spilled over as he saw what he took to be Patch's silent indifference; he lunged forward and began to punch and pummel the elf. Patch squawked with surprise and put up his hands, flailing back at the boy in self-defence; trying without much success to fend off the painful blows. He had not practised his elf-defence moves in far too long; and besides, this kid didn't bother to fight fair.

'Yeah!' Joe sobbed hysterically, kicking and swinging. 'He seen what you are – a big dummy stupid-head stink-face creep who made kids hate the best guy that ever –' As they struggled together, something dropped from the boy's pocket and clattered across the cement floor. Joe and Patch broke apart at the noise, looking down in startled surprise. It was a brightly painted wooden toy, of a kind very familiar to Patch's trained eye.

He moved away from Joe, their fight forgotten as he bent down to pick it up. Holding it in his hands, he saw that it was a carved wooden elf; and for the first time he saw its features clearly. His breath caught. '...what is this...?' he murmured, and his own eyes grew misty with sudden tears.

196

'Gimme that,' Joe cried, 'it's mine!'

He reached out to grab it, but Patch pulled it away from his grasp. 'Where did you get it?' he demanded.

'*He* gave it to me,' the boy said, his jaw jutting with stubborn pride as Patch's face changed. 'See? I told you I'm his best –'

Patch looked down at the carved elf again, seeing in its face a perfect recreation of his own, carved by Santa's own hands. He took a deep, tremulous breath as a profound, unexpected emotion filled him. 'He *does* like me,' he whispered. 'He *does* like me after all.' In spite of all his terrible mistakes, in spite of everything that has happened ... He looked up at Joe again, his eyes shining, and gently handed the wooden figure back to him.

'Huh?' Joe muttered, confused by the complete and completely unexpected change in Patch's manner. He looked down at his wooden elf in curiosity, cradling it protectively in his hands; noticing for the first time the resemblance between its face and the face of the elf before him.

Patch's face filled with resolution as his racing mind fitted pieces of a new plan together with lightning speed. 'Come on, kid!' he cried, gesturing to Joe. He started out of the room, heading for the stairs. At least it wasn't too late to set right his mistakes and make it up to Santa Claus –

'Where we going?' Joe called, hurrying to catch up with him.

'The North Pole,' Patch said decisively. 'We'll both go. And for once, we'll bring *Santa Claus* a present!'

Joe caught up with him on the stairs. Looking at the expression on the elf's face now, he began to grin. Everything was going to be all right after all!

Patch led him through the factory to the vast storeroom where a glowing mountain of magic candy canes lay at the foot of a huge chute, waiting to be wrapped for shipping. Patch held out his hand proudly, gesturing at the great pile of presents. 'There's enough here to take care of all next year's

Christmas orders.' He grinnèd, his enthusiasm infectious. 'Santa Claus can take a year off! His first holiday,' he said eagerly. 'Won't that be great?'

'Hey, yeah!' Joe nodded, grinning too as he gazed at the incredible display of candy; never dreaming, as he thought of the happiness it would bring to Santa, that instead they would be bringing him a mountain of potential disaster.

Patch swept up an armload of the candy canes, and started back towards the Patchmobile. He dropped the armload into the rumble seat and hurried back to the storage area for more.

Joe picked up an armful of candy, following his example, and trailed Patch to the car. He dropped his own load into the back seat and stared at the Patchmobile in open amazement. 'How's this thing work?' he asked, fascinated. He had seen a lot of really smart cars in his time, but he'd never seen anything like this. It was really awesome.

'It's elf-propelled,' Patch said proudly, and dropped in another load of candy canes.

TWENTY

Santa's sleigh soared over the wintry suburbs, silhouetted by the glorious red-orange of sunset over the distant horizon. Far below, the usual evening rush-hour jam was turning the main road beneath them into a river of light. Fortunately, no one caught in it bothered to lean out of the window of a car into the icy breeze to admire the sky, or notice the curious spectacle passing overhead. The six reindeer travelled more slowly than eight, and they did not have the time-stopping magic of Christmas Eve to help them along tonight. But with Cornelia's sure guidance, they were closing in rapidly on the B.Z. Toy Factory.

Not very far away, inside the factory, Patch and Joe had just finished loading the huge mountain of candy canes into the back of the Patchmobile. By now one of the things that fascinated Joe the most about the strange car was the seemingly infinite capacity of its back seat. The glow of all the enchanted candy canes was dazzling, making the darkened building almost as bright as day; the glow seemed to pulse with energy, as if the candy canes had a life of their own.

At last Patch climbed into the driver's seat and motioned to Joe to join him. Joe hopped excitedly into the car and settled down in its patchwork bucket seat, staring at the dials and lights of the instrument panel before him.

Patch picked up a small black box with buttons on it, which looked to Joe exactly like the kind of thing somebody would use to change channels on their television set. Patch pressed one of the buttons, holding it out at arm's length, and the big star-bedecked hangar doors at the end of the room began slowly to grind open. Outside the sky was indigo with twilight, glowing a deep red-orange at the horizon.

Patch glanced over at Joe. 'Fasten your seatbelt,' he instructed.

Joe looked down in surprise, realising that Patch was wearing one and he was not – in his excitement he had forgotten all about it. Obediently he pulled the strap across and fastened himself in. 'Can I drive it later?' he asked eagerly, remembering his trips with Santa.

'Do you have a driving licence?' Patch asked, looking at him sceptically. This kid hardly looked old enough to ride a bicycle.

'No.' Joe shook his head, his face falling.

'Sorry,' Patch said, shaking his own head with a shrug; not bothering to mention that he didn't have one either. Patch switched on the ignition and the engines roared to life.

The Patchmobile charged up the runway and soared out through the open hangar doors, rocketing away into the ozone.

Santa and Cornelia looked down over the side of the sleigh as a sudden distant roar sounded far below them. Cornelia saw her step-uncle's factory looming black and silent below. Then she saw, high above it now and still climbing fast, the rocketing Patchmobile.

'It's them!' she cried, pointing ahead. 'Both of them!' She was sure she could see Joe riding beside Patch in the car. She watched them soar away with very mixed feelings of relief, amazement and dismay.

Santa's own wide stare of surprise changed suddenly to a look of fear. '*Oh no!!!!*' he cried.

'What is it?' Cornelia glanced back at him in sudden fright.

'Look!' Santa raised his arm. Cornelia followed

his pointing finger to the rear of the Patchmobile, where the metal roll-top of the rumble seat was glowing a hot puce from the extreme concentration of volatile candy canes inside it.

'The candy canes! They're in the car with them!' Santa cried.

Cornelia's hands flew up to her mouth, as the realisation struck her. 'Patch doesn't know they explode,' she said.

Desperately Santa shouted to his reindeer, '*Faster! Faster! Come on boys, fly like the wind! Fly like you never flew before!!*'

The reindeer leaped to his command as they heard the urgency in his voice. They surged forward across the sky with fiery determination in their eyes, their nostrils flaring as they sucked in the icy air, their chests heaving with the tremendous effort of pursing Patch's rocket car as it headed north at unbelievable speed.

Completely unaware that Santa's sleigh was in hot pursuit of them, Patch and Joe watched the sprawling suburbs of greater New York fall away below them. Patch opened the Patchmobile up all the way, his foot pressing the accelerator flat to the floor; having the time of his life showing the awestruck Joe what his pride and joy could do.

'Man this is great!' Joe cried, the wind whistling past his ears. He wondered fleetingly if Santa would ever consider giving up his old-fashioned sleigh for something snappy like this.

Patch honked the horn exultantly and listened as it played his song, happier than he had been in ages. 'It does anything I want it to do!' he shouted. 'Watch!' He leaned forward and at the same time jerked the steering wheel sharply to the left, then to the right, and back again, like a teenage hotrodder. The Patchmobile lurched erratically and plunged downwards through the air, spiralling through great swoops, like a leaf falling from a tree, or a daring aviator's plane in an airshow. Joe laughed in giddy delight. Patch righted the car's dizzying flight again and shot up towards the stars once more, aiming directly for the North Star. They were already almost to Canada. He couldn't *wait* to get back to the North Pole and show Santa...

While behind them, Santa himself wanted nothing more than to see them slow down or turn around. The tired reindeer kept up their valiant pursuit doggedly, but he could see that they were already showing signs of exhaustion. They were only flesh and blood, they couldn't keep up this pace forever, like a machine... but, unlike a machine, they had noble hearts and that would make them give him their best efforts to the end. And that was the reason he loved them, and would never *ever* trade them in for a flying car.

'Can't they go any faster?' Cornelia cried, seeing the Patchmobile gaining on them once again.

Santa shook his head. 'They usually get a year's rest! They're doing their best!' Taking a deep breath, he shouted, 'Fly, lads, fly!' In the distance he could still track the car by its glowing back seat. The sinister pulsing puce light seemed to be glowing noticeably hotter now.

And inside the Patchmobile's boot, where no one could see what was about to happen next, the candy canes pitched about wildly as Patch put the car through another set of turns at Joe's urging. Patch and Joe whooped in ecstasy as the car rolled and pitched. And beneath the load of candy canes, a stress crack opened in the Patchmobile's groaning framework, revealing unprotected wiring. Another wrenching drive tore the wires apart. A spark flickered, and then another, as the short-circuiting wires began to sizzle.

Fat Blitzen's tongue was lolling from his mouth, the reindeer's heaving flanks were white with foam from their exertion; but slowly, slowly the sleigh was gaining on the cavorting Patchmobile.

Up ahead in the distance Patch and Joe shouted with laughter, too involved in their own antics to hear anyone else's shout, or even to look behind them – to see who might be following them, or even to notice the cloud of puce smoke and sparks that was beginning to pour from their own back seat.

But Santa and Cornelia saw it. '*Oh no!*' Santa cried.

'Joe! Joe!' Cornelia screamed, but her own cries were lost in the sound of roaring rockets.

Santa shook the reins, calling out in frantic concern to his labouring team. 'Come on, boys! It's *Patch* in there! If you love him like he loves you, then give me everything you've got!!!'

Up ahead, he saw the Patchmobile suddenly begin to shake violently in a way that had nothing to do with Patch's antics. The pyrotechnics going on in its rear end were beginning to have their own effect on the car's performance.

And now at last even Patch and Joe were suddenly, frighteningly, aware that something was going wrong. Patch struggled with the shuddering steering wheel, trying to get it back under his control, but it was too far gone to obey him. Joe looked worriedly at Patch, seeing the sudden fright on the elf's face. He turned in his seat, looking around him in confusion – and saw the billowing cloud of thick smoke, the fingers of flame curling up from the back of the car. 'Something's happening,' he cried, more horrified because he didn't know what. 'Patch!'

Santa's sleigh was close behind the Patchmobile now, gaining fast; but Joe could not see it through the smoke, just as Santa and Cornelia could no longer see the car's occupants.

'Do something!' Cornelia cried, barely able to keep her eyes on the car, so certain that it was about to explode that she could hardly watch.

Santa's brow wrinkled with desperate concern as he tried to think of some way to save them ... 'The Super-Duper-Looper!' he cried suddenly. 'It's the only way!'

Up at the front of the reindeer team, Donner's head flew up in panic as he heard the dreaded words echo from antler to antler down the line.

Seeing Donner toss his head, and knowing his lifelong fear of heights, Santa cried feelingly, 'Come on, Donner! You can do it, boy, I know you can do it!' He drew back on the reins, giving the fateful command.

The two lead reindeer ducked their heads obediently and started sharply downwards, pulling the sleigh after them as they swept below and beneath the smoking Patchmobile, gathering momentum to begin their tremendous loop. The reindeer and sleigh began to climb again, rising upwards more and more steeply, beginning their first crescent of the arc – rapidly approaching the critical point where Donner's nerve habitually failed him. Santa held his breath. With only six reindeer instead of eight, even the slightest hesitation would mean failure for them.

But this time, with the vision of the smoking Patchmobile above, knowing that his beloved Patch was aboard it, Donner gritted his teeth and made the supreme effort of a lifetime. He kept on climbing... climbing... never looking down but fixing his gaze on Patch's car.

And, with an awesome surge, the reindeer continued into their loop-the-loop, soaring triumphantly towards the stars, to dance on the ceiling of the sky.

Patch and Joe, looking out in desperate panic for some miracle to save them, recoiled in amazement as Santa himself, his sleigh and reindeer, suddenly rose straight up from beneath them like a cresting wave.

Patch jammed on the brakes in a frantic attempt to avoid a collison. And at the same moment, in the most awesome display of fireworks anyone had ever seen, the candy canes exploded, blowing the Patchmobile apart. Its chunky, oversized toy parts flew out and away in all directions like an exploding jigsaw puzzle – and its two terrified occupants were flung straight up into the sky, Patch still spasmodically gripping the sundered steering wheel. They reached the top of their own arc just as the looping sleigh reached its zenith; hovered there in a split second of incredible weightlessness... and then began to plummet down again through the air.

The flying reindeer and sleigh swooped down like a roller-coaster through the final arc of its loop, reaching the bottom at last, the only, possible second for a mid-air rendezvous. The plummeting boy and elf crashed down into the back of the sleigh, a human cargo more precious to Santa Claus and Cornelia than a hundred sacks of toys. The two sat blinking and gasping for a long moment, recovering from their bruising crash-landing, and the shock of finding themselves safe.

Cornelia flung herself across the seat back to embrace Joe, hugging him with joyful triumph. Patch, still shaken but filled with heartfelt gratitude, called out to the reindeer, 'Oh my boys, I've seen some reindeer in my time, but you're the best! The best!'

Looking back at his human cargo, Santa laughed for the first time in far too long, his great rolling *ho-ho-ho* of sheer happiness. 'We did it!' he cried. 'We did it!'

Grinning contentedly in Cornelia's arms, Joe looked ahead at the reindeer, realising what they had done so flawlessly tonight, and remembering another night when he had seen them try the Super-Duper-Looper and fail. 'Awright, Donner!' he yelled. 'You did it, boy!'

Up ahead, Blitzen leaned over to lick Donner's face in fond congratulation. Donner flicked his ears modestly, exhausted but triumphantly happy.

The sleigh and its rejoicing crew flew on towards the North Pole, and an even happier reunion.

TWENTY-ONE

The new day found B.Z. at his desk in his private
office, gloating over the latest figures on his ill-
gotten gains from candy canes. But all was
definitely not business as usual today. Outside his
window he suddenly heard the wail of police sirens,
the screech of cars braking to a stop. With the
sudden sick dread of the guilty, B.Z. leapt to his feet
and rushed to the window, peering out and down.

Outside, far below him, five blue-and-white squad
cars had surrounded the office building. There were
police everywhere, rushing from all sides towards
the building entrance.

B.Z.'s eyes bulged with pure terror. He had no way
of knowing, any more than Cornelia did, that the
police had indeed believed her story. Aware of her
step-uncle's shady reputation, they had decided to
act swiftly to nip the potential national disaster –
and international incident – in the bud.

But with the justifiable paranoia of someone who
was guilty as sin, B.Z. was sure that somehow the
cops must know everything about him, and everything about the fatal candy canes as well. While he
watched, Grizzard and Towzer were hauled out of
the building's front doors, already in handcuffs.

He looked around him in wild panic, searching for
some way out. Down below a police officer was
raising a loudspeaker. '*All right, B.Z.*,' the cop
shouted, '*we know you're in there. Just come out
with your hands held high.*' The words echoed
across the empty concourse, from wall to wall of the
silent factory buildings.

B.Z. pushed himself away from the window and

206

ran back to his desk. Yanking open the top right-hand drawer, he looked inside. Eight or nine of the glowing puce candy canes lay there, waiting for just such an emergency. B.Z. snatched them up with both hands and began to cram them into his mouth, crunching them up and choking them down as fast as he could. 'You'll never get me, coppers,' he mumbled unintelligibly.

A loud pounding sound at his locked office door. 'Open up in there!' a deep voice shouted.

Still gulping down the candy canes, B.Z. rushed to his office window and flung it open. He climbed up and teetered on the ledge, fearless with desperation, just as the office door gave way with a splintering crash behind him. Looking back he saw five police officers rush into the room, their guns drawn.

B.Z. leaped.

The crowd of policemen below began to point and shout; their warnings turned into disbelief in mid-cry. Instead of falling, their quarry was shooting straight up into the air like a rocket, propelled by a mega-overdose of magic candy canes.

The five officers who had come running into the office stood at the window now, looking out and up with mouths hanging, unable to believe they were actually watching a man disappear straight up, like a guided missile. They watched in awe as their escaping prisoner grew smaller and smaller, until he was no more than a bright puce speck in the heavens, and then not even that.

When B.Z. recovered his senses and found the courage to open his eyes, he let out a howl of outrage and dismay that should have echoed around the world. But somehow the earth had suddenly become no more than a vast, misty ball, unimaginably far below him. From where he hung, permanently suspended in orbit, he could do nothing but watch the world he had hoped to rook so royally slowly roll by, forever beyond his reach, forever safe from him now.

He had been sent into permanent exile by the very
magic he had planned to exploit and the greed that
had driven him to do it, a rare example of a truly
Higher Justice. From now on his only companions
would be the meteors and satellites and cast-off
NASA flotsam – the space garbage of which he had
become one more piece, different from the rest only
in the quality and quantity of noise he broadcast.

'*Get me down! Get me out of here!*' he bellowed,
and bellowed again.

But as they say, in space no one can hear you
scream... B.Z. rolled on through the blackness like
the harvest moon, literally hoist on his own petard,
kicking and screaming gracelessly into that good
night.

And at the North Pole, where it was night for only
half a year at a time, the elves' village was bright
with the artificial day of countless lanterns and
candles, as its inhabitants gathered in the Great
Hall for a noisy, joyful celebration. Patch stood in
the middle of it all, overwhelmed with the warmth of
his welcome home, feeling now far too undeserving
of it, but filled with gratitude and love for the people
and the place he had finally returned to after so
long. At the front of the crowd of welcoming elves
were the faces that made him happiest of all – Santa
Claus and Anya; his pals Honka, Boog and Vout;
Joe and Cornelia, who had saved him and the
world's children from a truly fatal mistake.

The humans and elves lifted their tankards of
mulled cider in a toast, all eyes on Patch as they
cried together, 'Good elf!'

But instead of smiling, Patch looked down with
unaccustomed elf-consciousness. 'I never knew the
candy canes would elf-destruct,' he said, looking up
at them again with a grave expression. 'I never
meant to hurt anybody.'

Anya reached out and hugged him, reassuring
him that they all understood that he had been a

208

victim of circumstance. 'You couldn't hurt a fly,' she said gently.

He hugged her back, grateful, and then looked at the others again. 'I just wanted you not to forget me,' he murmured, his voice filled with emotion.

Santa Claus shook his head, grinning ruefully. 'Patch,' he said, 'whatever else you are, you're unforgettable.'

Patch took a deep breath, straightening his shoulders. 'Santa Claus,' he said, and including all his fellow elves in his glance, 'starting right now I'm going to start a course of elf-improvement and make you proud.'

Santa smiled with deeply felt fondness. 'Proud?' he said, shaking his head incredulously. 'I was always proud of you, Patch, no matter what.' He put his hands on Patch's shoulders.

Patch beamed, letting the love and good will surround him, basking in the glow of the respect and recognition he had always craved, never realising that he had really possessed it all along. His eyes welled with secret tears as he smiled and smiled, while the other elves pressed around to shake his hand and pat his shoulder, calling out 'welcome home's and congratulations.

And Joe, watching everyone else, including Santa, swarm around Patch, found himself drifting further and further back into the shadows. Patch was back home with Santa, this was their world and everything he saw – the terrific cuckoo clock, the wonderful tinker-toy balconies – reminded him that it was not his own. Feeling suddenly lost and more like an orphan than ever, he began to wander away from the crowd.

But Santa, glancing up over the heads of the gathered elves, saw him drifting away. Always the most sensitive to the feelings of a child, Santa left the mob of celebrants and followed Joe into a quiet corner.

'You've had quite a night, eh, Joe?' he asked, a

friendly smile hiding his concern.

Joe shrugged, sliding back into his super-cool persona to hide his deeper, darker feelings. 'Yeah, it was okay...' He glanced around him again at the wonders of the elves' twinkling village, which made the lost Patchmobile seem boring by comparison.

'Can I get you a nice cup of hot chocolate?' Anya asked, coming up to stand with a quiet smile at her husband's side. She looked down at the thin forlorn little boy standing by himself in a corner, and her heart filled with a sudden yearning urge to take him in her arms and hold him close forever.

'Nah, that's awright, I don't want any, thanks.' Joe shook his head, suddenly feeling even more awkward and ill-at-ease, as the object of all this attention. He pushed his hands into his pockets, looking down and scuffing at the ground with his foot. He turned and moved a few yards further away, his shoulders hunched and his back turned.

Santa Claus watched the boy silently for a moment, his expression filling with love. 'You don't want hot chocolate,' he said, his voice tugging gently at Joe's shoulder. 'You won't ask for a present. If it wasn't for you, the world might never see another Christmas, and yet of all the children in the world you're the only one who didn't get anything. Joe –'

Joe turned hesitantly, pulled around by the words.

'Joe,' Santa asked quietly, 'isn't there *anything* you want?'

Joe kicked at the wide wooden floorboards again, started to turn away once more, feeling his tough-guy act crumbling. 'Me?' he said, with desperate casualness. 'Nah, I... I don't need –' And suddenly the words came bursting out in a flood, 'I want to stay with you. I want to be your kid.' Tears filled his eyes and he was astonished to see tears shining in the eyes of Santa and Anya as well, while smiles of overwhelming joy lit their faces. They held out their hands. Joe ran to them, losing himself in their

210

welcoming arms. They held him tightly, until he knew in his heart that they would never let him go, that he was theirs to love, and they were his, forever.

Claus looked up at Anya over Joe's head, their eyes shining as their gaze met, as the man and woman who had never had a child of their own at last found the son they had always longed for.

Joe came up for air, grinning and tear-streaked, and looked over at Cornelia, who stood looking on forlornly and a bit enviously at Joe and his new family. He looked up at Santa again, his smile fading. 'What about Corny?' he asked. He knew that she would always have plenty of everything, because her step-uncle was a very wealthy man... everything but love and friendship.

Cornelia's mouth quivered, then firmed with resolution. Blinking her eyes and finding her sweetest, most irresistible smile, she asked, 'Can I stay?' She rose up on her toes, her hands clasped and her eyes wide. 'Just till next Christmas? Please...?'

'You could give her a lift home next year...?' Joe suggested with eager helpfulness.

Santa turned to Anya, seeing the sudden shining eagerness in her own eyes. Dressed in her best red-white-and-green Christmas outfit, after all these years she was still the most beautiful woman he had ever met, and it amazed him how much he still loved her. How did that old song go, he thought, *A boy for me and a girl for you...?*

Hastily he considered the sudden logistics and added requirements of having two children at the North Pole. 'Well...' he murmured, stroking his beard. He glanced at the two waiting children again, and nodded decisively. '*Dooley –*' he called, summoning his trusted advisor.

Dooley, who had been standing silently behind him for the last minute or so, and had overheard everything, grinned and said with mock exasperation, 'As if I don't have enough to do, now I'm going to have to be a schoolteacher!'

211

Joe and Cornelia looked at each other in sudden dismay. '*School*?!' they chorused, their faces falling.

Santa Claus began to laugh, his merry 'Ho-ho-ho' ringing out across the hall until all the elves gathered there looked up and smiled in contented satisfaction. Santa was laughing again; things were going to be all right.

In their midst, Patch stepped forward to meet his old rival Puffy, and offered his hand. In both their minds now was a fresh understanding that the old ways and the new were not separated by an unbridgeable gap, but part of a vast spectrum of possibility. Patch's belief in change and innovation could make everyone's lives – both elves' and children's – happier; but only when it was combined with Puffy's respect for tradition and careful workmanship. The two elves shook hands, resolving in their hearts to seek a real meeting of minds and skills in the coming year. The elves around them cheered until the rafters rang.

Santa Claus smiled as he listened to the cheers and looked around him at the smiling faces, happier than he had ever been in his life . . . and that was a considerable amount of time. His family was complete, the elves' community was complete again. It seemed hard to believe that this time yesterday he had felt that all was hopeless, that the world's children had forgotten him and forgotten the true meaning of Christmas . . . just as surely as he felt that anything would be possible now. He had faith in the children who were the future of the world, and he realised now, looking down at Joe and Cornelia, that that faith would never truly fail, any more than the children would fail to believe in him. He thought back to his first Christmas here, and to all the countless Christmases in between. To-morrow he would begin to prepare in earnest for next year, for the most special and wonderful Christmas of all . . .

And just as Santa Claus never truly stopped

believing in Christmas, the children of the world had not forgotten him or stopped believing in him, either. Soon one letter after another began to drift northwards, carried on the back of the wind, letters filled with love and apology:

Dear Santa Claus, a five-year-old boy scrawled, with his mother's help. *My name is Jimmy. I'm sorry last year how I threw away your present. Will you be my friend again? This Christmas I would like a bicycle and a cricket bat and...*

Dear Santa, a little girl printed carefully.
I am glad you are all right. Really I didn't like that lollipop last year, it made me air-sick. Since then I have been a good girl and I would like a doll with curly red hair...

Dear Santa, wrote another boy, *Please don't be mad about last year. My little brother wants a guitar but my mum says...*

Santa sat in his easy chair, peering through his spectacles, reading letter after letter until his eyes brimmed and his smile spread from ear to ear. He seemed to hear the children's voices as he read, like a choir singing a song of joy and love, the most marvellous music he had ever heard.

He sighed and settled back, putting his feet up at the long day's end. Sipping his cocoa with marsh-mallows and watching the colours of the fire, he let their happy voices sing him a lullaby as he drowsed contentedly before the glowing hearth.

Anya smiled fondly from the bedroom doorway, where she had just tucked the children into their beds, as all around the compound the elves and even the reindeer were settling into their beds for another long winter's nap. In the perfect stillness of the polar night, the lights began to wink out one by one, the elves' village slowly melting into the greater darkness. But above the mountain where the peaceful town lay, aurora still twinkled and shone, its crystalline colours rising to form a great Christmas tree of light, crowned by the North Star, the brightest star of all in that magical place.

The shining tree marked the spot, as it marks it still, where the true magic of unselfish love has always existed, and always will. It is a place that few of us may ever see; but it exists, somewhere beyond the edge of our reality, all the same. And, gentle reader, if you believe in Santa Claus in your own secret heart – in the spirit of loving generosity, in the true and sometimes almost-forgotten meaning of Christmas – you may glimpse those twinkling lights in the darkness when you dream tonight.

He was afraid.
He was alone.
He was 3 million light years from home . . .

Now he's back – the most lovable Extra-Terrestrial in the
Universe.

THE BOOK OF
THE GREEN PLANET

A new novel by the bestselling author of E.T. the Extra-
Terrestrial.

WILLIAM KOTZWINKLE
based on a story by
STEVEN SPIELBERG

Things have certainly changed on Earth since E.T. left. Elliott seems to
have forgotten E.T.'s teachings of gentleness and peace. 'He is about
to become the most terrible thing of all,' observes E.T. from 3 million
light years away. 'He is about to become – Man.'

So begins E.T.'s mission to return to Planet Earth to help Elliott. But
he has been stripped of his powers, demoted from his distinguished
job, and is suspected of suffering from earthly corruption. Can the
gentle botanist outsmart the forces of his own civilisation? Can he
harness the powers of the Green Planet's plant kingdom . . . in a
daring attempt to elude the elite guard of the Starcruiser Fleet, and
escape to Earth?

FICTION   0 7221 5247 7   £1.75

Also available by WILLIAM KOTZWINKLE in Sphere paperback.

E.T. THE EXTRA-TERRESTRIAL STORYBOOK
E.T. THE EXTRA-TERRESTRIAL

A selection of bestsellers from SPHERE

FICTION

POSSESSIONS	Judith Michael	£2.95 ☐
NECESSITY	Brian Garfield	£1.95 ☐
JACK AND THE BEANSTALK	Ed McBain	£1.95 ☐
THE MIRACLE	Irving Wallace	£2.50 ☐
SISTERS	Suzanne Goodwin	£1.95 ☐

FILM & TV TIE-INS

THE CASE OF THE MISSING HAT	Gregory Williams	£1.25 ☐
BO SAVES THE SHOW	Jocelyn Stevenson	£1.25 ☐
INDIANA JONES AND THE CUP OF THE VAMPIRE	Andrew Helfer	£1.25 ☐
WIDOWS	Lynda La Plante	£1.50 ☐
THE RADISH DAY JUBILEE	Sheilah B. Bruce	£1.50 ☐

NON-FICTION

THE MATERNAL INSTINCT	Susan Hampshire	£1.95 ☐
THE QUEEN MOTHER	Anthony Holden	£2.95 ☐
THE SPHERE ILLUSTRATED HISTORY OF BRITAIN VOLUME 1	Ed. Kenneth O. Morgan	£3.95 ☐
THE SPHERE ILLUSTRATED HISTORY OF BRITAIN VOLUME 2	Ed. Kenneth O. Morgan	£3.95 ☐
THE SPHERE ILLUSTRATED HISTORY OF BRITAIN VOLUME 3	Ed. Kenneth O. Morgan	£3.95 ☐

All Sphere books are available at your local bookshop or newsagent, or can be ordered direct from the publisher. Just tick the titles you want and fill in the form below.

Name _____

Address _____

_____

Write to Sphere Books, Cash Sales Department, P.O. Box 11, Falmouth, Cornwall TR10 9EN

Please enclose a cheque or postal order to the value of the cover price plus:

UK: 55p for the first book, 22p for the second book and 14p for each additional book ordered to a maximum charge of £1.75.

OVERSEAS: £1.00 for the first book plus 25p per copy for each additional book.

BFPO & EIRE: 55p for the first book, 22p for the second book plus 14p per copy for the next 7 books, thereafter 8p per book.

Sphere Books reserve the right to show new retail prices on covers which may differ from those previously advertised in the text or elsewhere, and to increase postal rates in accordance with the PO.